Simple
Truths

Simple Truths

Sheila Levin

Crown Publishers, Inc.
New York

Note: The letters from Leonid Rabinovitz
are modeled after actual letters sent by
Soviet Jewish refusneks to various officials.

Inquiries should be addressed to Crown Publishers, Inc.,
One Park Avenue, New York, New York 10016
Printed in the United States of America
Published simultaneously in Canada
by General Publishing Company Limited
Library of Congress Cataloging in Publication Data
Levin, Sheila.
Simple truths.
I. Title.
PS3562.E889715 1982   813'.54   81-22217
ISBN 0-517-54718-X   AACR2
Book design by Camilla Filancia
10 9 8 7 6 5 4 3 2 1
First Edition

For my Uncle Benjamin Levin

1897–1981

Acknowledgment

I wish to acknowledge the creative collaboration
of my friend Phil Baum. His intelligence, sensitivity
and demanding editorial eye inform every facet of this novel.
It is a marvelous thing to have a book published; we share
that triumph.

Sheila Levin

Simple Truths

Prologue

LENINGRAD, October 9, 1973—*An audience of 2,000 Soviet citizens, including high-ranking Communist party officials, sat in stunned disbelief tonight as renowned violinist Leonid Rabinovitz ended a concert at the Philharmonic Society here with an encore by an Israeli composer—an unpardonable gesture, by Soviet standards.*

Standing alone at the stage of the ornate concert hall, Mr. Rabinovitz ended his recital with a work by Mordechai Ben-Zemer, entitled Nigun. Nigun *is the Hebrew word for melody.*

The concert violinist's action appeared designed to achieve maximum dramatic effect. He completed the Ben-Zemer composition, then raised his hand for silence and slowly identified the piece and its composer.

The antigovernment gesture was not lost on the patrons. After playing the composition, there was a second or two or silence, followed by scattered applause. However, almost immediately the applause was drowned out by angry stamping of feet and derogatory shouts, including denunciations of Israel.

Some observers, including admirers of Mr. Rabinovitz, who is Jewish, expressed amazement, and in some cases shock, that the

1

violinist, who has never been identified with the dissident movement in the Soviet Union, should have made so political a statement, particularly at this time. Since the USSR is strongly supporting the Arabs in the current Arab-Israeli War, Mr. Rabinovitz's action has been greeted as an especially outrageous slap in the face of Soviet officialdom.

The violinist, who is thirty-four and has played extensively in the West, was unavailable for comment after the performance.

Mr. Rabinovitz first achieved recognition at the age of fourteen, winning a scholarship to the Moscow Conservatory. He was selected for tutoring by the late composer Mischa Tchernovsky. Mr. Rabinovitz is married to Lucia Belkin, a cellist, who is not Jewish.

One Jewish activist who attended the concert but asked not to be identified, told a Western correspondent:

"Rabinovitz showed himself to be a brave man and a good Jew. In the time of crisis for Israel, many Russian Jews would like to make a similar gesture. We wish the world to know that, particularly in these black days of war, we stand with our brothers and sisters who are fighting and dying in our own land."

He added that he hoped the repercussions of Mr. Rabinovitz's gesture would not be severe. "In choosing to play Israeli music, he has placed himself in jeopardy." He said, "I fear now for his future."

As was the case during the 1967 War between Israel and the Arabs, many Jews in the Soviet Union, particularly those who have already applied to emigrate, are deeply concerned about Israel's fate.

The official Soviet press has limited news and radio broadcasts to reports indicating that Israel is losing the war. Radio Liberty, Kol Yisrael and the Voice of America have been jammed since the outbreak of fighting three days ago.

1

NEW YORK, February 1975

I'm frightened all the time.

It's difficult for me to listen, to concentrate.

I stutter slightly when I speak.

The palms of my hands are damp. Anxiously, I pat them against my clothes trying to dry them. I count my body pulses throbbing at my temples, at my throat, at my wrists. I listen to the pattern of my breathing, not entirely certain that even that most natural of reflexes would not stop if I didn't consciously track it. All these things distract me from thinking about the fear. I spend a lot of time trying to dry my palms, counting my beating pulses and making sure I am still breathing.

This fear is not altogether a bad thing. It may, in fact, be necessary. There is no way to back out of it. The only movement possible is forward movement.

In three days I leave for Leningrad. I am expected. In certain ways, the news of the trip has been communicated. Perhaps a gathering is planned. The message transmitted to the Jews was that "a special gift will arrive." I am that gift.

There are questions here of courage and responsibility. Perhaps questions of vengeance and retribution, certainly questions of vanity.

The fear must serve to move me. Without it I might well falter. I might even cry.

I coordinate all parts of my mind and body to restrain the tears. Tears no longer comfort me. They are not cleansing, not any more. Retracting my eye muscles, lids half closed, the tears are blockaded in their ducts. They are hot and painful and I can't see through them.

It seems as if all my life I've been afraid of one thing or another. Those other times of unnamed fear were not productive. Identifiable fear makes me feel foolish. It has no redeeming value. Being afraid, for example, of losing a job or being poor is just depressing.

But this pervasive fear animates; it has a life of its own.

There's no corner that I turn that brings relief.

Sleep. I've never slept well, but lately it's impossible. I have seen people, men, who sleep well. I have been with men who arrange themselves for sleep. They yawn, perhaps stretch, plump their pillow, smile good night. While I watch, they fall asleep. I've always considered it rather insulting. In the morning they ask, "Did you sleep well?" "Wonderfully," I reply in a husky satisfied voice.

And then they hold me.

It embarrasses me that I have trouble sleeping. I resent my insomnia, particularly when I am with a man. Sometimes they fall asleep when I'm talking to them. I try to arouse them sexually from their stupor, not out of any real interest in the sex, but so they will not fall asleep.

Casually, I have asked my lovers, "What do you think about before you go to sleep?" (All I can think about is that I am not falling asleep.)

This question startles them. Mostly, it would seem, they don't know what they think about. They don't consider it anything remarkable to fall asleep. One told me that he looked down a long dark tunnel and by the time he imagined the light at the end of the tunnel, he was asleep. I have looked down that tunnel. It didn't work. The fact is I've never slept with a man who didn't fall asleep before I did. If I ever meet one, I will definitely stay with him.

Even when I am not frightened all the time, I have trouble sleeping. But now it's all I can do to monitor my vital signs, listen to the ringing in my ears and try to swallow past the lump in my throat. I suppose I finally exhaust myself with all this somatic censoring because eventually I do sleep.

One reason I hate to fall asleep is that I hate to wake up. Frequently my eyes will not open. At first I thought I might force them open but found I couldn't move my hands either. So I wake, eyelids glued shut, hands paralyzed, and wait for it to pass.

Another bad thing is my dreams. In the deranged instant between sleep and wakefulness, I lie numbed and leaden, clawing my way out of my dreams. Lying very still, I fish around in my mind, trying to spear some details of the dream. But the dream trickles away and turns to dread. And I know only that I've dreamed some terrible dream.

The dread comes on slowly like a blush.

Last night Mother was in my dream. I remember nothing but her face. But I sense it was a terrible dream. I rarely dream of my mother or of any of my family. When I do it's always the same. Whatever the form of the dream, the meaning is clear. In the dream I know that she is leaving or dying or that they are all leaving or dying. I feel alone and helpless. I want to ask them not to leave me. Sometimes it occurs to me that they are waiting for me to ask them to stay. Nevertheless, I am indecisive. Jean, my dead brother, was also in the dream.

Trapped in my body, with only my mind working, I'm becoming impatient.

The clock radio has gone off and the weatherman is announcing "Cold, and possible storms." My bedroom is freezing.

There, one lid is unstuck. With my good eye—there's no particular rush to open the other—I glance at the clock: 7:15, as usual. I can see my breath in the cold room and blow a breath ring with perfect precision. Now the other eye wants to open. It can wait awhile.

With my one good eye, I survey my clothes lying in their seasonal piles around the room. It's 0° in Leningrad. I know that, but still I have laid out a spring and summer wardrobe. Everything I own is scattered around the room waiting to be packed.

My bedroom faces the street. In the morning, the sunlight streams in before the tall adjacent buildings block it out. I like winter sun; in its duel with the snow it seems brighter for its combat. A beam of sunlight moves slowly across the room, across the dresser where the pictures of my family are propped. One after the other. They are spotlighted by the beam until they disappear into the glare. Fascinated, I watch as the images become black places in the frame.

Damn, Mother was in the dream all right.

But all I have left is a tangle of images, as twisted as the tangle of my hair, which lies curled and matted on the pillow. It's a nervous habit I have, twisting my hair. I hate it. But the smooth strands that I crush between my fingers comfort me. I form the strands into little balls and push them in and out, in and out. What I hate is the snarls they leave. That, and the fact that I can't stop doing it. Sticking up all around me, they leave little curlicues of hair. I want to look nice and neat, and I never can because my hair is always in disarray.

Sam used to tell me that the sound reminded him of a mouse gnawing away. That made me shudder, but still my fingers love to rhythmically quash the silky threads. Many times I've tried to stop. No use, my fingers seem to long for it. I do hate it, but it comforts me.

My back aches. Although Sam has been gone eight years, I still sleep on "my side," back protruding off the edge of the bed. It aches in the morning from hanging unsupported. At night I center myself on the bed but awake crouched on the edge.

Sam was a sleep addict. It was almost a religion with him. He didn't fall asleep so much as he seemed to suck it in. Lying on his back, mouth open, taking small gasps of sleep, soon he would emit his light snore. It's one thing to be able to fall asleep easily—but how arrogant to revel in the process.

This room is really cold. I have to go to the bathroom. I always have to go to the bathroom when I wake up. That, and the fact that I am certain that I have bad breath in the morning, have prevented me from having morning sex all my life. I thought that this was another of my life secrets until one morning Jason, trying to hold me as I squirmed out of bed, said, "I like the way you smell in the morning." I turned to look at him and he was grinning. I wonder how many of my other secrets are known to others?

Now that I'm older, I regret having relinquished my secrets. There are just a few left. Secrets that seemed important years ago I let slip at various times. The impact was never very great, not nearly equal to the sweet, lonely possession of the secret. Some slipped through boredom, some through a need to shock. Others I told in a convivial rush of warmth and companionship. Some of my secrets I thought would bring me love. Others I knew would bring me pain.

It was all a betrayal. I should never have told any of them. If I hadn't, I would be a happier person now, more complete, less known.

But I was frivolous, sometimes desperate and always anxious to please.

There are people who confront me with a glance to remind me they know. Ordinary people who were once important to me. They diminish me. They know.

Still, I have some secrets left and I doubt now that I will ever give those up. I do wonder, though, if they are true secrets or if, like my sour morning breath, they are just ordinary things that people don't talk about. Of course, I can't find out without revealing more of my secrets.

When I was a child I tended to my own body. It gave me pleasure to bite my toenails, ripping them straight across, leaving the edges jagged. I would suck on the nail parings, sometimes spitting them out, sometimes chewing them to a fine grain and swallowing them. Now, of course, I can't reach my mouth to my toes and have to be content with tending myself in less agile ways.

I am not one of those people who think about the slow decay of my body, not at all. I like the smell of my farts, the odor under my arms, the look of my shit, the texture of my vaginal discharge, the stubble on my legs, the wax in my ears, my dandruff, the sleepers in my eyes, the fuzz in my belly button, the scabs on my cuts. I breathe in my odors and eat my excretions. They comfort me.

At the end of my labor with my daughter, June, immaculate nurses in an immaculate delivery room were urging me to bear down.

"Bear down," they said, "just keep pushing down. Don't be embarrassed. Thatagirl, just push down." Irish nurses in clean white uniforms. Were they surprised that I didn't care that with each push I had diarrhea, that I vomited without waiting for a bedpan whenever another wave of pain hit me? My labor bed was filled with urine and vomit and shit. I sloshed around in it gleefully, pushing out more and more until, finally, June was born into that first crib of human excrement.

One of the few thoughts that penetrates my present terror is the knowledge that I will be taking my body with me to Leningrad. Whatever happens there, I will have my own secret ways of comforting myself. My body has never been my enemy. I trust in it absolutely and rely on its familiarity.

This is not the case with my mind, where I am limited by those chronic human needs that must be served. Insidious quixotic needs, boring in their redundancy. I want to be loved, liked, stroked, telephoned, listened to, wined, dined, adored, respected—to be central.

My father, who viewed all emotions as banal, was not a man to indulge those needs. He told me shortly before he died: "We are, all of us, both observer and participant. Well-meaning people will tell you that life is meant to be lived, that you should fling yourself into it. Now I see this as a conspiracy. The participants have to seduce the rest of us because most people have limited imaginations and limited intellect. For them, participation equals existence. They will

urge you to get involved, commit yourself, dedicate yourself—to care. Hypocrites. They are hypocrites. Worse, they
are wrong."

And then in a gentle way he cautioned me, "They
proselytize well, Susan, but don't be misled. Stay out of it,
Susan. Make your own circumstances, don't get trapped by
others. The closer you come to maintaining your observer
status, the happier you will be."

My father was an infrequent commentator on life and, of
course, one tends to put more stock in the pronouncements of
taciturn men.

My mother was quite the opposite. Eventually, my
mother told me everything.

2

My mother told me everything.

Until the day she stopped talking, my mother told me all the facts, thoughts, dreams and horrors of her life. She spoke extravagantly, compulsively, not seeming to care whether I was listening or whether my mind was wandering. She built a fortress of words around her—the words were everything. Meaning was nothing, a casual consideration.

After a while I would confront her with her own conflicting stories. But even I came to see that simple truth was nothing.

She couldn't stop talking. Sitting restlessly in a chair or pacing a room, she was like a playwright. She set the stage and played all the roles. She spoke in dialogue. In that way she did not have to describe the particular tone of voice, or the nuance of a phrase. She was writer, actor, director, master producer.

At first I was flattered that my mother confided in me. Later, I was shocked, nauseated, and became cruel myself, trying to stop her stories. Later, when I was older, the words took on meaning and emotion; the contradictions corroded all reason. I crossed my eyes and constricted the muscles in my inner ear, but still I heard it all.

MOTHER: I blame your father for Jean's death.

SUSAN: What should he have done?

MOTHER: He should have ordered Jean to go with us where we at least had a chance of being safe.

SUSAN: Jean was twenty. How could Father have ordered him to hide with us? Jean wanted to stay in Paris. He wanted to fight for France, to be part of the Resistance.

MOTHER: From the time Jean was born your father always took him from me. Even when Jean was a baby your father would come home from work and immediately take him from my arms. He was so proud to have a son. Jean was sensitive, almost fragile, but your father only cared that he behave like a son, like his idea of a man.

SUSAN: It was all so long ago. Thirty years. Why do you go over it again and again? I know how much you suffered but can't you put an end to some of your suffering now?

MOTHER: It doesn't seem long ago. You were two. Every day I listened to the reports. Storm troopers and fallen countries, as if countries could be felled like trees. What did I care then for these strange countries, Poland, Czechoslovakia? What did it have to do with me, with our lovely home in Paris, with our family and friends? Finally I stopped listening, but the men listened. All the time it was getting closer. I could hear them arguing in the next room, what to do. It seemed inconceivable that France would fall. But your father was the smartest of them all. He had made arrangements for us to go to the farm house. I begged him to leave with us. He wouldn't do it. Hypocrite. Poseur. Everything for appearance, even abandoning his family. He ignored me and made Jean stay with him.

SUSAN: What else could he have done? Did you expect him to go and hide with us?

MOTHER: Well, he was so smart. The only one of his friends to make arrangements for his family. Such a smart man, your father. I begged him and Jean to come with us. I told them I wouldn't go unless they did. Do you think I didn't love France? Did you think I wanted to leave? But even I could see it was hopeless. We had begun to hear the stories of the death camps by that time. It was so difficult to know what to believe. Finally I left with you. Your father convinced me he would join us soon. I went for your sake. If it hadn't been for you I would have stayed with him.

SUSAN: Father saved our lives. Because he refused to listen to you, we're alive today.

MOTHER: So is he. Of course it doesn't please him to be alive. But there it is, he survived.

SUSAN: Has he ever told you what it was like? I've asked him but he never speaks of it.

MOTHER: No, he doesn't like to speak of it. They were all so smart, all the men. Your father and Jean joined the underground. Meetings at night, secrecy, hushed voices. I think they enjoyed that really.

SUSAN: Father tried to do the right thing.

MOTHER: I know it's the fashion now to think of all those dead boys as heroes, but that's not the way it was. If he wanted to stay, perhaps that was his business, but he should have demanded that Jean go with us.

SUSAN: But no one else in the family listened to him either. They all stayed.

MOTHER: Yes, it's true. My father didn't believe him. For that matter neither did his father, not that I ever liked him. They were convinced they would be all right. After all, a banker and a shopkeeper. Your father was a very sarcastic man then. 'Banker,' he laughed, 'do you think the Nazis will not kill a Jewish banker? What is it to them? They will kill you and steal the gold fillings from your teeth and then they will be the bankers.'

SUSAN: He knew from the underground that they were coming. Can't you be grateful that he saved us at least? He tried to save the others. They wouldn't listen.

MOTHER: Underground? What romantic notions you have. The underground was a propaganda machine for young boys. How many did these undergrounds save? In Berlin? In Warsaw? I spat on the underground. I told Jean he would make no difference. One boy makes no difference. Not one, not a thousand. In the end everything was smashed. By that time we were gone, the two of us, leaving all the family still in Paris. And when the Paris tree was felled, the underground watched and took a few pot shots from behind the tree. Nothing. It did not change one thing.

SUSAN: I don't understand. Maybe looking back it seems as if father should have acted differently, but how could he know that then? Whatever else, he did save our lives.

MOTHER: You make too much of that.

She spoke about Father in the third person, even when he was sitting in the room. Did he hear her? Was he listening? Sitting at night in the large easy chair reading, the dim light sealed him in his own shadow.

He said nothing. Sometimes he would glance up, his

forehead creased in thought and, a moment later, return to his book. Was he so engrossed in his book he didn't hear her?

I know that he had body wounds. His number from the camp printed into his forearm was half exposed when he rolled up his shirt sleeve. Oh, I was so curious about his body wounds. How could I ask? She told me everything. What would have been his answers?

My childhood was only an extension of the birth process. Desperate to hold onto my mother, she pushed me, writhing and squirming, out of her womb. Then, a doctor cut the cord. Later, there would be many hands with long knives cutting me off. Kind hands who warned: "Forget her. Take care of yourself. You can't help her. No one can help her." And cruel hands that taunted:

"Mrs. Weill is a weirdo,
Mrs. Weill is a weirdo."

I felt ashamed. My mother, ranting, smelled of rotting fruit. My father had a number on his arm. I was ashamed. I held on as long as I could, burrowing into my mother's soft body. Walking up behind her in the kitchen, I kissed her neck, lingering over her sweet smell. A drop of sweat fell from her brow. I caught it with my tongue.

Once, only once I touched his number. He looked at me surprised, and shook his head as if to say, "Don't ask me."

I held on as long as I could. I didn't want to move away from those small comforts. There were too many hands and their knives were sharp and long. They told me then, those conscientious cleavers, that it was, after all, for my own good.

3

I am beginning to relax a little now that my eyes are open and the first wave of dread has abated. I wish I was still a list maker, neat check marks next to an inventory of what I will take to Leningrad, like packing for summer camp. I want to be certain I come back intact.

My bedroom has a transient look. Clothes are strewn around, as if I am not certain whether I am staying or going, just moving in or leaving.

My telephone has a loud ring; the gizmo on the bottom that is supposed to turn it softer is broken. Long before the first ring is over, I feel a new panic. Little good comes of the telephone, particularly lately. It's 7:31. There have been times when I haven't answered the telephone—just watched it ring, faintly curious, but sufficiently detached not to pick it up. Today, as I reach out for it, my arm is stunned by the cold reception it receives from the room.

"Hello." My voice is hoarse. I clear my voice and say hello again.

"Hi. How are you?"

Marge's voice makes me smile; it's so safe. "What the hell

are you calling me at seven-thirty-one for?" I sound harsh but she knows I am relieved.

"I'm worried about you, Susan."

"I'm worried about me, too."

"I tried to reach you all day yesterday."

"I was at the hospital."

"All day?"

"Except for a brief drink with Jason."

"Oh?"

"What kind of an 'oh' is that? A critical 'oh,' a skeptical 'oh,' a judgmental 'oh'?"

"Just an 'oh.' Did you call him or did he call you?"

"How could he? I was at the hospital."

"So you called him."

"What the hell difference does it make at this stage? For Christ's sake, you sound as if we were all in high school. 'Did he call you? Did you call him?'"

"Okay, so you called him and he took you for a drink. He couldn't afford dinner?"

"He was tied up."

"With What's-her-name?"

"I guess so; I didn't ask. Listen, it was comforting to see him."

"Was it? It isn't for me. Not with Gary. Not for an hour anyway. And then knowing he was leaving to see What's-her-name."

"Crumbs, I like crumbs. Confucius say: 'People who insist on whole cake get icing in their eye.'"

"Pardon me. God forbid you should get icing in your eye."

For a moment there is an uncomfortable silence.

"How is Sam?" Marge asks. "I meant to get up to the hospital yesterday but got tied up."

"He was the same. Terrified. The same. God, he looks lousy."

"Well, when are they going to know something definite? Can't you pin them down?"

"No, I talked with Dr. Rappoport late yesterday. He admits they are all totally stymied by Sam's symptoms. The pain is excruciating, but nothing shows on X-ray. They think it may be a pinched nerve, or some kind of virus attacking the spinal cord. He said if things didn't get any better they would do exploratory surgery. In the meantime Sam is on double doses of morphine."

Marge sighs and makes a small throat sound. Her sigh is for me and what I'm going through, not for Sam.

I reach for a cigarette, light it and take a long drag, blowing smoke into the holes of the telephone receiver.

"What the hell are you going to do, Susan? About the trip, I mean."

"I want to do the right thing. I really do, Marge. For once I want to do it right."

I have lived my life just missing. A myopic shooter, my sight lines are always skewed. Inevitably I miss the mark. I am cautious now about my own judgments. I have miscalculated too often. Wounding and being wounded with arrogant impetuosity, certain at the same time that I would get what I wanted. It hasn't worked out that way. It seems prudent now to try to get those sight lines true.

"Right? Right for you, you mean?"

"Yes, right for me. I am tired of having to regroup, of picking myself up off the floor. You know the way I am. Deluding myself, too lazy or scared just to let the chips fall. I'm always way ahead of the other guy, figuring out what they want and then giving it to them. One step ahead, all the time. Believe me, it's hard work. Even when Jason used to ask me what movie I wanted to see, I was frantically trying to figure out what *he* wanted to see. I used to sneak into the movies I wanted to see in the afternoon, never telling him, of course. The laugh was that often he would then want to see it, too. You want to know how many dumb movies I've seen twice?"

"Hell, we all do that, a little at least."

"Well, I don't do it a little, I do it all the time. I'm very considerate that way, protective, you might say."

"Who are you protecting?"

"Them. Me. They must never think they've disappointed me, or that I'm hard to please. If I'm difficult or contrary, they'll leave. So in the end I guess I'm protecting me. The important thing is not to get left. To that end I will compromise everything. Amazing, isn't it, considering how accommodating I am, that my lovers find me entirely resist-able?"

"You're thinking of Jason, I assume."

"Yes, Jason, certainly Jason. My track record with men will not exactly win gold medals. That's why this trip is so important to me. I have the feeling that if I can do this one job right, cleanly, without manipulation and deceit, maybe it will spill over into the other areas of my life."

"Do you remember what you said last night?" Marge asks.

"No. Did I say something important?"

I don't remember my middle-of-the-night talks with Marge. When I tire of my struggle for sleep and see it's getting on to one in the morning, I take a sleeping pill or two. Lately I have taken to calling Marge just as I get sleepy and liberated from my panic. Sometimes I fall asleep while we are still talking, leaving the phone dangling. Last night, I guess I managed to replace it.

"Well, one thing, you were crying."

"Oh, lordy. About anything in particular?"

"You weren't very coherent. Something about Sam and going back with him, and Jason. Leonid got into the act, too."

"Oh, shit. Listen, I'm sorry. Why don't you just hang up on me when I make those calls?"

"Not a bad idea. I can't stand them. I really can't, Susan. It's like talking to a zombie."

"So hang up. Really, I mean it. I'm not in my right mind anyway."

"As opposed to your waking hours, like now when you are in your right mind? Are you packed?"

"Packed?" I glance around again at the uneven piles. "No, I'm not packed. I can't seem to get my shit together enough to pack."

"Christ. You want me to come over tonight and help? If you can't even get yourself packed . . ." But she lets her thought dangle. Her voice becomes softer as she says, "You're scared, aren't you? I know you're scared, and it's making me scared for you. Can they hurt you over there?"

"I don't think so. I'm sort of scared, but I don't think anything can really happen to me. What can they do to me?"

"I certainly don't know. You're always telling me how dangerous it is for Jews there. You're in the Jewish business; my trade is advertising, remember? They must know who you are. Why'd they give you a visa in the first place?"

"Well, David thinks they just slipped up, or they know who I am and hope they'll get something more on Leonid."

David Hirsch is the executive director of the International Committee for Soviet Jews, of which I am the public relations director. "The Israelis aren't offering any opinion, just a lot of advice about what to do when I get there." Suddenly I am annoyed with myself. "The whole thing is ridiculous. Can you imagine me the victim of an assassination plot?"

"Don't go," Marge says sharply. "Just don't go. You have no obligation. You don't have to go. You're scared shitless. You can't pack, for Christ's sake, just don't go."

"They expect me."

"You're going because they expect you?" she asks incredulously. "That doesn't jibe with what you were saying before."

But she's wrong. It does fit in. At times I wonder if I'm going only for the effect it will produce. I would go farther than Leningrad if it secured the image I would like people to have of me. But maybe this time it's not only that. It suits my purpose to go now, and the fact that it enhances my standing is not the primary reason. It's terrific, but not primary. Whatever happens over there, I know I won't do much good and can't do much harm. The task is simple enough. The thing is to do it right. What's in this for me is exactly that, to restrain my need for centrality. This time I just want to get the job done. To remember I'm not in trouble, the Soviet Jews are, it's not my neck at stake, but theirs. I'm an outsider to their struggle, an observer of their plight. I am not one of them, and cannot really experience their fears. I don't expect to laugh and cry with them, I just want to get the job done.

Also, the idea of leaving appeals to me. For once I would like to be the one who leaves, particularly Jason, particularly now. I think Marge is wrong, but I hesitate to explain further, afraid that I will succumb to her natural skepticism, that my resolve will weaken, that my good intentions are invented.

"Listen, Marge, it's complicated. But I think it's right, for a lot of reasons, among them that they expect me."

"You're doing it again."

"What?"

"Just fulfilling other people's expectations, or what you think are their expectations. What the hell difference does it make? You don't really think you're going to get Leonid released while you're there. There's no good reason for you to go. Except maybe a quick fix for your ego. You'd be amazed, Susan, how little people notice: you seem to think everybody is watching you all the time. Nobody gives a damn. So they expect you. So what? That is not the ultimate criterion most of us are guided by. Other people's expectations are unreliable; you just finished telling me that."

"This is some conversation for seven-forty in the morning. Stop preaching at me."

"Never mind the time. How do you know that Leonid even wants you to come?"

"Well, of course he does. Why wouldn't he?"

"I don't know. Maybe it will cause him more trouble if you go. Maybe you'll get yourself in trouble and then what good will that do anybody?"

"I can't not go because I'm scared."

"Why the hell not? What do you have to prove?"

"It isn't a question of proving anything. Leonid and the others matter to me now. I'd like to do something that transcends Sam and Jason, that is not just an extension of my own problems."

"But do you really have to go to Russia to extricate yourself from Sam and Jason? There's got to be an easier way, I mean, you could just say goodbye, for example."

"I'm not going because I'm running away."

"Well, that's what you make it sound like."

"I can't help how it sounds. I know it's not just running away." Before Marge can answer I change the subject. "Now that that's settled, let me tell you something that will really make your day. I've been thinking about asking Sam to come back."

Marge is silent for a moment. "That's what you said last night, but you're joking. You must be joking."

"No, I've been thinking about it."

"He's really not your responsibility any more, Susan."

"Oh, it's not a question of my feeling responsible. Although I do feel awful for him. No, it would be because I want to. Because Sam may be, in the end, the best of the compromises I can make. Anyway, I'm just thinking about it."

"Well, don't do anything rash, for God's sake. Look, dinner tonight or tomorrow night? I'd like to talk more, but I can't now. Goddammit, it would be nice if one or two of your crises could be settled. I've got a few things on my mind, too."

"Gary?" I ask.

"Gary."

"But I thought everything was terrific with Gary."

Gary Franklin is Marge's married lover. I've met him a few times, seems a nice fellow. Crazy about Marge. Sends her flowers, calls her half a dozen times a day, long lunches, cocktails, presents. Like all married lovers, he keeps running in place.

I have had a few of them myself. After the first one or two, you get used to it. Agonized protestations of love, but how can he leave his wife who is too deeply in love with him, too dependent, too vulnerable, too fragile, would surely fall apart (perhaps kill herself) if he were to suggest life with her was less than ideal. Nodding, I marvel that all those wives, in sexless marriages (they never, never sleep with their wives, of course, haven't for years), fail to notice that their marriages are perhaps slightly flawed. But no, according to Married

Men, they, the innocent wives, are far too . . . well . . . nice to mention, notice, such a minor matter. "But," I would reply, "it's so unfair, you're making the decisions for both of you and only you have the facts. Tell her about me, or at least tell her you're unhappy, and let her be part of the decision."

"Madness," they say sadly, shaking their heads. She must be protected at all costs.

"But maybe she won't want you if she knows; maybe she will find someone else."

"Never, not her. No, she loves me. God, how I wish she were unfaithful. But she isn't, she is wonderful, she hasn't done anything wrong, it's all me."

"Oh, come on, nothing's all that one-sided."

"This is. She'd never make it if I left her."

"Maybe she would."

"Never, not her."

"Well, then give me up. Go home, try again."

"No, I can't give you up. Give me time, a little more time."

And so it goes, with the first few. But Marge and I survived the first few, the endings are equally predictable.

"You deserve more," he says, sipping his martini at lunch. "You know I love you, but I can't keep on making you miserable."

"It's okay. I'm not so miserable."

"Yes, you are, what kind of life is it? Saturday nights, holidays—all alone. I'm never there when you need me."

I shudder. "Listen, I love you, I'll wait."

"No, you're too good for me." (I must have become too wifelike.) "It kills me to say this, but I'll understand if you find someone else."

This conversation occurs only when the ball, for some reason, is definitely in his court.

"I don't want anyone else," I insist.

"Not now maybe. But you will. You'll see, you'll forget me, in time."

How much time, I want to know. A couple of weeks, okay. But I have the feeling he thinks it will be years, years of yearning for him. Anyway, as it turns out, we're both right. I do find someone else, and I don't forget him. How can I when I'm having the same damn conversation all over again? Different husband, different wife, same conversation.

But Marge and I are too old for this now. We know the rules. We don't have those conversations any more. Quite the opposite, those anguished protestations are now met with compassion. We're on *her* side. Married men who find themselves in this position are doubly cursed. Their wives do not care enough to demand a showdown, neither do their lovers. Occasionally they become desperate at this double rejection and make little administrative errors that they hope will force the issue. She is too fragile, and we're strong. The proof of this is that we're the ones with married lovers. All women with married lovers are, by definition, stronger than wives. Even wives with married lovers are stronger than wives without married lovers. Gary and Marge had, I thought, a perfect understanding. No questions about his leaving Marsha, his wife.

"So what's the matter with Gary?"

"He's busy, very busy. Too busy to even celebrate my birthday on the day—a few days later, he says. Well, dammit, I want to celebrate my birthday on the day of my birthday. It's a Monday, for Christ's sake, a Monday. Now that's not breaking the rules, is it?"

"I guess not, but why can't he?"

"Because they have theater tickets."

"Well . . ."

"Fuck the theater tickets, I told him. Get out of it. It's the first birthday in the three years we've been seeing each other that didn't fall on a weekend. A Monday, that's fair."

"He won't?"

"I don't know yet. But it started me thinking about a lot of things. And we're having drinks later. I'm going to present him with a bill of particulars."

"Such as?"

"Such as, I want at least six sleepovers a year, and two long weekends, and one week, one solid week."

"My God, you drive a hard bargain."

"I'm serious about this. That's it. Those are my demands. Take it or leave it. God knows I don't want him to leave Marsha, I like Marsha, I don't even want him for a husband."

"You don't? If he asked you tonight to marry him you'd say no?"

"Yes. No, who knows? Anyway, he isn't going to ask me and I'm going to get some of what I want. You think it's too much?"

"No, just about right. Except for the week. How in hell is he going to manage that?"

"That's my negotiating point."

We both laugh. "Good luck. I'll bet he buys it. Marge, do you love him?"

"Love? Him? Yes, I love him. Too damn much, I guess. Sure I love him. I'll tell you this, it's the best sex I've ever had."

I wish I could ask her to explain this. I wish I knew what Marge's idea of "best sex" was. Can it be that she and Gary have what Jason and I have? I wonder about Gary's lovemaking for a moment, trying to picture him making love to Marge. But Jason appears instead. It is impossible to imagine sex without Jason appearing.

"You know, Marge, I think he really loves you. Don't be too hard on him."

"Oh, I know he loves me. But I'm hurt, I wanted that birthday celebration. It is a Monday."

"I'm sorry, Marge, I really am."

Marge is in no mood for sympathy, however, and brushes it off. "Oh, I'm all right. Fine, really."

A few times in the nearly twenty years I have known her I have seen Marge lose control of herself—just a few. Even then it was controlled, a crisp handkerchief dabbing at her tears, neat hair. Altogether, Marge is a very tidy person.

"Well, Susan . . ." She sounds tentative. A kind of awkwardness has set in between us. "I'll call you later. I've got nothing but meetings, so I'll call you."

Marge owns an advertising agency that she inherited from her father and it, too, is neat. She has built it into a successful business by being decisive and hard, which is nothing at all like the Marge I know.

Predictability is a necessary ingredient for a close friendship. People stake out territorial imperatives. So it is that ceded to Marge are: being richer, smarter and emotionally stable. I got the leftovers. Causes: sex and being Jewish.

I have often worried about the inequities in our friendship, but it's tempered by this memory: Ten years or so ago, when Marge was still married to her first husband and I was married to Sam, we drove to the Cape for a vacation. It was fall and we had not expected to be able to swim and Marge had not brought a bathing suit. We stopped at a small dry-goods store on the road so that she could pick one up. She was in the dressing room, which had a curtain to shield it from the rest of the store, trying on bathing suits, when I slipped in to see if I could help. She didn't see me, but I saw her agonized face reflected in the mirror, tugging and pulling at the bathing suit that wouldn't stretch over her ample hips. I slipped out again before she knew I was there.

I light another cigarette. It tastes terrible.

Maybe Jason will call. I have to go to the bathroom. I'll wait awhile. I don't want to miss his call.

I should call the hospital to see how Sam is, but I don't want to tie up the phone in case Jason calls.

Maybe Marge is right. Why should I go? If Jason calls right this minute I won't go. For a moment I am filled with the magical anticipation of Jason's call canceling the trip. The phone does not ring. Of course, it's not Jason's pattern to call this early in the morning. I used to log the times he called me. No, it's not his pattern to call this early.

The phone rings and I wonder if I've tricked Jason by being so certain he wouldn't call.

"Susan, honey, did I wake you?"

It's Joel Simmons, television producer, recent lover, and benefactor of this trip.

"No, I'm awake." (It's a silly question. Does anybody ever admit they're sleeping?) "What's up?"

"I want you to meet me today to get the cameras and I've got somebody lined up to give you a quick course in eight-millimeter film. What time can you make it?"

"I'm not sure. I have to go to the hospital and then I'll have a better idea of what my day looks like. Suppose I call you as soon as I know."

"Yeah, okay, but listen, Susan, you've got to take this seriously. It's not easy; you have to know how to load it and hold it so you get us some decent footage."

"I think I can master that all right, Joel. I'll call you as soon as I know I'll be free."

The trouble is, I am a marginal person. I try too hard and

it shows. I don't know enough about practically anything and it seems too late to catch up.

I talk good and I fuck good and I've come to rely on talking and fucking to manipulate all of the other things in my life. Either on my feet or in bed, I feel secure.

A month ago I talked and screwed my way into this situation and now I can't even pack my suitcase.

In room 1472 of the Barclay Hotel, Joel Simmons, producer of TV documentary specials for CBC, and I were enjoying a shared joint after a companionable fuck.

I had met Joel a couple of weeks earlier when I called to see if I could be of help in the documentary he was making on Leonid Rabinovitz. It was the kind of call I hate most. Joel is important, a power in the television industry. Much of my job is to see to it that the name of the I.C.S.J. gets before the public. It seems a feeble way to help. I introduced myself as the coordinator of the Rabinovitz campaign in the United States and it was on that basis that I got through to Joel.

From the first he seemed interested and I met him several days later, taking with me my files on Leonid and several pictures. Because Leonid is a violinist, we had been able to mobilize many people in the entertainment world in an ad hoc committee. I was to be the link between Joel Simmons and Paul Newman. Well, Paul Newman was on the committee, had signed his name to the petition. But at the times I tried to reach him, his wife explained to me, "He's in the sauna."

I was not, however, inclined to disabuse Joel about my connections in the entertainment industry and we sat for several hours trying to decide whether Paul or Dusty or Hal or Clive would be best for the program.

By the time that afternoon was over, I was practically a

consultant on the program. I do talk well. I am good.

So there we were, musing about the special on the Rabinovitzes when I said, "It's too bad we can't get current film on them. Film shot now, in their apartment."

Joel sat up and replied, "Why can't we? We've got enough time. We'll send someone in and let them take some home movies."

He was really excited about the idea. (More excited than he was about the fucking.)

"It has to be someone they can trust. Someone they will talk to," I replied. There was a moment of silence when it struck the two of us that I would be the ideal person.

"You?" Joel asked, passing me the joint.

"I would love it," I said. "It will cost a lot of money."

Joel smiled. "What's a lot of money, Susan?"

"Oh, two thousand, I guess."

He laughed out loud then. "Susan, dear, two thousand dollars for a prime-time television show is coffee-break money."

So, I'll go. I am expected. What I know of Leonid and the others I have learned from their letters and appeals. Several times before Leonid's phone was disconnected I spoke with him. His appeals have a voice. I can hear the desperate tone behind those written words. It's all I know about them and the others. Perhaps they are not nice people. Maybe selfish and mean. I don't know. I only know what they have written in their letters and appeals. What does it matter anyway? For all the Soviet Jews, we have only their appeals and perhaps a blurred picture or the memory of a voice on the phone.

Because Leonid is famous there has been much attention focused upon him. He is observed by international organizations which, occasionally, in polite tones, ask for his release.

There is conversation about him in high places in our government. He is becoming a political thorn in détente. Sometimes I wish he would just go away, preferably quietly. Other times I have worked day and night to coordinate letters and demonstrations on his behalf. Always having to call people to ask for help and being turned down:

"Sorry, I'm too busy."

"Sorry, I'm helping the Chileans."

"Sorry, I don't want to get mixed up."

"Sorry, this is my month for Bangladesh."

"Sorry, I'm planning to go on tour to Russia."

Who can blame them? We all have our our own lives to lead.

I blame them. I hate them.

I'll give Jason five more minutes. If he calls in five minutes, I won't go.

My mother told me everything:

MOTHER: Don't forget, Susan, today we light a *yahrzeit* candle for Jean.

SUSAN: It's always so painful for Father. Couldn't we just not do it this year? It hurts Daddy so much.

MOTHER: Jean must be remembered. Even after I'm gone I want you to swear to me that you'll always light the candle. You know your father was in the room when Jean was born. Of course he didn't assist with the delivery but we had such fun. He was wearing his white coat and a mask and joking with the doctors and nurses. I think he wanted very much to deliver his own son but of course that was just not done. The moment Jean was born I heard someone say, "It's a boy." I was so relieved. I wanted to please your father and I knew he wanted a son. He came and kissed me and thanked me for giving him a son.

SUSAN: Don't light the candle this year, Mother. It hurts Daddy too much.

MOTHER: He was there when Jean was born and he was there when Jean died. I think until that last roundup they all thought it was a game. A war game. They were together when the S.S. came. Your father had made himself conspicuous with his daring in the underground. He was not content just to tend to the wounded. No, he was one of the planners. By that time the S.S. knew who he was.

SUSAN: It must have been terrifying for him. Think about *him.*

MOTHER: I think about it all the time. I think of nothing else. First herded and jammed into trains, trying to keep their spirits up by singing, telling stories. Except after a few days no one sang any more. They just tried to avoid stepping in the filth and vomit and find some place that hadn't been urinated on to rest. They were all professionals, you know, that particular group. It was a reprisal for the activities against an important German officer. Even the doctor who delivered Jean was there.

SUSAN: Do you think Jean would want to be remembered this way, causing Father more pain?

MOTHER: It was a mistake that Jean was there at all. They were rounding up doctors and lawyers but they took Jean, too, because he was with your father. When finally they arrived at Auschwitz they realized their mistake. Jean would be no use to them. He couldn't serve as a doctor. The train doors opened. Your father had linked arms with Jean but still they were pushed out by the rush of the others desperate for fresh air. It's pretty country there. It must have been a relief to see the trees and the grass and be out of the stench of the cars. In the pushing and the shoving they became separated but still your father could see Jean and called to him, "Come stand by me." Jean tried to move to him but was stopped by an S.S. officer. The officer demanded to see his papers. "What? You're not a doctor?" Your father ran to Jean. "Sir, this is my son. Here are my papers. I'm a physician. This is my son." He linked arms again with Jean. The Nazi said to him, "Your son is puny, small. He is of no use," and ordered Jean, "Go there. Go in that line there." Your father tells me he clung to Jean, refusing to be separated from him, pleading, "Please let him stay with me. He is my son," but it was no use. Jean disengaged from your father's grasp and said, "Don't worry, I'll be all right. Take care of yourself. Kiss Mother for me when this is over. I'm not afraid," and walked away to the other line. Your father could see that the other line was filled with old women, small children, weak boys. He knew that it was the death line. The line of those who were of no use to the S.S.

SUSAN: What could he do, Mother? How can you blame him? There were so many on those lines. Why do you torture him all the time?

MOTHER: I don't torture him. I don't have to; he wanted to participate in Jean's birth and he did, and he participated in Jean's death.

SUSAN: Father must have been crazy with grief after that, seeing Jean marched away in the death line.

MOTHER: Perhaps, but not so crazy that he didn't survive. He was, after all, a doctor. He did what they told him to. Can you imagine what those things were, what he did? He doesn't speak of that, even to me. But I have read. I know what he must have done to survive.

SUSAN: Father probably saved many people. Maybe many people lived who wouldn't have because he was a doctor.

MOTHER: I have no doubt of it. Once we had a letter from a man whom your father had saved. I've no doubt he saved many people or at least helped them die more easily. But what difference did that make if he couldn't save his own son?

SUSAN: He saved us, Mother. Doesn't that count for something?

34

5

I was not in this work when Leonid first applied to leave Russia.

It was several months before he could actually make an application. In order to do that he had to receive an invitation from a relative in Israel. An aunt was found for him.

It was then that he began to send out his letters and appeals. I have them all. In those first months he was hopeful. But I was not involved then. Now jammed into my wallet are his latest letters. I take them out and reread them frequently. Am I afraid that I'll forget what they say? Impossible. I have committed them to memory. His letters comfort me. At first they were so hopeful.

Mrs. Lena Rabinovitz
Tel Aviv, Israel

Dear Aunt Lena,

We are rejoicing. At last we have received your invitation to be reunited with our family in Israel. Immediately we began the long process of applying to emigrate. So many papers! At first the papers were refused by the OVIR. It is necessary to obtain character references. One would imagine that this would be an easy matter for me. However, this is not so. All of a sudden, it seems, I am "uncooperative" and "unreliable." This, after so many years of acclaim.

Already Lucia and I are shunned by former colleagues. They are frightened to be associated with us, now that we have declared our intention to emigrate.

I have been informed that I will not be allowed to perform publicly. It has been hinted that I am not of sound mind. All of this troubles us but we are determined to keep our spirits high. We hope you and the family are well and that it will not be too long before we are with you.

Leonid Rabinovitz
December 4, 1973

6

After Sam and I were divorced, there were many men, many jobs. I had no talent for holding either. I drifted from man to man, from job to job.

I often walk around the house replaying conversations with Jason. There was a time when all I had to do was to remember what he said the evening before or the moment before to feel happy. But now that I'm losing him I look further back in time in order to comfort myself.

There were moments in time when I was completely happy. They bear remembering. When I recall them, I breathe slowly through my mouth, hugging myself, my arms around my shoulders, sucking my body inward. A coward's stance. Those moments in time have nothing to do with the present reality. I will preserve and cherish them intact. There are some who, if the promise of a memory is not fulfilled, deny it.

I will not. They are my memories. I keep them safe, cradled.

There, just in front of the dresser, while he was straightening his tie, I, laughing, asked him, "When are you going to marry me anyway?" He raised his eyes to look at my reflection in the mirror. "Soon, sweet girl," he said, "soon."

I met him on a job interview. After Sam and I were divorced, I had several jobs. I did not do well at office work. Often unemployed, I was afraid to stay at home. I went on any interview the employment agency set up, no matter how ridiculous. This one sounded particularly promising: French-speaking assistant to the legal partner of a large brokerage firm.

It was April but the weather was unusually warm. It was the first day I had not worn stockings and I could feel my skirt rubbing against my legs. I had bleached the dark hair on my arms. In the sunlight they appeared to have a golden tone. I shaved under my arms, my legs, up to my crotch. My hair was freshly shampooed. I was smooth all over. Conscious of the panties cupping my buttocks, I felt laundered.

(This is it. I'll get this one, it feels right. I wonder how much to ask for. How could anyone refuse a girl with such lovely blond hair on her arms?)

He stood to greet me, a medium-sized, sleepy-eyed, slightly bending man with a round face, thin lips, and horn-rimmed glasses.

"Mrs. Warner, I am so sorry. We tried to reach you but you had already left."

(Oh, shit, here it comes.) "I suppose this means the job is filled," I said, sitting down anyway.

"Yes. I am really very sorry if we put you out."

"Oh, no. I was going downtown anyway." (How polite I am. He seems like a nice man. Why don't I tell him how much trouble I'm in?)

His name was Jason Lampert and he was acutely uncomfortable. Later I would learn that he suffered greatly from a fear of disappointing people. "Have you been looking for a long time, Mrs. Warner?"

"Oh, a few months. It isn't easy. My credentials are a little difficult to place. That's why I thought this was so perfect." I looked at him half expecting that he would reconsider and tell me that the job was mine.

"I really am sorry," he said. "I know that job hunting can be brutal. Why don't you let me have your résumé in case I hear of something?"

"That's very kind of you," I said pulling out a couple of résumés from my folder. "Really, this is nice of you." We smiled at each other, the tension of the disappointment behind us. He looked at me with what can only be termed frank appreciation. I am not unaccustomed to this look.

There is a certain kind of man who confuses my Mediterranean complexion with his fantasy, the promise of dark, intense sensuality. At the first sign that I have met such a man, I give it all I've got. Large eyes become "riveting," a generous mouth opens slightly, I suck in those cheeks ever so slightly. I do not avoid their eyes; these men are not interested in coyness. And not in blatant sexuality either. They would like me to be the embodiment of raw sexuality (unfulfilled yet of course). They will bring it out in me.

I do not avoid their eyes, but rather seem to ask the question "Are you the one?" I appear to them innocent, unaware of my own vulnerability (they sense, of course, that I am extremely vulnerable). It's a terrific combination when it works, all that untapped sexuality in a disarmingly guileless (but curious and trusting) woman. I wish it worked all the time, but it doesn't. I know perfectly well I can't possibly appeal to all men, but still it smarts a bit when I realize it isn't working.

Jason Lampert was one of those with whom it worked.

Jason looked at his watch. "Mrs. Warner, Susan, if I may, I can't give you a job at the moment but perhaps you would allow me to take you to lunch. Not an equitable substitute, of course, but . . ."

My God, he was beginning to aspire to me. Why not, I am better looking than he is.

The captain called him by name, inquired after his health, and gave him an approving nod for having such an attractive luncheon companion.

Jason guided me through the dimly lit room of an expensive restaurant. I began to feel confident. Metamorphosed from a job applicant into a woman. He, a potential lover rather than a potential employer. I noticed the way he walked: his shoulders slightly stooped, an old man's walk for someone not yet thirty-five. I liked his looks. He sustained his air of gracious formality. We ordered drinks and I began to notice more details about him. He was fair-haired, had freckles on the backs of his hands. Perhaps the most extraordinary thing about him was his voice. He spoke in a careful, well-modulated voice, gliding melodiously over the words. I couldn't imagine him ever shouting. His diction was precise. It was as if he never used contractions. He did, of course, but I didn't hear them. He ordered a bottle of wine, by year, vineyard and importer.

"I'd like to know everything about you, Susan, but I don't want to begin our relationship by asking you to tell me about yourself. Too conventional, too banal. Instead, I'll tell you about yourself. And then, perhaps, you will do the same for me."

I laughed. "Well, I don't know that I require such unconventional beginnings . . ."

"It is a beginning, isn't it?" He smiled, nicely though, not a hint of insolence.

"You were going to tell me my life story, I believe," I said, breaking a breadstick.

40

The waiter hovered.

"Shall I?" Jason asked.

"By all means," I replied.

He ordered superbly, unfalteringly. Whatever the food would taste like, I'd never forget his style.

"Now, I'll begin." He straightened his shoulders; his face turned serious.

"You speak French. So, you were born twenty-eight years ago in a small remote area of Alsace-Lorraine. Your father, an Italian prince, was traveling through the village on his way to Paris when he stopped at a farm for driving instructions. The door was opened by the daughter of the house, a young woman whose beauty was famous throughout the countryside. Although married and an upstanding man, your father could not resist the girl. He fell immediately and profoundly in love with her. Without disclosing who he was, he arranged to lodge at the farm for several days. Your mother, who was as modest as she was beautiful, admired him from the start. Each day they walked the fields, he helped her with her chores, they talked about their dreams. After several days, your mother was in love as well. And finally, one evening, unable to restrain himself any longer, he knocked upon her door. They were friends now and, although a virgin, she was unafraid. Their coupling was exquisite; after, they both wept. That night you were conceived.

"Your father left shortly thereafter, determined to return as soon as he could obtain a divorce. Alas, he was killed a few days later in a motor accident. Before he died, however, he wrote to his lawyers in Italy and told them of his intention to divorce and marry your mother. Upon his death, your mother was notified by one of his lawyers, who took pity on the unsuspecting girl. He turned over a sum of money to your mother when she wrote to him that she was pregnant and you

41

were therefore able to go to school and travel. Your mother, of course, never recovered from the shock and died a few years later from a broken heart.

"Her letter to you upon her death revealed the circumstances of your birth and you traveled to Italy to see your natural grandparents. They received you coldly, but acknowledged you as a grandchild. They explained that they wished to set up a trust fund for you, but you would have to live in America, and never return to see them because your presence caused them embarrassment. You were then sixteen, and even more beautiful than your mother. Too proud to accept money from these grudging relatives, you nevertheless emigrated to America. Once here, you obtained full scholarships to a university, attending to your studies and remaining aloof from other students. You were much sought after, but discouraged suitors. The bitter lesson your mother learned was not lost on you. Your natural talent for writing and drawing flourished and you developed confidence in yourself. Finally, a few years ago you succumbed to the charms of one of your professors. A renowned man in his field, he seemed to adore you. The marriage was pleasant, but you knew something was lacking. You wondered, and still do, if there is a lack in you. You became irritable and discontented. Finally, you left him, as kindly as possible under the circumstances." Jason paused, sipping his wine.

"And then," I asked, "what happened then?"

"Then you came to New York. It is too painful to describe the exploitation you suffered over these last years. Suffice it to say that I understand. Your beauty and pride remain untouched. Like your mother, however, you wait for your prince to come."

"But she died from the princely love," I reminded him.

"But you won't, Susan; you will live happily ever after."

The waiter arrived with the food, and set the plates before us, cautioning, "Hot plates, very hot."

Jason poured more wine. "Well, am I close?" he asked.

I was wrong about this man. I had been deceived by his deferential, almost humble manner. Whatever else, he was no fool.

"I think you've got the essence of it; the details don't matter all that much, do they?" I replied.

"Well, just to set the record straight," he said politely.

"As a matter of fact," I said seriously, "you have got the essence. Early abandonment, death of both parents, crummy marriage, a little exploitation here and there, but waiting for my prince to come."

"Good," he said, satisfied. "Now it's your turn."

I took a sip of wine and began.

"You were born thirty-eight years ago to a family so wealthy even now you use another name so that you will not be a target for kidnapping or, worse, philanthropic solicitation. You resided until you were twenty in one of the many homes your family owned throughout the world. Your private tutors traveled with you. At twenty, you entered Harvard, the only student in its history to be permitted to skip the first two years. You graduated with highest honors, first in your class. You insisted on doing three years at Harvard Law School, although they, too, would have exempted you from the first two years.

"When you were twenty-five, you had a shock. Your father was on the verge of losing all his money. The only way he could be saved was for you to marry the daughter of the family to whom he owed the money. She had long been in love with you, but you had no interest in her. Nevertheless, you married her. Your father was saved, and for a few years you lived compatibly. Because you had not really loved her in the first place, she eventually took a lover. Upon learning this, you divorced her and implored your father to watch his future business deals more carefully.

"You live quietly, building an empire, going to the opera and ballet, and still see your old friends from Harvard. Lately, you have become acutely aware that although you appear to the world to have it all, something is missing. How am I doing?"

"Pretty good, the essence as you would say, a few minor alterations on the details."

"Jason, why are we doing this, I mean all this fantastic storytelling. If it's a line, it's new to me."

"It's not a line, Susan. I like you very much. I won't say more now. It would be foolish. But you sense it, too, I know you do. Simpatico. Let's start with that. There's plenty of time for the real stories, which I assume in both our cases are fairly interesting but not entirely novel. Anyway, as you aptly put it, we've got the essence already."

The restaurant had cleared; we were among the last there. He glanced at his watch. "My God, do you know what time it is?" he asked me. "Two-thirty. I think this is the longest and most pleasant lunch I've ever had. My partners will think I've gone mad. I never do this."

I could sense his ambivalence and half expected him to ask me to spend the afternoon with him. I wanted him to. I almost suggested it, but was not that certain of my hold on him.

"I must get back, and what's worse, I'll be away for several days. I'll call as soon as I return."

We were on the street. I didn't want to leave him, I had no place to go.

44

"Susan," he said, extending his hand, "I'll call you the minute I get back. And good luck with the job hunting, I'm sure you'll find something."

"Thank you, Jason, thank you for lunch."

Stay with me now, I thought, please.

I turned and walked away, counted to ten to make sure I was out of sight and then hailed a cab.

Late that afternoon flowers arrived. As I looked at the card, I realized that they were the first flowers I had ever received. On the card he had written: "These flowers will perish but others will grow. See you soon. Jason."

Sweet thoughtful man. I wrote several thank-you notes, none quite right, and finally ended up sending him one that said: "Dear Jason, Those were the least perishable flowers I have ever received. Thank you. Susan."

Dear Susan,

At·the moment I am on an airplane to Europe. It is not glamorous, but actually a nuisance. Unexpectedly, one of my clients seems not to be able to do without me. So it's Geneva, Paris, London and then home. I have been wondering what present to bring you.

As the plane flies into the darkness, I wish that you were sitting here. I would buy you some champagne, and tell you about all the lovely things to see and do in Europe. Perhaps you've already seen them? No matter, I'll show you them again. Maybe this letter is strange, but hopeful; don't you think?

Fondly,
Jason

Dear Jason,

Of course you won't receive this until you are already back in New York, but still, I feel an urge to write. It keeps the line between us flowing, yes?

I would like to have been on that dark plane. I'm a little frightened of planes so perhaps you would hold my hand. Then, soon, I would be tired (too much champagne) and drift off to sleep on your shoulder. No, I've never really traveled in Europe. I was born in France, but that is another story entirely. It is so splendid to know you think about me. I think about you, too.

Sincerely,
Susan

Jason was a troubled man when I met him. Divorced even more recently than I, he was uncertain of himself. Because he was clever and intellectually facile, his emotional insecurity was a poignant counterpoint to the rest of his life, about which he was arrogant.

We walked in Central Park late at night after dinner on our first date. The dinner had gone well. Because he had sent the flowers and his courtly note, I felt sure of myself. I acted like the woman I wanted to be. We were companionable with each other.

"My wife was crazy," he told me. "I made her crazy. For fourteen years all I cared about was being successful. I left her alone. One day, just after our son was born, he was sick and had a high fever. Clarissa had been up all night with him. I got a call from the office and I left her. She was screaming at me to stay but I left anyway. I wanted to stay; I wanted to take care of our baby, but I had to go to the office. That was just one time. There were so many others. She needed me to love her and I did love her but I couldn't give her what she wanted. She thought I was ashamed of her. She asked me to draw up reading lists and she went back to school. I thought that was what she wanted to do but somehow it got turned around into an accusation. I wasn't ashamed of her. I certainly didn't care about her college degree but I could never convince her of that."

We stopped and spread our coats on the grass. It was a dark night and in the distance we could hear traffic sounds. We sat not touching, peering through the mosaic of leaves above us. The more he told me about himself the stronger I felt. In the telling he was appealing to me to understand. I felt honored, as if he were bestowing in his plea some kind of prize. I didn't want to say much. It was enough that I nodded occasionally or smiled. Although he never once said a word, I knew he thought I was beautiful. I had never really felt beautiful before. Attractive sometimes, but not this kind of beauty. This was the kind that gave me power.

"The thing is I am always fragmented," he said in a restrained way. He always spoke so that the words had to have meaning because there was no special tone attached to them. His restraint made me even more eager to touch him. I would change that passive, melodic voice.

"Whatever I do, whatever my own expectations are of fathering or husbanding or lawyering or loving, if I chose one, the others suffer. There is no way to cover all the ground. I feel like a poor man's Clark Kent rushing around changing feelings and attitudes, trying to please everyone. It doesn't work."

"Do you ever try to please yourself?" I asked him.

"Oh, sure, except that I am not very certain what pleases me. The things that used to please me are not so wonderful any more. But when I find out what pleases me, I am going to please the hell out of myself. Listen, I must be boring you stiff." Reaching out to touch my cheek, he said with some amazement, "What a sweet girl you are to listen."

"I'm not bored. Finish it, tell me the rest."

"There isn't much more. She started to drink. Whatever the reasons, whether or not I drove her to it, before long she was a drunk. During the day I was a civilized, respected, successful businessman. At night I went home and fought with my wife. Frequently she wasn't there but over at a neighbor's drinking. She used to hit me, slamming her fists at me until I had to grab her arms to stop her. I did not hit her back but the things we said to each other . . ." He shook his head. "All I could do was leave. She was glad, I think, except at the end, that last day. We had not fought that day. I was packing. The house was peaceful. She sat on the bed watching me pack, sober, in clean jeans and a checkered shirt and said, 'Jason, I never believed you would abandon me completely.' It would have been better for me if she had been drunk then and crazy. I almost stayed, but it was too late."

I felt sorry for his wife but then very quickly felt jealous that perhaps he still cared for her. Whatever the simple truth of Jason Lampert's marriage was, it couldn't matter to me. He was asking me to choose between him and his wife. His words were self-accusatory, but invited contradiction. I understood that completely, having rehearsed my own dismal marriage many times. I, too, seemed to blame myself, but sought relief in the predictable response of a solicitous suitor.

If I had met her, Clarissa, in some casual way and she had told me the same story in the same words, I would have been entirely sympathetic to her. But if he was to be my new love, I would have to conspire with him to assuage his guilt.

I did not love him then. I did not feel much sympathy for him or even much attraction. If I hadn't been so beautiful that night, so sure of myself, I might have stood up and said, "That really is a dismal story and you are a dismal man. A lady like me wouldn't have anything to do with the likes of you."

If I did that, of course, I wouldn't be beautiful any more. An answer was required. "You blame yourself too much," I said. "Fifty percent. That's all you're entitled to. It's really quite arrogant of you to assess yourself more than fifty percent of the blame."

"You don't think I am a monster?" He was lying on his jacket and I bent over and kissed him.

"Listen, monster," I said, "it's very late."

"Come home with me?" he asked.

"No, not tonight."

We kissed again. He held me close to him; a button on his jacket was pressing against my nipple. I felt stirred, if not aroused. Gently pulling away from him I thought, So that will be good too. Even that will be good.

8

Once I accepted the premise that Jason was the man I wanted, the one who would save me, the rest was easy. Like adjusting to a new pair of glasses, I was soon able to see him as I wanted him to be.

There was no courting period. No gradual deepening from affection to love. We set each other up. Our investment in each other was, at first, simple. He made me beautiful and I made him right. The instant I was beautiful, I believed in my power.

By the end of the week we were seeing each other every night. He stayed over, making friends with June, singing her lullabies with lyrics he made up. Maybe he made June feel beautiful, too. Anyway, she seemed to care for him.

It was power I discovered that first night we went to bed. We were at his apartment and I went directly into the bedroom, taking off my clothes, flipping back the covers on the bed and sliding in to wait for him. The time for modesty was over. I could see he felt awkward as I watched him taking off his clothes. Boxer shorts and long hose. I had been married to a peasant in jockey shorts and short socks. He sat on the bed, bending over to kiss me and I pushed him gently down onto the pillow. "You just lie there," I said. "Jason, you just lie there." I began to kiss his mouth, little small biting kisses. He put his hands on my face. "No," I said, "you just lie there." I was a beautiful woman with my first sense of sexual command. I knew exactly what to do. There was no hesitation. No embarrassment.

I moved my mouth over his eyes and closed them with my tongue, slowly moved to lick his cheeks and over the bridge of his nose, leaving a trail of wetness. My hands were stroking his shoulders and I moved my mouth down to lick his shoulders. I left him covered with faint dew. An endless supply of moisture flowed from my mouth. Licking down his arm I stopped to suck at the inside of his elbow. I pricked his skin lightly with my teeth as I sucked. The inside of his elbow was a place, all right, tripping nerves in the rest of his body. He moved a little and moaned a little. "That's a good place, Jason, right?" Before he could answer, my mouth was on his again, sucking his tongue and biting a little harder. My hands moved to his crotch, my breast rubbing against his cock. He tried to position me so he could enter me. "We've just begun, Jason, just begun," I said in a chiding tone.

"I want you now, Susan."

(There, that's what I was looking for. Not so restrained any more, are you?) "Sure you do, but not yet. Soon. You just lie there and relax."

I moved my mouth down to his chest, drifting over it, leaving that moisture on his chest hair. Pausing for just a minute I contemplated my next move and then quickly, like an eagle after prey, began to lick and suck his left nipple. How did I know that? I had never before thought about men and nipples.

52

But I did know it. I knew it would make him wild. I knew he would have to have it. "Do you like that, Jason?" I said, biting the nipple hard and then swallowing his whole breast. He grabbed my hair. Was he afraid I would stop? I shook myself free and admonished him in a quiet voice. "Jason, now I told you, you just lie there." I toured his body. I felt his nipple. It was still hard.

He was squirming under me. "Susan, I never felt anything like this. What the hell are you doing to me?"

"You just remember it all, Jason. I want you to remember it. Then you can do the same to me." I moved my mouth to his right nipple and forced his hand down over to his own left breast. He didn't want to touch himself. But I held his hand there. Soon, he was playing with his own nipple.

Every part of him was swollen. I saw him move his hand down to his cock. "Not there, Jason, I'll do that." And I forced his hand down to his balls. "Now you just play with them and I'll do the rest." I slithered down his body—wet mouth leaving tracks of wetness—and slipped my mouth onto his cock. Gentle and easy, my mouth its natural shield, I took more and more of it until my face was pressed to his groin. My tongue was working his cock. My teeth had a life of their own, scraping against the sides. I held his hand over his balls and soon he was clutching at them.

I shook my hair loose, the skein like a net covering us.

Every time he wanted to come, I pulled back and he, having no words, made animal noises that I wanted to hear.

I wasn't tired, I wasn't particularly sexually excited. I wanted him to make more noises, to want me even more. With one final sucking I left his cock and moved my mouth over his hand which was still fondling his balls. I started to kiss his hands. He wanted to stop touching himself, now conscious of what he was doing, but I held his hands there and moved my mouth to his thighs. Each time he tried to move his hands away I pushed them down until he relented and I no longer had to force him to knead his balls.

Down his leg to his feet, there a long time licking the arch, I moved my hand up again so that, together, our hands touching, we could both play with what he probably used to call his private parts.

I knelt at the edge of the bed taking inventory to see if I had missed any parts of him. I arched my body and slid over his, my cunt closing in on his cock. Lying on him, my mouth over his nipple, teeth gripping, sucking again, I held myself to one side so that he could not push his cock in me. I wet my fingers and was back sucking one nipple, squeezing the other with my damp hand.

I could feel his hands clutching at his own cock. I was smiling a half-crazy smile. Excited now but still in wondrous control, slowly I lowered myself over his cock, my hands still pulling at his nipples. He sucked in his breath. It was an inverted scream. As harsh as the way he was tearing at his balls, he was pushing them now against my ass, wanting them to be inside me, too. Very softly, I said, "Now, Jason, now!"

After he came he moved for minutes like a snake that had been beheaded but still wriggled on after death. Even his cock was still hard, although there was so much wetness between us he soon slid out.

"Are you all right?" he asked.

Still astride him I began to move again. "Fine," I said.

"What are you doing?" His hands were moving over my ass. "It's impossible. You'll kill me. You want more? Hey"— he was laughing now—"you really want more?"

I slid off him and onto the bed, not touching him. He leaned over me, kissing me gently.

"You didn't really want more, did you?" he asked.

I began to shiver.

"Are you cold?"

"A little," I said. He pulled the blanket up over me, up to my chin.

"You really are shivering. Let me hold you. What is it, Susan?"

"I'm afraid."

"Of me?" He looked so alarmed. I willed myself to relax.

"A little. A little of you but mostly of me. That I could want more. After all that, how could I want more?" He was holding me, warming me.

"That's all? Don't be frightened of that. Susan, you must know that even if it never happens again, what we just had was very special."

"You mean the sex?" I asked.

"The sex was special. Wasn't it for you?" he questioned.

"Of course, but it was more than just the sex. I wanted things I've never wanted before. It was always enough before to touch a little and he would enter me and maybe I would come. But now I want more. I want us to touch everywhere, deep inside. I don't want anything held back. Everything between us must be open. Do you understand what I'm saying, Jason? I want everything."

He was stroking my hair.

"You sound so desperate. Why shouldn't you have everything?"

"Can you give it to me? Do you understand what I'm talking about?"

"Some kind of voyage. You want to pass back and forth between the sex and the feelings; you want to translate that sex into emotion."

"That's it. That's right. I want to stop in the middle of

some sexual peak and still feel what we feel for each other, even though the sex has stopped."

"But they're different feelings. That intensity. That sexual intensity sometimes gets lost in translation."

"We mustn't let it. All my life I've comforted myself. I've stroked my cheek and held myself. I never believed I could have that comfort from anyone else."

"Are you asking me to become you? How can I do that? I can only comfort you in my way. The way that I know. Perhaps that won't be adequate."

Slowly I began to twist my body over him. I kissed his mouth. "Now you see why I'm frightened," I said.

"Christ, you're making me hard again," he said. My knee was rubbing against his cock, my fingers playing with his nipples. "Jesus Christ."

"We could do it, Jason, if you want to. You could give it all to me. I know that because I can give it all to you. I think you're the one who's frightened now. You know I can give it all to you, don't you?"

His hands moved me on top of him. "You want so much," he said. "I'm afraid I'll always lag behind."

"No, you won't. If you'll hold my hand I'll take you with me on our voyage. All you have to do is hold my hand."

"What do you want, Susan?"

I suspended myself above him, my hands against his chest.

A puppet with strings attached to another master.

Poised there, his hands were on my back pulling me toward him.

Tell him you love him. Tell him, Susan.

(I'm afraid.)

Tell him.

"Susan, let me come into you. Come down now, hard on me. I want you."

For a second more I resisted, puppet strings holding me back.

Tell him, Susan.

"I love you, Jason."

"Yes," he murmured.

9

TO: INTERNATIONAL COMMITTEE FOR SOVIET JEWS, JEWISH PEOPLE OF ISRAEL AND THROUGHOUT THE ENTIRE WORLD

Dear Friends:

Can you imagine what hope we have in learning of your work on our behalf? Where once I was a respected artist of the USSR, I am now treated like the worst traitor and enemy of this country. In one month since my application to emigrate, my wife and I have learned all too well what the thousands of other Soviet Jews wishing to leave have always known.

We crouch now, alone in our apartment, an apartment to which we were moved after we made our application to emigrate a month ago, and which we share with the vermin who inhabit it, both inside and outside of our flat as well, and wait for some word that our situation will be improved.

I ask myself all the time what crime I have committed to be dealt with in such a fashion. As a child, I always listened. Even before I studied music, I heard the sounds of the street in howling storms of Leningrad winters. I heard, rather than felt, the gentle good-night kiss of my mother. I was a strange boy who heard things the way other people see them, smell them or taste them. If a sound was unpleasant—the neighbors quarreling next door— I constricted the muscles of my ears and made of these sounds an atonal symphony. I couldn't bear ugliness and so perhaps I refused to see that it existed.

My music and my studies were everything and I can remember my teachers telling me that my talent was a responsibility. I did not experience the commonplace growing pains of life. I was sheltered and isolated because I was talented. When I first began to perform I felt the audience's response. I could not bear to disappoint them. For myself, I could have heard the music in my head. It was for the audiences that I played. I would watch them move forward slightly in their chairs to be a fraction closer to me. I could see their faces, sometimes damp with tears. I was a totally fulfilled and satisfied man and when I married Lucia, my dear sweet wife, my life was truly complete. It seems important now to confess to these sins of ego. I was a small man.

Although we are harassed, now I'm filled with pride at the thought of joining my relatives and fulfilling my life as a Jew.

Leonid Rabinovitz
January 1974

10

I knew Jason wouldn't call. It's not his pattern to call this early.

I like being in bed. There was a time when I liked it so much I didn't get out of bed. Sam used to say that I used our bed like a command post: telephone near at hand, books and magazines on the night table, calling out orders for cold drinks, warm food. It sometimes seemed as if there were no reason to leave the bed.

It's 8:10. I dial the hospital and ask for Sam's floor. The nurses all know me. I'm told he is the same.

Sliding out from the covers, I dash to the radiator. It bangs regularly through the night with a promise of warmth. The wind whips off the Hudson River to find this room. I warm my hands on the radiator and stand for a minute musing on the day.

My bladder is full. I like that feeling. As a girl I used to sneak into the hall closet and caress my father's overcoat when I had this feeling. I pretended I was being kissed. Now I feel my nipples harden and touch my breast with my warm hand.

The thought of the day depresses me. If I call in sick they'll believe me. At least I think they will. Phyllis who is the program director of the I.C.S.J., will go into David's office and tell him I'm sick. He'll look at her doubtfully, but Phyllis will say, "Come on, David, Susan wouldn't call in sick unless she was sick." He'll nod in agreement. At least that's what I think will happen. What do they know anyway? It depresses me even more to think they believe me above feigning illness.

This bedroom in which I spend so much of my life has fit itself to me, like an old sweater that retains the shape of the body after years of wear. It is the one place in which I need not stumble around in the dark. Everything stays where I put it. The mattress is queen-sized and rests on its box springs. On one side of the bed there is a small table, covered with the evenly broken pieces of an Italian marble table I once used in the living room. On my side, on the marble piece, there is a jar lamp filled with shells I collected on various beaches. Under it and around it, the telephone, books, tissues, an ashtray made by June in kindergarten, chipped but service-able. Once a week I take everything off the surface, wipe it shiny with lemon oil and carefully replace it. The marble is slightly stained with water rings from glasses left too long. It needs to be sanded and I mean to get around to it.

Opposite the bed is a long dresser upon which I keep perfume bottles. I use only Chanel, but have somehow collected a dozen or so other brands of perfume. I like the shapes of the bottles, but not the aromas of their contents. A large mirror hangs over the dresser useless both for vanity, since the light is poor, and for voyeurism during sex since the angle is wrong. My desk admittedly is an eyesore. Inherited from Sam's family, it is modern and has a white Formica top.

Piles of bills and circulars adorn the utilitarian plastic; the drawers are stuffed with receipts and old checks.

I have not painted since Sam left, and there are odd colorations on the wall where pictures were removed. The curtains were a mistake. Light and airy, they do not block the light. I would prefer shutters.

I decorated this room in my mind from *House and Garden* and *House Beautiful* when Sam and I moved here. I knew exactly what I wanted. A four-poster bed, Queen Anne furniture. An area with a small table and two chairs for Sunday brunch. A wooden valet for Sam and a dressing table for me. White sheets with lace trim, four really good pillows. A plush wine carpet, a chaise with a tea table next to it. Onyx cigarette box and teak lighter, alabaster ashtray. In the end, it was necessary to cut a few corners. I did the best I could, and now it suits me. There is no chaise, no area for brunch. But I have covered the windowsills with soft padding and occasionally curl up there, to read. By leaning out the window you can just see the river.

The alternatives are not good. If I stay home from work, I'll probably end up going to the hospital and spending the day there. That ought to settle it. Not another day in the hospital. I've lingered too long already.

I walk carefully across the room, along the borders of the area rug (and even that is freezing) and wonder why I can't get more heat in this room. Goddammit, I pay the rent; why can't I live like a regular person in a warm bedroom? Letters to the landlord, pleas and threats, have been greeted by his treating me as if I were an eccentric person: "Imagine, she wants heat in her bedroom." One thing you can be sure of, Marge would have gotten them to install a fireplace if she wanted it.

My bathroom is blue, the sink and the toilet seat are blue.

On the way to the toilet, I glance in the mirror. Jesus. My hair is sticking up in those curls I make to comfort me.

I relinquish my bladder water. It drains out of me along with the pleasant sex feeling.

The scale is several pounds off. It doesn't matter, of course, because as long as it remains constant I can always calculate my weight correctly. I'm experienced at compensating for incorrect premises.

Pushing back my hair, I examine my face. I suck in my cheeks and create planes. High cheekbones would have made me a classic beauty. When I smile broadly, which I only do in the privacy of this exclusive blue room, the space between my two front teeth gapes back at me. Stuck haphazardly in my mouth, they refuse to touch, like a quarrelsome couple each going its own way.

I wish I could really see my face. Mirrors always distort. No one really sees his face. Is that part of some important cosmic scheme or just a structural dilemma? Some prehistoric creatures had a third eye. Where did it go to? With all the miracles of science, surely it should not be too difficult to arrange for an eye that would turn inward, so one could actually see one's face. God created eyes, and they can see everything. Everything except the face itself.

Watching old women on the bus, when I was young, I wondered if they saw themselves. Was it possible that they had to live with the knowledge that their faces looked like that, wrinkled and flabby? Maybe their reflections were kinder. Maybe we all see ourselves reflected differently from the way we are and no one knows it because there is no way to really see your own face. God could have put the eye in a finger, say, or had it protrude like a visor from the forehead.

I'm thirty-seven years old and have never seen my face. Not likely to either.

Splashing water on my face, I search for blemishes. This morning, my skin is so smooth. But there is, of course, the puffiness under my eyes. Gently, I push it in a little.

I can remember how much I wanted to be twenty-one. Now twenty-one has passed and thirty-one and I can't remember too much about the passage.

I used to have a secret trick. Touch a leaf and I'll always remember the moment. Or hold my breath and that moment will fix itself forever. But there were too many leaves, I guess, and I don't remember the moments, only the trick. I'm still hurling myself forward.

An old lady on the porch, long white hair neatly fashioned in a bun. A glider and fern growing over the railings. Hot biscuits and cool tea. Melted butter and honey.

My fingers smooth the smile wrinkles and I wonder where that image comes from. I've never lived in a house, except those years in the basement. But the fantasy cheers me. Hot buttered biscuits seem, at least, to be within the realm of possibility.

Back in bed, I'm suddenly filled with a sense of dread. Have I forgotten something else? Some awful thing that I'm afraid to remember, besides Sam. I'm cold even under the layers of covers. Quickly now, riffle through the checklist of my life. Must be some old dread, plenty of that around.

So, I'll call in sick and take a breakfast tray back to bed. Maybe go to a movie later. But, already it's souring; even with my hair freshly brushed and lying in the center of the bed, I feel too anxious really to plan a day at home. Turning on my side, I slam my eyes closed. It is intolerable, this suspense. My hands are turned to fists and the nails bite my palms. I conjure up the past to alleviate the dread.

TO: COMRADE N.V. PODGORNY, CHAIRMAN OF THE PRESIDIUM OF THE SUPREME SOVIET OF THE USSR.

TO: COMRADE R.A. RUDENKO, PROCURATOR-GENERAL OF THE USSR

I wish to protest a search of my apartment that was made two days ago.

The so-called reason for the search was my "interest in Zionist affairs." The search took place shortly after my wife and I applied for permission to emigrate to Israel. The following materials were confiscated:

A Bible in Hebrew and Russian
Several cartons of sheet music
14 recordings, 2 in the Hebrew language
My entire library of tapes of my music, which were recorded during concerts

I don't believe that any of these materials can in any way be considered anti-Soviet. Or has the day arrived when the Bible is to be recognized as a part of the Zionist conspiracy? Since I have been refused permission to perform concerts it is extremely important to me that I have my music at home. Both the acts of searching my apartment and confiscating my personal belongings represent the type of discrimination and oppression which I seek to avoid. Indeed, I believe it to be against the specific law of the USFSF Criminal Code, Article 131, which deals with the "deliberate belittling of honor and personal dignity."

Since my application for permission to emigrate has been unjustifiably refused, I beg to apply for reconsideration of my application for permission to go to Israel as well as for the return of my confiscated belongings.

Leonid Rabinovitz
March 1974

Like a well-thumbed book of poetry that opens automatically to a particular verse, my memories begin out of order, nonsequential but recurring. I begin midstream and then crisscross the waterway, touching all the other memories.

It always begins with a day in fall, my second year in college. There was so much before and so much after but that day is my starting point.

I played with my hair then, too, but of course not in public. Standing in line, waiting to register for a course on what passes for a college campus in New York, I had just met Marge. She was taller than I and had long flowing hair, which was quite beautiful. I can remember feeling almost petite next to her. She was complaining in some desultory fashion about the long line and what courses we would be taking. Complaining? What, indeed, was there to complain about then? But still, we griped in the way of young women with nothing better to do.

Some words were spoken, I can remember her mouth moving, but I was distracted by a hand on my shoulder. I turned to see the dean, Dr. Denton. "Susan, I wonder if you would come along with me to my office?"

"Sure, anything wrong?"

"Let's wait until we get there, Susan."

We walked across the campus, I struggling to keep up with Dr. Denton's quick pace. Alarmed, confused, I tried to comfort myself. *Whatever it is, you'll know soon. What could it be?* I'm a good student, unobtrusive. My stomach was cramped. *Take it easy, you'll know soon. Maybe it's something good. But what?*

We entered the administration building and I told Dr. Denton I had to go to the bathroom. "Certainly, just come right into my office when you're finished," Dr. Denton said softly.

She's speaking so softly. Dr. Denton, whose booming voice was as much her trademark as her sensible walking shoes and her steel-rimmed glasses, was speaking softly.

I dropped my books on the bathroom floor. In a cold sweat, my body drained itself frantically. I flushed the toilet and picked up the books. *For God's sake, take it easy, you'll know in a minute.* A book fell, and while I stopped to pick it up, another slipped from the stack I was carrying. *The hell with it, leave them there.* But I patiently forced myself to balance them. As I stood up, the books now secured, I saw my frightened face in the mirror. Placing the books on a ledge beneath, I held my face in my hands, stroking my cheek. *Hey, what could it be? Some silly school thing, calm down, you don't want Dr. Denton to think you're frightened of her.*

I have always been my own observer. For as long as I can remember, there was a separate presence. Someone who would comfort me, chide me, alert me to danger, appease my loneliness and, most of all, note and record my actions and thoughts. By not moralizing as a conscience would, this observer never caused me pain. And finally, when all else failed, it was the way I knew I really existed.

Straightening my blouse, neatly loading my arms with

school books, I walked into Dr. Denton's office on the second floor. It was paneled. The trees brushed against the French windows. The room was sparsely furnished; several framed diplomas were hung discreetly on one wall.

Dr. Denton was sitting behind her desk, holding a pencil. She stood up when I entered, thought better of it and sat down again, motioning to me to sit in the club chair opposite her desk.

"Susan, there just isn't any easy way to do this. I wish . . . there just isn't any easy way." She waited for me to respond, to ask a question. Easier to answer a direct question, than cruelly volunteer this. But I was silent.

"I've just had a call from the police. It's your mother, Susan."

"My mother?" I inquired politely. *At last.*

"I'm so sorry but the police say there is no doubt, they have a positive identification. A neighbor saw her fall from the window."

"A positive identification of my mother?" I sounded dumb to my own ears.

"I'm afraid so, Susan. Your mother is dead."

I looked out the window. The trees were swaying fecklessly in the fall breeze. A leaf dropping here and there. Mother dead, the suspense over, I knew there would be more. I would have to know the details of her death. But it hardly mattered now. First I must be consoled a little. There, another leaf just fell. It wavered a little, caught up by a rush of wind, perhaps it wouldn't fall after all. No, there it went, gliding downward. Pointless.

Dr. Denton was talking again, but I was too busy counting the falling leaves to hear her. *This is bad, really bad.*

I wished I could reach out and catch one of the falling leaves; I would dry my tears with it. Except there were no tears. I noticed that as I touched my face.

My mother was dead and I wanted to be crazy with grief. I forced myself to think about her body splattered on the sidewalk. I wanted to see, in my mind's eye, her broken, crushed, frail frame darkening the cement. Hairpins sticking out of her soft graying hair, her blood seeping into the cracks to be washed away by the next rain. My mother deserved to be mourned the way she could mourn. The best I could do was to sit and watch the falling leaves.

I knew they would treat me gently, the way they treat a child who has just lost her mother. I wanted to be treated gently. Let this lie serve me as well as all the others.

12

I had left Mother that morning, as usual having her second cup of tea. Little more than an hour ago, I had left the small apartment we shared on Ninety-fifth Street and Broadway, kissing her goodbye, wishing her a good day.

We had been living together for four months this time. All through the summer we took long walks in the park and went to movies to escape the heat. At night, pulling down the Murphy bed, we turned on the radio. We didn't talk much; there wasn't a whole lot to say. All through the summer, I watched my mother waiting.

At night I would awaken and see Mother at the window, staring out of it, holding one of the photographs. The small room was filled with them. Framed images of relatives on a picnic, my brother Jean at various ages.

My father, many of father; a handsome man, he had photographed well. The pictures were yellowing slightly and curling a little within the frames. Dusted daily, they were spread out over every surface of the apartment. No other ornaments were necessary. Mother would pick them up, sometimes favoring one then the other, talk to them, caress them, laugh a little as she remembered some good times.

I had not known any of the people in the pictures except Father. The rest—grandparents, aunts, uncles, cousins and my brother, Jean—had died in the war. Some claimed by the ovens, others mangled in the crowded cattle cars which took them to the camps, another shot as he tried to prevent them from entering his house. One infant cousin strangled by his mother who could not stand his hungry crying. Stealing a knife from another prisoner, she gratefully opened her veins and bled to death, still cradling her dead infant. Two shot, strung across the barbed wire, while trying to escape. My grandfather, Mother's father, died from madness. Only Father the survivor had died a clean death. The rest of them died in filth, confused by the multiple horrors, their last breaths smelling of decay and excrement. I had heard the stories of their deaths many times. It was not something that needed repeating, once would have been enough. Never having known them, when I looked at the pictures I had only their death tales.

Time had attenuated some of the details, but the overarching horror made the pictures sharp and precise. Like shards of glass in my memory, glinting and painful, I was stuck with memories I had not witnessed. I knew nothing of the Bible, of the Prophets, of Hebrew or Yiddish. Jewish history began with the story of *Kristallnacht*. It was a purely negative legacy, this catastrophic connection to my people. However, in the very horror of the tales there was opportunity for romantic revision of the past. This allowed my mother to take nurture from her recall.

Father had seen what was coming and believed it. In Paris, in 1940, he tried to warn them. He argued and urged them to flee. They would not leave. My mother, the most adamant of all, refused to go. Rumors, they said, and one called him a coward.

By then it was too late. Gentile friends of my fathers who

led a simple farm life hid my mother and me. Understanding the consequences, they were nevertheless unwilling to be a party to that evil. We lived in the basement. Sunk deep in the ground, the chill of the earth that surrounded it seeped through and we were never warm. Two cots, a short-wave radio, cans of food, supplemented by fresh vegetables and occasional meat from above, a makeshift toilet emptied daily by the wife. My child scribblings decorated the walls, and the photographs of the family, their fate of course not known then, were propped on a trunk.

We rarely left the basement; even a passing neighbor could be dangerous. Never a word from Jean or Father. Mother taught me to read and add. I was two when we began our subterranean life and five when we emerged. I remembered little; steaming caldrons of soup, a pattern in the ceiling formed of mud which frightened me, and the cackling of the radio which sometimes disturbed my sleep. Other noises, strange and frightening.

When the war ended, we returned to Paris. The light hurt my eyes and I was afraid of the crowds on the street. Later Father methodically searched for our relatives. A name on a list, a survivor who remembered, a neighbor who admitted knowing; it took a year but finally we learned it all. Our dreams of reunion were a cruel hoax; they were all dead.

With the help of a refugee organization, we located distant relatives in New York and were eventually allowed to leave France. On the ship we met others who had escaped. No family was intact, and at night the ship glided through the water adding its own lament to the dirge of the survivors. There were children on the ship and I, overcoming my shyness, made a special friend. I refused to be separated from her, even for meals, and finally begged my mother to let her sleep in our cabin. I who for three years had been the most cooperative of children was now greedy for my childhood.

It was during the time that Mother and I lived in the basement that I first discovered my observer. Satisfying my various child needs, my observer was reliable.

Later, when I saw that my parents' grieving would not be interrupted for my childish whims, my observer comforted me. From the little I knew of God, I was unwilling to trust that He would provide me with what I needed. I had asked my father about God. Where exactly was *He* when our family was being killed? Father had no answer, looked into my child eyes and murmured only that there were some things beyond human comprehension. It wasn't good enough. My own observer stood apart from me, validating my existence.

On our arrival in New York, the distant relatives were kind. We found an apartment in the Bronx and Father went to work for a cousin. I began school, speaking French now only at home. I hated to come home; it was a world of unassuaged grief. My parents were single-minded in their resolve to enshrine the dead; they would allow no distractions. Uncertain as to their own claim on life, they preferred to let it pass them by, only watchful that nothing penetrate their despair.

When I was nine, I asked my mother why she would not enter into our new life. "Don't you want to put it behind you, to forget just a little?" Startled, Mother replied, "No, I only fear that I may forget."

"Would that be so bad for you and Daddy to forget just for a little, to live now? We could have such a good life."

"You don't understand, Susan," she explained. "To forget would be the final defeat. I have no choice, no more than they did who died. It is not something you decide. There is no way to resolve, 'Today I will forget my family was murdered, starved, tortured.'"

"But why did we survive then?" I persisted. "Why did we survive?"

"Each of us must answer that for himself. For myself, I think perhaps I survived just for this, so that they would be assured of being remembered."

Father seemed more forgiving. Father seemed not to hate anyone. The radio in the kitchen was always tuned to WQXR. When any music of Wagner's came on my mother would turn it off.

"What's the difference," my father said to her. "Leave it on. Let at least the music stand by itself."

"No!" she replied. "God, how weak you are. Too lazy to turn off those beasts even now when it's too late."

"It's only music," he insisted. "You can't blame the music."

"Perhaps," my mother said, "if you knew how to hate, Jean would not have died."

There were many survivors in our neighborhood. In their homes they had other questions and other answers. On the High Holy days I was ashamed that we didn't go to synagogue.

"Maybe this year we should go," my father said.

"Yes, let's go this year," I said. "Everyone goes. It's fun."

"No," my mother answered. "We will not go to syn-agogue."

"Martha, let the child go. Let her be with her friends. What harm can it do?"

My mother turned to me. "You want to go to the synagogue? Why?"

"Well, we're Jewish," I answered.

"You want to go because we're Jewish? Go then, little Jewish girl. Perhaps you will sit next to some nice Jewish

74

woman. If you do, ask her what it means to be Jewish. Ask her where she was when your brother walked in the line to the oven. Ask her why she didn't help us. Remind her who you are. See how quickly she recoils from you."

"Martha, you shouldn't talk that way to her. Susan must be allowed to make her own choices, to find her own answers. God knows we have none to give her."

"You talk as if you hate the Jews, Mother. Do you?"

"No. I don't hate the Jews. I have no time for their hypocrisy. They go to synagogue to remember. Imagine. They have to go out of their homes to a special place to be blessed by a rabbi so that they may remember. By the middle of dinner of the same day they will have already forgotten. Let them come here to this home. I'll give them a lesson in remembering. The witnesses are excused from synagogue. I won't go."

"Am I a witness, too, Mother?" Then, I too wanted to be a witness, a victim. Anything but part of the enemy.

In my second year of high school, my father shot himself. He was found by a cleaning lady late one night at his office. He left no note for me, but I understood. He had survived only to be tormented by the memory of his choices. His death was not surprising. Because he venerated life, he was not a man to live only in pointless, incriminating retrospection. And so, he would not live at all.

When Mother learned of his death she stopped speaking. She had no words for me, but I understood. From my mother's eyes, I could see that only her inner voice could save her. I tried to explain it to the doctors but they called it something else. I was powerless to stop them from sending Mother away. I pleaded with the doctor, "Is it some virtue to mourn out loud? Can't you see she is shielding herself from more pain, saving her life by withdrawing into the comfort of herself?" The doctor told me that Mother was sick and could be helped.

"No, she is not sick. Maybe in your world she is sick, but in her world it is the only sane thing to do."

Mother, allowed to take her collection of photographs, did not seem to mind much and smiled at me as she left for the institution. I visited her twice a month, every other Sunday. For three years, I took the bus and then sat in a small room, bars on the window, bringing sweets and books, waiting. Gradually Mother began to talk again. She did not speak of the dead, but of how nice the doctors and nurses were and how much she was looking forward to leaving and making a home with me. No mention that we were the last ones left; we sat and planned for the future . . . my mother's hands still caressing the pictures said all there was to say about the past.

Pronounced well, because she could talk again, she left the institution and moved into the apartment on Broadway and Ninety-fifth Street. Free now to plunge herself back into her world of perpetual bereavement.

For four months, I had watched Mother, both of us living with the anxious understanding that something was still incomplete.

Mother had fallen from our window, twelve floors above the ground. She would not have flung herself or thrown herself, that would have been too great an effort. No, Mother would have been sitting on the window ledge, looking down at the grime of Broadway and beyond to the calm of the Hudson River and, perhaps satisfying herself with a last look at the pictures, would have just fallen down. It was her final retreat from anguish, the only real break with the past.

Perhaps she felt she had borne enough, the time was right, and she could allow herself this surrender.

Once, there must have been some hope that it would be bearable or else she would have fallen years ago.

Later when people would ask, I would say my mother died of a disease or an accident. I didn't know what else to call the sorrow that had destroyed her.

I was uncertain whom to blame. The enemy as well as the victims were too vast. Ephemeral villains haunted me. In small fumbling ways I blamed myself. Imprecise wonderings on how I might have eased their burden. I had failed them. Although I saw no clear way to have saved them, someone must be blamed.

I didn't want to be a victim like them. I didn't want to be part of a family or a people who were so hated. Sometimes I hated them myself because they had died. Of one thing I was certain, both had been victims. Was being a victim inherited? Was I joined to them in their remorse? Now that they were dead, was I to take up the banner of hate and guilt, of their memories? What did those memories have to do with me? Now, I had memories of my own, gnawing and anguished memories of my own. My father shot off his head, my mother splattered herself on the sidewalk. Now, I too was afflicted by memories.

I would not be a victim, too, not from their memories and not from my own. I would will myself to forget. Not one drop of memory would pollute my life. I would dwell no longer on death, morbid images of camps, cattle cars, inevitable suicides. I would not be seduced by small reminders that would lead only to more death. Just as stubbornly as my parents had embraced them. I would reject them.

Only the pictures were left as token keepsakes of my past.

Until Leonid, I was satisfied to remain on the periphery of

my own history. I've learned a great deal from Leonid. We are part of a continuum.

TO: SENATOR HENRY JACKSON AND HONORABLE MEMBERS OF UNITED STATES CONGRESS

I appeal to you to assist my wife and myself to be permitted to leave the Soviet Union. Our condition is worsening; we are in great distress.

I have heard of the interest you have in securing the basic right to leave for Soviet citizens who wish to do so. I know we are all special cases, mine no more so than others. Except that perhaps because I am well known, it is more difficult for me. Perhaps an example is to be made of me.

Those of us who wish to leave have great faith in your work.

We hope you will remain firm in your resolve to influence the Soviet government. We are certain that the great leaders of the Soviet Union will act wisely and adhere to international law, which ensures the rights of all people to emigrate if they wish.

We are grateful for your interest. Please do not forget us.

Leonid Rabinovitz
April 1974

13

My mother told me everything:

MOTHER: Your father likes young girls, you know, Susan.

SUSAN: Oh, really, Mother, please. I don't want to hear about that.

MOTHER: He always liked young girls. I was only fourteen when he met me. And he took advantage.

SUSAN: Mother, you weren't fourteen when you met him. You were nineteen.

MOTHER: Of course for years I was too young to understand that he had a sick perverted nature. Then, after we were married he would brag to me about his conquests.

SUSAN: Look, Mother, I really don't want to hear about this. You weren't fourteen when you met him, you were nineteen and I don't think he took advantage of you. You told me so many times how you admired him and loved him.

MOTHER: Oh, well, those are just lies that mothers tell their young daughters. Now that you're fourteen, just the age that I was when I met your father, you should know the truth.

SUSAN: All right, all right, you were fourteen when you met him and he was a terrible lech and he took advantage of you and ruined your life. If that's your story this week, okay.

MOTHER: He liked to tell me about the young girls he treated. Of course, his patients all adored him and then he would force them to—well, to do things to him.

SUSAN: Oh, for God's sake, Mother.

MOTHER: It is important that you know these things. You think he's such a hero. It's time you understood what he really is.

SUSAN: I don't want to be rude, Mother, but I really don't want to hear all this.

MOTHER: Well, of course things were different in those days. It was his right to come home and tell me those dreadful stories and I didn't complain. He thought they excited me, telling me all those disgusting stories of how he would feel up those young girls and force them to do terrible things to him. He had no decency at all. He would tell me his stories and then expect me to make love with him. He still likes young girls. That's why I don't like you to bring your friends here. It's not that I mind, it's just that I'm afraid that he might—well, he might take a fancy to them. He's really capable of anything.

SUSAN: Why do you make up such lies, Mother? Why do you want to lie so about Father?

MOTHER: I haven't told you the worst thing yet. Mind you, it's no great pleasure for me to tell my own daughter these things about her father.

SUSAN: Well, then, don't. Don't say any more.

MOTHER: I always knew one day it would be my responsibility to tell you these things. I don't shirk my responsibilities. I don't expect you to shirk yours. No one else knows these things but me.

SUSAN: I don't want to hear it. Whatever it is I don't want to hear it.

MOTHER: After the war, when your father got out of the camp, he told me what happened to the women there. They raped small girls, made prostitutes of the teenagers, experimented sexually on the women.

SUSAN: Please, Mother, please stop. I don't want to hear any more.

MOTHER: There were so many stories. There was nothing foul and evil that the Nazis didn't do to women. Sometimes the women welcomed it because it saved their lives. Of course all men always have power but these Nazi men were special. There was nothing to stop them from using women however they wanted. He saw it all. He pitied them but in the end he was a man, too. He used them, too.

SUSAN: What do you mean? You don't know what you're talking about. Don't tell me any more.

MOTHER: I suppose he couldn't help himself. It was in his nature. He should never have told me, of course, but that was part of his excitement. At first he tried to help the women. Comfort them. Perhaps there was too much brutality around him. In the end he became like them. Excited by the screams of the women. Using them. He became just like the other brutes.

SUSAN: I don't believe you. I can't believe you.

MOTHER: It's for your own good. Of course he felt guilty afterward. God. I remember when he first came out of the camp and told me the stories; he cried, begged me to help him. He was sick of himself then. Disgusted. What comfort could I give him? Do you think I should have comforted him?

SUSAN: Yes. You should have comforted him. Anyway, I don't believe you. Maybe it's you who was excited by the stories.

MOTHER: What! You think I enjoyed hearing it? You think I liked hearing about how night after night he walked into the women's section and selected whomever he wanted for that night? Walked between the rows of young girls and women and pointed "you" or "you." And the woman, probably terrified, got up and followed him because it was a way to survive. All those nights I lay alone, he had someone.

Was it possible? Had my father done those things? Had he told her about them? Mother wanted me to know the particulars of the tragedy. She wanted me to hate, perhaps to fear, as she did. And that was right.

But it was not all.

Mother rehearsed again and again stories of unspeakable acts. There was no form of brutality unimaginable to my mother. She would look at him, my father, defiantly, as if to say, "Do you have anything to add?"

His lips moved slightly; he glanced at me. His eyes seemed kind in contrast to the burning holes in my mother's face.

There was something he wanted to tell me.

I did not believe her, not about my father. I could see even then she was crazy from grief. From guilt. She blamed everyone, drawing no distinction between victim and torturer.

Of what was she guilty? I was not kind; I knew her terrible secret.

SUSAN: You weren't always alone. I remember that much.
MOTHER: Oh, you do, do you? Well, yes, it's true. You think I invited him to come down, that stupid, fat farmer? You think I asked him into my bed? No. It was the price for

your safety. I hope you never have to pay such a price. I couldn't help myself.

SUSAN: You did it for survival. Is that it?

MOTHER: Yes.

SUSAN: Father wanted to survive, too.

MOTHER: Always you defend him.

SUSAN: If it's true, if, then I forgive him.

Was it true? My mother's mouth should be wrapped in a plain brown wrapper.

"What is worse than death?" I asked my father.

"Erosion," he answered, for once moving out of his shadow. "To be nibbled away at, day after day. Not just from the beatings, the starvation, the fear of death. Worse than that is the mutilation of the spirit. The body can endure what the mind cannot. The brutality was unendurable because it was incomprehensible.

"The world accuses us of being passive. Passive in a world of perfect evil. We were not passive. We fought in the ways we could. In a world of absolute horror, it is an act of resistance to scheme to stay alive for one more hour; to wish to stay alive at all. It was enough to dream of deliverance, to fantasize retaliation, to retain some small sanity.

"The choices that that world allowed were a masterpiece of evil. Civilization was gone. Boundaries, parameters, limits, all canceled. 'Shall we send these hundred-and-fifty boys to the ovens, or these? Tell me, sir, would you prefer us to rape your wife or your daughter? Which twin shall we castrate?' Those were the choices. Madness. Those were the choices. Not once, but every day, every hour, day after day. Every day was the end of the world. There has never been such a catastrophe before, not even to the Jewish people. There was no relief from the choices. If you refused to make a choice, you were killed. If you made a choice, you were a collaborator, a member of the *Judenrat*. The world has convenient labels now for what it did not have to endure. Who knows what one will do in such a circumstance? Who can define that moment when men do things they never dreamed they were capable of doing? What is brave or moral in such a world of perfect evil? Most men do not have to do more than idly speculate on such matters. But for us, after our bodies were numb from beating, cramped from starvation, our minds were still assaulted by the unremitting cruelty of the choices, and of the answers. Our world was flooded with grief. Personal grief; for sons and daughers, mothers and fathers, for ourselves, and finally a kind of collective grief for all victims. That's all there was, sorrow and anguish. How do you comfort people in a world where everyone needs to be comforted?

"I did not make that world, I fought against it, I saved many lives. But still, I cannot escape a sense of shame and guilt. I wanted to transcend evil. In the end all I did was to survive.

"I did not do those things your mother speaks about. But it could have happened. Anything could have happened. But I did not do those things. It is true that I made some choices, of the kind I spoke about before. Many of us were capable of acts which saved lives, perhaps at the expense of other lives. But the Nazis had no such rationale. No rationale at all. They annihilated us, millions of us, and left those of us who survived with the constant anguish of our choices. And that anguish continues to distort our lives."

A friend of Leonid's came to the office the other day. A strong, handsome man who finally had been allowed to emigrate after waiting two years. He was a prominent scientist who lived together with his wife, two children and old mother in a small flat in Leningrad. We tried to call

84

Leonid but the Russian operator told us that the line was out of order.

We spoke for many hours about Leonid and his situation.

"He doesn't trust anyone, you know," Ilya said. "It's very hard to trust anyone over there."

"I can imagine it, I think."

"Everyone is a spy." He shuddered as if to rid himself of some memory. "Two months after I applied to leave I was called in suddenly by the KGB. The proposition was very simple. If I would supply them with the names of the Jews who were thinking of applying to leave, they would guarantee I would be permitted to leave with my family in one year."

There were always rumors of course, of this one or that one being untrustworthy. This was the first time I had ever had such a conversation with a Soviet Jew.

"What did you do?" I asked.

"I walked for a long time, and then I went home. My mother was in the living room. I told her what the proposition was. 'What should I do?' I asked her. 'What do you think?'"

"What did she say?"

Smiling broadly, Ilya stood up, picked up a poster I had been preparing. "Nice work," he said, "very nice."

"What did she say?"

He looked at me as if trying to judge if I could believe him. "Oh, she said to me, 'Ilya, I would rather see you in your grave.'"

"And that was the end of it?" I asked.

"Yes," he said. "Now you see the way in which a man becomes brave. It all happens at the mother's knee."

I believed him. He had been mocking himself with his talk of brave men. Perhaps he was right to do so. Another man with another mother might have behaved quite differently. Sometimes I think men choose what they do only because they cannot do the opposite. Who sets these standards for survival by which we are judged?

I believed him. I remembered my father's words. I believed that on such a mother's judgment, his standard for survival was set. Another mother, another judgment, another standard.

And if he had collaborated? It makes no difference to me. They gave me what they could, my father and my mother. They gave me what they had left, after the catastrophe.

My mother, crazy with grief, wanted to protect me, to teach me to hate and fear.

My father just wanted me to understand. I have found, in this work with Russian Jews, a place for both those lessons.

I used to think I would have to move from this apartment, from the memories of Jason, here, in this bedroom, in this bed. People do move after a theft or a rape.

But I learned soon enough that I carried the pain of Jason with me wherever I went. I looked for him in unfamiliar restaurants, in darkened movie theaters, on lonely stretches of beach. At least here in my bedroom there could be no promise of a casual meeting.

Of course, he might call; people do call after a lovers' quarrel.

The piles of clothes around the room present me with too many decisions. If I don't pack in an orderly fashion the whole trip will go wrong.

I know how to lead an orderly life. I've watched others. I can imitate stability.

I must seem to others to live a noisy life. The noise is all external. Inside, there is only silence. Now that I'm afraid all the time, my mind wanders. I fasten on the form of things. The glitter of lights, shapes. I stare. I observe.

I am too far forward in this theater; my nose is pressed against the screen. Life images are grainy, frighteningly large.

I sit in the middle of the circus. Focusing on the center, my peripheral vision is poor and I miss what is happening around the edges. Who's to say I have not therefore missed the point? What's happening on the fringe may be crucial. Without it nothing makes sense. But I focus only on the obvious, the center, and miss the acrobats in the other rings.

Put me in your pocket, bury me in your grave, attach me surgically, let me live like a louse tangled in your hair, swallow me, dangle me on your watch chain, tattoo me on your chest, gulp me down whole, let me crawl into every crevice of your body. Yes, I want to be that close.

I crave intimacy. Is it only for others? I, who would allow any bloodsucker to have it all, strike any bargain God would allow, find no hospitable living person to infiltrate.

When Sam called two days ago at two in the morning I was still awake. He sounded frightened and his voice was weak. "I'm sorry to bother you, Susan," he said in his apologetic way, which makes me feel guilty, "but something's terribly wrong. I can't move my legs."

I knew immediately that it was true, that he was in some kind of serious trouble. I woke June and took her to a neighbor, assuring her that everything would be all right. I dressed quickly and ran the block-and-a-half to his apartment. I found him lying on his bed sweating and ashen. I tried to help him stand, but the pain was too great and he couldn't manage it. He began to cry, a helpless, piteous kind of crying.

I called the police and got Sam a glass of water. I kept telling him it would be all right thinking all the time that he was probably dying and furious with him for that.

"I wet the bed, Susan. I wet the goddamned bed."

"It'll be all right. Sam. Don't worry about that. Do you want an aspirin?"

"Aspirin?" he said, his voice mocking me now. "How very like you to offer me an aspirin at a time like this."

We waited together for help to arrive. He had no shirt on and I could see the hair on his chest had turned gray. He looked like an old man; he smelled like an old man. Still, it was not depressing. In some odd way, we were together again and there was some comfort in that for both of us.

I was twenty-one; I liked Sam; we had been dating for several months. Because he was stocky, we appeared to be the same height, although actually he was two inches taller. Sam was twenty-eight then, the only son of a poor family who had hounded him all his life to make good, while at the same time convinced that no son of theirs could ever be successful.

He believed he had a speech defect and was shy and reticent. I tried to reason with him, because the truth was he spoke quite normally. Sam, wounded from years of thought-less taunts, heard a lisp where none existed. He valued certainty and was delighted by my capricious and impulsive nature.

Slow-moving, slow-speaking, slow to anger, seemingly slow to grasp a point, at first I valued his measured response. Later, his hesitating manner and silences would frustrate me and drive me into wild furies.

Even at the beginning, we didn't have much to say to each other. I used to be nervous waiting for him to pick me up, wondering how we would spend our evening and greatly relieved if we had planned to go to a movie or see other people. Sneaking glances at other couples in restaurants or waiting in line at the movies, I wondered what they all had to talk so much about. But when the tension of silence became too great, Sam would put his bear arms around me and hold me tight and tell me he loved me, and then I knew I was a lucky person and was grateful to have him.

During the first months of our marriage, I would argue with myself, beginning already to feel cheated.

"He's good to me, considerate and kind, brings me breakfast in bed and helps with the marketing. He calms me in the night when the fear of death is worst."

Those nights—when I would wake him because it was so unbearable to think of life continuing after I was dead. Those nights—when I would grab my hair and pull it as hard as I could trying to cause myself some pain other than knowing that one day I would die.

"Sam, wake up, please."

"What is it, Susan, what's the matter?"

"I'm afraid. I'm afraid to die. I lie here and try to imagine what it will be like, coffin, earth, but I see myself frightened in the coffin and I don't want to die. Sam, aren't you afraid of death?" And he would hold me, stroke my hair, and in his calm way, always give me the same answer.

"Susan, were you afraid before you were born? That's the way I think of it. I wasn't afraid before I was born. That's what death is like. Susan, it's long time away; don't rush it so. Years away."

I loved him then, for my terror abated and I slept in his arms.

Other times, watching him fold the laundry, methodically arranging the piles of linen and underwear, I did not love him at all.

"Talk to me, Sam, let's talk."

"What about?"

"Anything, anything, but let's talk."

I had married Sam in the hope of acquiring a present and

a future that would completely obliterate my past. If only I could be in love enough, consumed by passion, I could escape the past. I would not be another victim.

Sam married me for a similar reason. Insecure and tormented himself, he was trying to escape failure. Between us, failure and victim, we did not at first understand our mission. We sucked at each other, cloying and childish, each desperate for a transfusion of vitality, of courage. What little energy I had, I wasn't about to give away. I needed it myself. I assumed he felt the same. I wanted him to fill me up first, then, belly stuffed, I would gratefully deliver him from failure. "You first," he said. In our hunger, we competed for each meal, each scrap of sustenance.

Now I saw that he was short and humorless, more a stranger to me now than before. His bear hugs were revolting. I wanted more precision. And especially in bed, I wanted some precision. I wanted him to move his tongue with unerring accuracy into my cunt. To plunge his tongue in, my legs spread open, sucking and licking with his mouth while his tongue created a whirlpool of exquisite sensation. I wanted to drown from all that, eager to be a victim to such lust.

His mouth, like a fish mouth, nibbled away, barely touching me, barely ruffling my cunt hair. I could feel him lick his lips after delicate pecking, to see if any cunt hair had attached itself, perhaps. To wipe away my smell, to replace my taste with his own mouth juices. I wanted to be a feast, his feast; he regarded me as a mere morsel.

Fastidious and polite, he would ask, "Are you ready down there?"

After, turning on my side, I stuck my own, reliable fingers into myself. They, at least, knew exactly what to do.

Being married to Sam was making me feel like a victim

91

again; I began to think about divorce. Once again, I would put this dismal memory behind me and start over. Sam never knew I was considering divorce, because I became pregnant with June and, at last, we had something to talk about.

I was stunned by the news that I was pregnant. Having been my own child for so long, I had never given a thought to a new life. Delighted and excited, I loved Sam again, this time determined to hold the feeling. I carried large, was huge by the time June was born and spent most of my pregnancy in bed, resting. Sam insisted on it, although there was nothing wrong with me.

As I lay in bed, waiting to be a proper mother, I reflected on what I knew about motherhood. Not much.

Leafing through magazines, I saw plenty of mothers. It looked easy. Tidy Moms, with well-scrubbed children except for the artistic smudge of chocolate around their lips, a sure sign of Mom's loving indulgence, hugging, laughing, holding hands. Was it my imagination, or did all those Moms have a certain look in their eye? Pride and love and fulfillment.

I liked these Moms—a better example than my own, sparse mother. I remembered her eyes. Dark caves lit by an occasional burst of fire. Seeing through, beyond, and always backward. Eyes which disappeared as they swiveled so that she could see more clearly the savage images warehoused in her brain.

These guileless magazine Moms had no such stockpile of garish memories.

For a couple of weeks after June was born, we had a baby nurse. June was brought to me, a tidbit on a salver, to be occasionally fed and petted. With a weary motion of my hand, she was removed. Friends and relatives visited, paying homage to the newborn child, while I, resplendent on my inner tube, graciously accepted their accolades. I heard June cry in the night and listened for the shuffle that meant Mrs. O'Hara was off to the kitchen to warm her bottle. Sweet child, I thought. Soon the crying ceased and I drifted back to sleep.

Then, one Monday, Mrs. O'Hara was at the door, bags packed, good wishes on her lips, backing out of my front door, out of my life. "Don't go, for God's sake," I wanted to cry. "Stay here, I like it this way. You take care of her. I'll love her, but you take care of her."

I pressed another $20 on Mrs. O'Hara and kissed her cheek.

"Don't worry, don't worry, we all get used to it."

I walked into June's room; she was starting to stir. Well, I thought as I picked her up, it's you and me, kid. Boy, do we have a lot to learn. I sure hope we like each other.

I was not born to be a mother, that much was certain. I wanted to talk to my child. Talk, have a conversation, intelligent discourse about books, maybe, or politics. It would be years before I could talk to this baby. Of course, I had wanted a child, but a child who could at least read. A child who could sit across a dinner table and hold a civilized conversation. A daughter to shop with, to lunch with, to take to the theater. I was quite ready for all that.

What I was not ready for was this baby who, after all her primitive needs had been administered to, still screamed; who spit up an endless stream of seemingly innocuous white slop, which could never be completely cleaned out of my blouses. I was stained from head to foot with all matter of baby excrement.

What in God's name did she want, I wondered. "What do you want?" I screamed. "Fed, dry, loved, what do you want?" Still, she screamed. I pick her up and she falls asleep on my shoulder. Tenderly, loving her, I place her in her crib. But this princess feels a pea. And she screams again. I love her when she's quiet, when she looks up at me (who knows if she can even see yet) with bright, dependent eyes. But when she screams, I go into the bathroom, lock the door, turn on the water, and drown it out.

No natural mother am I; such exalted traits must be acquired. And, sure enough, pretty soon, we are getting along, June and I. The rhythm of motherhood begins to set in. A whimper tells me she wants to be turned, is bored with her mobile. A sigh and I know she is ready for a bottle. I am attuned to her. And she to me. She settles into my body, her head in the crook of my arm, wriggling her torso until she has found just the right angle, pressing against my breasts and stomach; we breathe together, I feel her long sucks on the bottle; I suck with her and the air tastes of milk.

She was born into my world, but we live in hers. Baby smells are everywhere. Baby powder, formula, white sputum and delicate mocha shit. I adapt. I understand we must inhabit that baby world for a while. And though I do not yet know the full meaning of mother love, I am passionately protective of June. She is never left alone on the sidewalk while I run into the butcher for the meat. Oh, no, not to be kidnapped, or perhaps to have the carriage brake fail. In the afternoon, she takes a nap, and I too lie down. Listening for her, I touch myself. Ah, at last another smell, a grown-up smell. I suck my moist finger; June and I are not so different after all.

Sam adores June. At night, she lies in his arms and her hand lies just under his ear. He lifts it gently, tears in his eyes. Watching from across the room, I marvel at what a natural father Sam is. He is ostentatiously proud and grateful to me for this baby, and he loves us both.

For me it is not a question of pride or love. I hope all of that will come later. It is a question of resolution, of determination, and of utmost obligation. June is mine. It is no different from when she was in the womb, no different at all. She is part of my womb still. I know nothing of pride or that adoration Sam seems to feel. I know she is still growing in my womb, still drawing on my lifeblood, still part of my body. Implanted in my womb forever, they will never be able to hurt her, to separate her from me. So we feed each other, June and I, stumbling through those early years crooning to each other our separate songs, drunks in the uncertain night.

I told Sam about my family, about their deaths. "I'll tell you this just once, Sam, the whole thing. And then I don't want to talk about it again, ever. Promise me that." He promised at the time, not knowing what to expect. But after, he said, "Susan, you can't just pretend it didn't happen." "Yes, I can, Sam, I can do whatever I want with it. Don't make me sorry I told you, you promised we would not talk about it. I only told you because you have a right to know, but you have no right to make me think about it or talk about it."

He had been very quiet then, nodding his head in agreement.

After June was born, I suffered from a severe case of hemorrhoids. The labor had been very long. Nothing helped; I took baths, used creams, took painkillers. The pain was not eased; it made me nauseous and I could not eat and began to throw up my own bile. I lay in bed at home and prayed it would go away. Sam took me to a specialist, and I got a different cream and a stronger painkiller.

One day, while Sam was helping me into one of the many

baths I took daily, he could no longer stand to see me in such agony. As he began to apply the cream—I was bent over holding onto the toilet—he gently began to push those balls of distended veins back inside me. At first, I was alarmed, and withdrew from the pain. But we both knew I would suffer less if only they could be pushed inside. He was sweating as he opened my rectum and manipulated the large hemorrhoid inside me. He carried me back to bed; I had nearly fainted. He held me and I cried a little, too exhausted even to thank him.

It was the single most intimate experience of our life together.

15

TO: COMMISSION ON HUMAN RIGHTS, UNITED NATIONS

Through this letter to the International Commission on Human Rights I hope to influence all of the free peoples of the world to act on behalf of myself and other Soviet Jews who are being illegally detained. In the great halls of your organization where you debate the rights of human beings and decide what inalienable rights are legal and which are arbitrary, I beg that you consider the inalienable right of human continuity. The right of the perpetuation of one's heritage, the right of one's own religious faith. I have considered these questions and believe that these are inalienable and legal rights. For all of the history of my country, Jews have been persecuted. As we rose to defend this country, we were shot down by our neighbors. Every promise made to Jews was subverted or broken, for the goal of this government is to dominate all of its people and to have them all assimilate as Russians.

It is true that there is no mass slaughter of Jews now taking place as there was 30 years ago. It is even true that some few synagogues remain and it is true that if a Jew will assimilate, will deny his heritage, his birthright, he may live peacefully. But history has shown us that wherever a spark of honor will remain,

97

total assimilation is impossible. Even if one wished for practical reasons to become a Russian, indelible memories of what it means to be a Jew and of what it means to break the chain of Jewish continuity are impossible to overcome.

History has entrusted to the United Nations a great responsibility. It is the world forum to help people, to get for them their inalienable human rights. There is much injustice in the world today. Perhaps it exists in every country, but surely these injustices must be dealt with too. I have been waiting now for five months for permission to emigrate to Israel. That is my stated inalienable legal right. If you do not support those of us upon whom these terrible violations are being perpetrated, who will you support? I will continue to wait and respectfully demand, as a man must, from such a great organization, that you do everything in your power to assist me and the thousands of others who are waiting to leave the Soviet Union.

Leonid Rabinovitz
May 1974

Dear Leonid,

I am one of the many people in the United States who are trying to help you and Lucia emigrate to Israel. As you know, there is very great concern for you. In the Congress of the United States there is a petition for your release. Your case has brought the plight of Soviet Jews to the attention of the world. I hope that the Soviet authorities will soon let you leave.

I have been trying to telephone you, but each time the Soviet operator says your phone is out of order. I will place a message call to the post office in Leningrad later this month and send you a cable. In that way, perhaps we can talk on the telephone.

Many visitors to Leningrad are anxious to see you. Probably

they have already visited you. The main thing is not to lose hope. We are all certain that you will be allowed to leave.

I will place the message call on July 1 at 8:00 your time, in the morning. I look forward to speaking to you.

Sincerely,
Susan Warner

16

I'd grown up with Sam. The girl in me was gone now; I was wife and mother. Depressed most of the time, I planned dinners. Outings to the park with June, the lending library, the marketing, the laundry, the essential trivia of mothering occupied my time.

That is, all the time I didn't spend in bed.

Soon after June was born, I fell into the habit of taking long afternoon naps. Closing the door to my bedroom, I would undress. Putting on a nightgown and taking up one of my endless supply of books, I'd read for a while then doze off.

Because I slept so much in the day, I was wide awake at night and it was then that I began to take sleeping pills. The pills made me dopey, and Sam, frustrated, began to make love to me while I was half drugged in sleep. I would awake in the mornings; the soreness between my legs alerted me to the fact that he had done it again. I asked him not to do it. "It's like making love to a dead person," I said. "Then stay awake, Susan, don't take the damn pills." "I need sleep, Sam, you know that, I don't sleep well without them."

I hated to be touched by him. Sometimes I just stayed in

bed after my afternoon nap. Sam would find me there and bring me a tray for supper. Sam attended to it all; there was really no need for me ever to get out of bed. He whipped around the apartment, setting it straight, feeding June and me, never tiring of his dual roles. Baiting him, I'd say, "Sam, you'd make someone a wonderful wife."

"Susan, don't be like that. What's wrong? I want to help."

"Help." I laughed. "My God, you do help. You're the perfect husband, everyone says so. I don't want any more help. I think if you help me any more, I'll disappear altogether."

"Susan, listen to me, no, don't turn away, listen."

"Is this the serious Sam, now," I asked. "Just tell me, are we about to have a serious talk?

"Yes, damn it, we are, Susan. You need help."

I screamed at this. "I just told you I don't need any more goddamn help."

"Calm down, please, don't get upset. I mean professional help."

I glared at him. "You presumptuous bastard. So now I need professional help. What about you? Mental health is just around the corner for you, I suppose. You're okay, with your sanctimonious self-righteous stupid values. Oh, sure, I need help. But you, the great fixer of them all, you're just fine." I spewed this at him, momentarily sorry, then glad. I waited for his retort. I had more to say, but wanted to let him have his shot first. But there was no more, Sam could never respond in the face of verbal onslaught. He patted my shoulder and went out to fix dinner.

At night he watched television. All a blur to me—I read or dozed. Sometimes he would stand up, usually during the commercial break, and take off his pajama bottoms, never the tops, just the bottoms. Very polite he was about it. Did I mind if he entered me? He knew I hated to be touched. He would lie on top of me and move quickly to relieve himself. Sometimes I would demand from him the payment of a fantasy. Grotesque fantasies that pleased me all the more because they revolted him.

When he came, he would say, "You all right?" and not waiting for an answer, he pleaded, "This one was for me, okay?"

"Leave me, Sam," I said to him in one of my alert moments. "We really are destroying each other, can't you see it? Leave me."

"Susan, I'll never leave you, we're just going through a hard time."

Between his denial and my stupor, years passed and the dreary pattern of our life was a mosaic of frustration and misery. The day Sam got his promotion, I asked him for a divorce. I had cleaned the house and made dinner. A bottle of wine was opened and Sam was excited about his future. "I'm going places, Susan, I know it. God, it's good to see you up, you sure you feel all right? I can't tell you how it felt; of course I knew it was coming but still, when he said it, he said, 'Sam, you've done a fine job here and you deserve a promotion,' well, I felt terrific, Some things have to be said, I guess. You know, Susan, you look terrific—a little thin, but really good. You're awfully quiet tonight, usually you complain I don't talk. What are you so quiet about?"

I hadn't meant to spoil it for him; I was happy he'd been promoted. But I believed now would be the best time, when he was strong from his success at work. "Let me check and see if June is asleep," I said. Returning from June's room, I poured myself a little more wine. "Want some?" I offered.

"No, I'm fine, just perfect."

"Sam, I'm really happy for you. . . ."

"You mean for us," he interrupted.

"No, I mean for you. You've worked hard and you sure as hell deserve it. Long past due, if you ask me."

I put my wine glass down, looked at him. We had been married for eight years. I felt like a squatter in my own home.

"Sam, we have to talk now. It's important."

"Well, sure, honey, we'll talk, make plans, you know we can do more now that there'll be more money."

"Sam, it isn't that. Oh, shit, Sam, I want a divorce."

His body seemed to crumble, and then I saw his eyes. He blinked for a second, as if to shut out my words. He closed his eyes, then, and shook his head, "No," he said.

"Sam . . ." I started to say something. But what? I had known he would react this way. Known from the beginning that he believed he was not a failure because I married him. That was all the proof he needed. Of course I didn't have to do anything, be anything, it was enough that I had agreed to marry him. To live with him, to be wifelike. I looked right, I sounded right, I was more than just acceptable, I was better than he believed he deserved, or could get. In the years we had been married, he was not a failure, not to himself. I had destroyed more than our marriage by asking for a divorce, I had extinguished his image.

"I knew you would ruin it for me." He was grim. "All day I knew you would do something to spoil it. When I came home and found you up and dinner made, I was still apprehensive. You've spoiled so much. You're incapable of just enjoying something. And now this. Today."

His face hardened; his voice was bitter. "Susan, I won't talk about it, not today, not ever."

"You'll have to, Sam, because I mean it, this time I really mean it."

"What do you want, Susan, what the hell do you want?"

"I want to start fresh. I guess I want to live alone."

"Do I disturb you so much? Hell, I've tried to give you everything you want. This is crazy. You're not normal, Susan, you know that, you're just not normal."

I was relieved that he had raised his voice, was angry.

"I'm not normal? And you are? If I'm a junkie, you're a supplier. You expect nothing from me, so you can feel yourself a man, and I give nothing, except my litany of phony illnesses to satisfy you. That's why I want out. I don't want to be sick any more."

"I'll say you don't give anything. Go ahead, be well, behave like a normal person, get the hell out of bed, cook dinner, take care of June, I'm not stopping you."

"Yes, you are, anyway, that's the way I feel—that as long as we're together I won't ever get out of bed."

Sam got up to pour himself another drink. "You're not right. I don't want you to be sick. No, that's not it. You can't help yourself. You need protection." He shuddered slightly. "All you've ever known was remorse and hate and destruction. What else do you know?" Sam paused for a minute. "Look, Susan, let's be rational. We don't have a perfect marriage. But we have June. She's my daughter, too. Have you given any thought to that, to June, to what it will mean for her?"

I had given a great deal of thought to June. I had, after all, turned into a magazine Mom. She was five now, eager, bright, vulnerable. We still lived in her world, most of the time. To accommodate her child needs, I had reduced my own to the bare minimum. We were a couple of cute kids, in matching check shirts and jeans. Sitting at the kitchen table, eating chocolate pudding, we read Dr. Seuss together and marveled at the pop-out pictures in the newest Raggedy Ann picture book.

We each had our dolls; she tended to hers with loving care. I tried to follow her example. Sam seemed to find her child world intriguing, I found it tedious. He thought it adorable when she said "Fusketti" instead of spaghetti. "June, baby," he would urge in front of company, "say 'fusketti' for Daddy." And June, nobody's fool, obliged with a shy smile. Everyone applauded. Kisses all around and then her small hand in mine, I went to tuck her in. "June," I said, "it's spaghetti—spa-ghet-ti."

We measured her growth with the obligatory marks on the kitchen doorsill. Red lines across the white paint edging upward. Inside me she grew as well. Still somehow implanted in my womb, I needed no ruler to measure that growth. Bored and irritated as I was, I would never be whole without her. We would take our chances together, without Sam.

"Very few marriages are perfect," he said softly, "but at least we understand each other. We have that."

"We do not have that. You don't understand a god-damned thing. You never have. I know you've tried, I'm not blaming you, I blame myself, if anything. But really, Sam, it doesn't work at all. It's not a good marriage; it's a lousy marriage."

"The goddamned trouble with you, besides the fact that you're never satisfied with anything, is that you think you're so special. Nobody could possibly understand Susan. Special. Go ahead, smile, but it's true. You're even too special for an ordinary marriage; maybe you won't be satisfied until you achieve greatness, a special greatness like your family."

"That's terrible, Sam, really terrible. Don't throw that up to me, don't use that against me. They were victims, don't twist it into something else."

"You're the one who twists it. Trying not to feel anything about it, not even to think about it. How can you expect to have any human feelings when you won't even allow yourself to feel anything about your parents' suicides. Anger, you must be angry and sad and God knows what else."

"Stop it. I don't want to talk about it. You know that."

"Maybe it's time you did. You're a victim, too. They dehumanized your family, exterminated them and twenty-five years later you're a still a victim. It never ended for you. Maybe if you would just let some feeling in, you could deal with it."

"Sure, just like my mother and my father did. I watched them for years. They had an inexhaustible appetite for remorse. Everything else was superfluous to that. They carried their death lode proudly, as if it could breathe life back into the dead. They were intoxicated with their own grief, drunk on their gallant gestures of remembering their dead. They were ashamed that they lived. Why did they live when all the others died? They had feelings all right, they never stopped feeling for one single second until they died from it. Not me—let the experts dissect it now. Experts in war, and genocide, and suicide with subspecialties in matricide, mourning and death-camp paranoia. Let them analyze it, philosophize about it, justify it, deplore it, let the experts who know it all write the history. It won't kill them, they'll live to write another day. But the victims, they must not have this mania for remembering."

Sam shook his head. Putting his glass down, he went to put his arms around me.

"Don't, please, Sam, just don't. I told you, you don't understand. Please leave me alone. I told you I just want to live alone."

"Don't do this, Susan. It won't be easy for you. Maybe I don't understand, but at least I care. What do you think you'll find out there? Not many people will care."

He was kneeling in front of me and I touched his hair.

"I know you care. I'm sorry. It's so inadequate just to be sorry but I am."

"You'll only isolate yourself, Susan, you know you will. Even more than now, you'll withdraw and shrivel up."

"Maybe not, Sam, maybe I'll be strong and healthy and useful."

"Can't you see what you're doing to yourself? You're running away from reality. Not the reality of your past, maybe you're right about that, I don't know, but the reality of the present. Can't you see what that will lead to?"

"The reality of the present stinks, Sam. What it will lead to . . . I don't know. I'd like to give it a try though. You're doing it again, you know, even now. Making me out to be a cripple. You want some reality, all right, how's this for reality? I can't stand it when you touch me. I pretend to be sick, any kind of sick, so I can be alone, away from you. You bore me, you drag me down, you make me pity you, we have nothing in common any more except my various sicknesses. That's the reality."

Sam stood up, and stared down at me, still curled up in the chair.

"That's how you see it, that's really how you see it. Everything I've done for you, and that's what comes out." His voice was cracking; he was near tears. "Susan, please, Susan, I'll never leave you, you know that. You don't have to be afraid. I'll never leave you. Please don't do this."

"I'm sorry, Sam, I'm sorry."

There wasn't really anything else to say, but we continued to have such conversations for months. Finally, with our words echoing off the walls, Sam gave up and moved out.

June was heartbroken when Sam left. It was the beginning of her voyage into my world, the world into which she was born. I would have sacrificed anything to shelter her from the bitterness of divorce, if only I could have endured that malignant marriage.

I had entered motherhood with a kind of religious fervor, determined always to place my child before myself. For years I lived a monastic life, isolated with my child, a long retreat of silence, and like all zealots, the deprivation had its own rewards. As long as I was sacrificing, I knew I was a good mother.

If only it had remained simple. The early trade-offs were not so bad. Long days of solitude, boredom. The only sounds those of baby June and the whirring of machines that cleaned. But some conflict set in. While I seemed to gratify all her physical needs, she did not do the same for me. We both needed stroking, but her small arms around my neck, her wet kisses, her tiny body curled into mine for an afternoon nap did not quiet other urgent desires. June fell asleep with a smile on her lips. I disentangled myself and softly closed the bathroom door. Uncomfortable on the cold tiles, I was ashamed and angry that I sought such relief.

I remembered other times when I had crept from my bed. Sam was asleep. I chose the thicker towels and arranged them artistically on the bathroom floor. The light was harsh but, covered with a washcloth, it produced a soft glow. It was cramped in there; my position was, of necessity, always the same. Knees drawn up, my head barely touching the piping under the sink, I closed my eyes. The view of the toilet did not suit my mood. The towels became disarranged as I moved; the unfriendly tiles stared back at me, disinterested in my autoeroticism. In a moment it was over. I had no wish to stay there, to rest in that place of temporary passion. Quickly, alert now to Sam's breathing, I folded towels, replaced the washcloth, checked for evidence. Of what? Who, after all, was deceiving whom? I slid back into bed, no more satisfied than when I left. Why then did I do it?

Later, when I was angrier still, I did not bother with the elegance of my bathroom. I turned on my side, the bed slowly undulating, rippling with my stroke for sexual release.

Was this desire? This need to intrude myself into myself. To stroke my membranes, to scratch and tease that soft inner lining, those small raised knobs?

My back touched his, surely he could feel me move. It is a quick business and lacks variety. The grand finale tensed my body, a soft cry stuck in my throat. Wet now, I turned around. Oddly grateful to Sam for still being there after this massive insult to his manhood. I fell asleep then, my hands, smelling of sex, curled my hair.

Again, Sam gone at last, I was still performing this hungry act of loneliness.

Alone with June, I saw that she too was a creature of impulse. Her demands were not eccentric. Her simple kindnesses were touching. A breakfast tray, with charcoal toast, and eggs congealed on the plate. A cup of instant coffee made from warm tap water slopping in the saucer.

"Surprise, Mommy, I made it all for you." She watched me while I ate it.

Her favorite pastime was trying on my clothes and shoes. Did she want to be me? I wanted to be her. I wanted me for a mother.

I sat there, waiting for the police, holding Sam's hand, his face grimacing in pain; he was a model of martyrdom. I could never hope to compete with this emotionally broken and now physically stricken ex-husband.

It had been a long time since Sam aroused any emotion in me except anger and pity. The anger is real enough but the pity is detached, filtered.

In the wake of our divorce Sam became a solitary person, living alone, unable or unwilling to restructure his life. I imagined him alone in his apartment, waiting for something to happen, waiting for the phone to ring. I thought of us as friends who had had a falling out; we could not be enemies, we did not hate each other. There was no sexual tension between us, as there had been none in our marriage. I did not understand how he could have felt sexually betrayed, since he had never aroused in me a feeling of sexual commitment. Surely he knew that, could feel it in my dry, parched cunt. Never wet for him, never moist, he pushed into that arid territory nevertheless. But surely he knew. He was the injured party; what defense did I have, after all? I left him because I craved wetness, wanted a dripping, drooling, lusting cunt.

Sam physically incapacitated held out some promise, however. Now I could be noble, grand. I would never be disappointed because I would have no expectations beyond his ability. The things Sam did well, he could still do as an invalid. He was marvelous at things like gratitude and respect. A born supplicant, being bedridden would fulfill his dearest fantasy.

And what would I get from my new role as nurse-wife? Someone to come home to, to share the day's gossip with, to admire me, to debate the trivial decisions of life with. Someone who cared for me, dependent and reliable in his debilitated state.

Perhaps my affair with Jason had dampened my appetite for a wet cunt. And I had to face the fact that nobody, not even Jason, could irrigate it as profusely as I could myself.

When the police arrived at his apartment I shared begrudgingly those critical moments with Sam. (How do I look to the police and to the young intern? Do they think I'm attractive?) Even as they wheeled Sam out of his room I had to catch myself from looking in the mirror to see if the appropriate expression of concern looked well on me.

I would like to feel some purity of sadness or grief independent of how it appears to others.

Hospitals in the middle of the night are silhouettes in slow motion. Doctors congregating in the halls cast long shadows on the walls, heads bobbing, whispered words echoing through empty corridors. I sat outside his room, smoking, waiting. Equipment had been moved into his room and doctors with clipboards and nurses with trays walked in and out.

Always before, someone had told me the news of death. This time I would have to be the one. I would have to tell his parents, and June, everyone. This time I would be the announcer, a position of some importance, as I recall it, these messengers of death. They themselves to be respected and consoled.

I sat and prepared myself for the role of harbinger of death. Every now and then, when no one was watching, I relieved myself by curling my hair. Then, furtively patted it in place so as not to look too odd. I wondered if people would feel sorry for me, but feared that the general reaction would be "Well, after all, she did divorce him, no sympathy for her. Now the child, that's different." I wished I hadn't divorced him; how different all this would be. I would be a legitimate wife, soon to be widow, instead of ex-wife with no standing. Of course as June's mother, the child's mother, there might be some leniency.

The hospital corridor was chilly. I had smoked too much and been ignored for hours while the doctors came and went, taking blood samples and ordering tests for Sam. Finally, the chief neurologist stopped to speak to me. He started to explain what he thought was wrong with Sam but I stopped him.

"Dr. Rappoport, please, just one question first, is he going to die?"

He looked surprised, but what other question counted? "Mrs. Warner, I have to be honest with you, we don't know what it is but I don't think he is going to die." He smiled protectively as he said this as if he were indulging a frightened child. "I have scheduled a series of spinal taps. It looks as if he has a tumor that is pressing on the nerves and causing him great pain, but we can't be sure until we see the results of the tests. Why don't you go home? We won't know anything until tomorrow afternoon at the earliest and I'll call you if the situation changes."

I didn't want to go home. I couldn't bear to be away from the hospital, but not for love of Sam.

"Should I call his parents?" I asked. The doctor thought a moment and said that he thought that would be a good idea.

Now, at least, there was something to do. I exchanged a dollar for ten dimes and went into the phone booth. I hadn't spoken to his parents since the divorce. They were bitter and blamed me. His mother answered the phone. When I told her I had been with him all night, she resented it. It was her place to have been with him. "We'll be right there as soon as we dress," she said. "Is June all right?"

I had forgotten all about June. I called my neighbor's house where I had stowed her away. I tried to explain without frightening her that Sam was sick and I would be staying at the hospital for a while. She wanted to know if she could visit. I told her not yet but soon, when Daddy was better.

At nine o'clock I called the office. David was in and I explained about Sam. I told him I would be in some time during the day. David was sympathetic. I imagined during the course of the day he would say to people in a hushed tone, "Susan's ex-husband is gravely ill and she's with him, of course." That made David important. Just being close to the ex-wife of the gravely ill is important. And then there would be the extra burden of my absence and he would perhaps have to stay late to finish some of my work. This would work out quite well for David, who enjoyed being a martyr.

The more people I called, the less reality Sam's illness had. Everyone was concerned for himself.

More doctors arrived now with papers which Sam had to sign. The papers said essentially "We are not responsible if you die." Sam signed the papers (not wishing to offend the doctors who would not be responsible if he died) and was swiftly removed to another floor for spinal taps and X rays.

Shortly after, his family arrived; two short parents and Sam's mother's sister and her husband. They were a close family. In the beginning that was what I envied about them. There were many cousins, more than twenty, and they seemed to have good times. I wanted to be part of that but from the start I didn't fit in. There was never anything wrong with any of his family. They had perfect teeth, no one had acne, no one miscarried, no one divorced. They were an enclave of family perfection. If I could have, I would have made myself over to be like them but all my instincts were wrong. If I tried to dress like them it ended up gauche and if I tried to sound like them it ended up phony. During the years we were married they were not cruel, just disinterested and perhaps frightened that I would get close to them, bringing with me my messy family history. They never asked any questions and, of course, I never volunteered any information. Considering how they ignored us during the years of our marriage, I was amazed how they rallied round Sam at the time of the divorce.

I had called one of his cousins, Dorothy, to whom I felt closest, to try to explain that I hoped we could still be friends even after the divorce, but she was cold on the phone and said, "I'm sorry, Susan, I don't have much sympathy for you, I think you're making a terrible mistake. Naturally you can understand that all my sympathies are with Sam."

I didn't understand. I said I did but I really didn't. She'd rather liked me before. What did it matter to her that Sam and I would be divorced? That was the last time I spoke with any of them, and now his chirping little mother was fluttering down the hall toward me.

"Where is he? Is he all right?" she asked. I explained what the doctor had told me. "Oh, God, he is going to die. I know he's going to die," she shrieked.

"No," I said, putting my hand on her shoulder, "no, he's not going to die."

She stood rigid and stared right at me saying, "How do you know, you tramp, you with your divorce and your men? How do you know anything?"

Sam's father was overweight and sick himself. Coughing and spitting, he seemed too weak to absorb much of what was being said. Turning to him, I said, "Listen, Hoard, sit down. The doctor will be back soon, you don't look well."

"He doesn't look well," Sam's mother shrilled, "and why do you think he doesn't look well? He hasn't slept one minute since you left Sam. All night he lies awake and cries for June. Get out of here. We don't need you. This is our business."

"Oh, for God's sake," I answered, "this isn't the time for all that crap, and I'm not leaving, I'm staying."

"Crap! That's all you are, crap! Get out. I hate the sight of you. I will never forgive you for what you did. You should be lying in that bed instead of Sam."

Sam! Poor Sam was getting more lost with each encounter of his loved ones. Who cared any more about Sam?

His aunt and uncle, who had always disliked me, were being coldly cordial. "Ruth," her sister said, "calm down, this isn't helping. If Susan wants to stay, let her stay. Let's get some coffee."

And the five of us, an uneasy truce declared, had coffee. Many cups of coffee.

From other rooms on the floor we could hear a moan or sometimes a patient begging for medication. This is a very sick floor, I thought, they must put the worst cases here. The morning passed and Uncle Nat went to get sandwiches. I was hungry but rather ashamed to eat, so I tried to nibble unobtrusively.

I called the office again and David got on to tell me that there had been a roundup of refusneks. Some in jail, others under house arrest.

"It's all right, we are handling it."

But now I was torn between the two scenes of action. The one at the hospital with my, maybe, dying ex-husband, and the one at the office with Leonid's hunger strike. I knew the press would be calling for background material and pictures, anything I could give them. There was no question about it, I was a terrifically important person.

I was getting tired of sitting around at the hospital, but I didn't want to leave the field to his mother.

By noon, Sam still had not been returned to his room. Other relatives of patients came and sat in small groups in the waiting room area. No one had a book or knitting or crossword puzzles or anything that might distract from the interminable waiting for news of their relatives. It was as if there was some virtue in waiting for hours on end without the relief of any diversion. What difference would it have made to those ailing relatives if one were engrossed in a book? Was it that the fear of what might happen was so great that no distraction was possible? Or was it a kind of mystical belief that if we agonized enough, worried enough, there would be a reward and the relative would be all right? I had no bargains to make with God as I had done when I was a child. God was not making any bargains with me then and I doubt very much that he would be making any such arrangements now. If it would help Sam, I would have been willing to sit with the rest of them and wait. I doubted that this medical dilemma could be resolved spiritually and certainly not mystically.

Dr. Rappoport finally appeared in the early afternoon. Grimly shaking hands with all of us, he sat down to explain that they were still trying to draw spinal fluid for a simple spinal tap. Sam's muscles were in spasm.

Ruth was trembling. "He'll be all right, won't he?" she asked, begging for a kind of reassurance the doctor was not really able to give.

"I think so, Mrs. Warner," he answered kindly, "but I think we will have to operate if we can't get a clear picture of what's going on. He's really in a great deal of pain and from the tests we've already taken, we feel pretty certain that there is a tumor pressing on the nerves."

"Oh, my God," Ruth said, "operate? Please don't cut him!" Dr. Rappoport was distinctly uncomfortable with Sam's small hysterical mother and I could see him grimace when she used the words "cut him." Was he, after all, a butcher?

"Well, Mrs. Warner, let's see what the next few hours bring. Try not to worry, we will do the best we can for your son."

Dr. Rappoport had looked at me during this exchange a couple of times in a kind of conspiratorial way, as if to say, "You and I are the only intelligent people here. I can count on you not to get hysterical." He really was rather nice looking; each time I saw him he got better looking. His long white doctor's coat covered an expensive business suit and I noticed particularly that he had well-groomed hands and long fingers. He spoke with his hands stuck in the pockets of his white coat, occasionally drawing them out to pat Ruth on the back or scratch his head.

Those were the hands that would cut Sam open; I wondered how they would feel playing with my cunt. I liked the idea of those long fingers moving inside me, giving me pleasure.

As we were talking, Sam was brought back. We saw him being wheeled to his room. They all rushed to the door, abandoning Dr. Rappoport, while I stayed to thank him and to let him know that I would be delighted to be his conspirator. I would in fact be delighted to go to bed with him. I leaned toward him as I spoke words like, "I'm so grateful for all you've done for my ex-husband. It's good to know that he is in such good hands." I wished I could take one of his hands and put it on my breast. I don't generally like to have my breasts touched. Sucking pleases me but most men are clumsy touchers. A surgeon, I thought, must have very sure hands.

There was a slight commotion going on as Sam was being wheeled into his room and his mother was trying to move alongside the bed he was being wheeled in on. This caused something of a traffic jam in the doorway and the nurse politely asked her to step aside and said, "He's really not allowed visitors but his wife can come in for a few moments."

"Wife!" Ruth screamed. "She's no wife. Let me in. I'm the mother. Let me in that room."

The nurse, unaware of the politics of death in this family, looked to me for guidance. I nodded and motioned for her to allow Ruth to go in.

"All right, you're first, but please remember he is tired and don't stay long."

Ruth came out a few minutes later, walked straight to me, her eyes black holes of hate. "He's going to die," she said, "I can see it on his face, so now, lady, you go, go to your husband, you go and help him die."

I went into Sam's room. He was huddled in the bed. His face was contorted trying to smile, but twisted instead with pain. His voice was thick and dry. His tongue seemed to be falling out of his mouth.

"Jesus, Susan, you wouldn't believe it. They tried four times, four times they tried to do the tap. What's happening to me?"

I didn't want to sit down. That was too much of a commitment. I bent over his bed and said, "Sam, you have the best doctors. This hospital is known for its fine doctors." (What crap is this?) "Hey, Sam, this is some way to get attention."

I had to keep talking, whatever banal words they were. I could see he was close to crying. I didn't want him to cry and, God knows, I didn't want to cry, not here.

"Sam, really, they have the best here." Why the hell did I keep telling him that? I couldn't think of anything else to say.

He closed his eyes, "I'm so tired, Susan, but I can't sleep, I'm afraid to go to sleep. It's always you that's been afraid to sleep. If I go to sleep now I'm afraid I won't wake up. You were right, all those nights you couldn't sleep because you were terrified to die, you were right. Dying is shit. I don't want to die. I never felt such terror before. How's June? Does she know?"

"I told her you were sick, Sam. Don't worry, go to sleep, I will stay. Do you want me to stay?" (Oh, how I wished he would tell me to leave. Please Sam, tell me to leave.)

"Yes," he said anxiously, "please stay, just stay where I can look at you, you don't have to talk, just go and sit there near the window."

I pulled the chair over by the window and he seemed to drift off to sleep. The nurse came in, taking blood, checking other things, glancing at me sympathetically. More doctors came and asked me to leave briefly. I called the office again but there was a meeting in progress and I could not speak with David. I called Marge and asked her to pick June up and keep her at her house.

"After I get June," Marge said, "do you want me to come by the hospital?"

"I don't know, I don't know how long I will be here. I

hoped I wouldn't be here this long. This whole hospital scene is beginning to drive me a little crazy."

"I'm really sorry. What can I do to help?" Marge asks this politely; she will have nothing to do with the intensity of this life-and-death matter. She would do anything I asked of her but still, whenever she speaks about anything that has strong emotional overtones, she sounds only polite. That's her style just as mine is a kind, ubiquitous intensity about practically anything that has an emotional component.

We have in a sense adopted each other's external life claims and made them a legitimate concern of our own lives. It doesn't really matter what the issue is, it only matters insofar as our lives are affected. So, by proxy, Marge is concerned for Soviet Jews because it affects my life and, in the same way, I am concerned with art directors and copywriters with whom she works because they affect her life. We are a dependable couple, Marge and I. There is no problem too trivial that either of us may have that the other will not concern herself with. Only we know where the real boundaries are. To others it must seem as if we have almost identical interests.

"Nothing more than taking care of June. I have got to get to the office eventually," I said.

"Well, you know if there is anything at all that I can do. . . ."

"I know, Marge. Thanks. Sam does look deathly ill; I'm afraid he really may die."

"Susan, he won't die, Sam won't die."

I can see it's hard for her to take in that it's really this serious. Death is not a part of our lives, we're too young, it's not time yet for death to be anything but shocking. We don't even read the obituaries regularly.

"He might die," I said, "and the worst part is, I'm afraid

for him to die for all the wrong reasons. I won't even be a proper widow, although I suppose I will call myself that. If I had known he was going to die, I never would have divorced him. You'll have to help me, I mean about the funeral, and if I should go, and what I should do. If he dies, Marge, you will have to tell me what the proper conventions are."

"Susan, stop it. He isn't dead yet. If he dies we'll figure it out. You can be a widow if you want to."

Rejoining the relatives (who stopped talking as I walked toward them), I sat down on those terrible, cold plastic couches in the waiting room and accepted another container of coffee from Uncle Nat, who seemed to find a purpose in supplying us with this symbol of sustenance.

I sat apart from them, hoping that they would feel free to talk among themselves and let me think my own thoughts.

I had an affair eight years after we had been married. Sam had brought him home. Stuart White was an old friend from Sam's Greenwich Village days. We so rarely had company, except for the small group of married friends we rotated weekends with, that I was both nervous and excited. Our entertaining consisted of spaghetti dinners, salad, French garlic bread and chocolate mousse. I had begun to notice that the other couples in our group were branching out to roast beef and quiche. It struck me that Sam and I would be spaghetti people all our lives, eventually going to grand homes of those same friends who, in private, joked nostalgically about their spaghetti days.

On this occasion, I made duck. And when Stuart walked in, I knew my day's efforts were worth it. He preceded Sam into the apartment. Tall, tan, lean, hands outstretched to greet me, one handsome cheek curled into what he knew was a winning smile. He dressed expensively. Black blazer, ivory shirt open at the throat, a flash of a gold bracelet on one wrist, on the other, a Cartier watch. He looked like a man who would have a valet. Sam shuffled along behind him.

"You must be Susan," he said, his voice deep, seductive. I began to wonder if he was already in love with me. Surely he didn't talk that way to everybody.

"Indeed, I must be," I replied, glancing around the apartment to indicate that I was the only one there.

"Sam," Stuart said accusingly, "you didn't begin to do her justice."

Stuart now lived in a suburb of Los Angeles. A stockbroker, "doing all right, no complaints." Rich, clearly very rich. He did not talk much about his marriage, no pictures of her and the children. Good. Probably breaking up with her. Conversation at dinner was divided between Sam and Stuart reminiscing and Stuart and me finding common ground about books and movies we liked. Sam kept trying to intrude himself with questions that began "Whatever happened to . . ." but it was our evening, Stuart's and mine. The apartment looked better with him in it, almost elegant. The food tasted delicious; I was beautiful, and slim and gracious. I didn't do the dishes, not wanting to give up being with him for even that short time. I wished Sam would go do the dishes, but when I kiddingly suggested it, he gave me a dirty look.

Stuart left with promises to get together again before he went back to California.

"Like him?" Sam said as he was undressing for bed.

"Sure, he seemed nice." I yawned. "I'll clean up in the morning."

"He's changed," Sam said thoughtfully, "I guess that's what the Coast does to people."

"How do you mean, how has he changed?"

122

"Sort of phony, Christ, did you notice that gold brace-let?"

"Well, he seemed very genuine to me."

"You're easily impressed. I'm telling you he's a phony. Shame what happens to people. He bored me to death."

Not me, he didn't bore me to death. Sam's maligning him made him more attractive.

Stuart called at ten the next morning.

He didn't say hello, he said, "One o'clock, lunch at the Four Seasons."

I said, "Yes."

We astounded each other with the uniqueness of our interests: Bach and Beiderbecke, Proust and Agatha Christie. We both hated fish, loved pasta al pesto, could take ballet or leave it, but would kill for opera. Marriage. Sam was sweet, but insensitive. Paula was wonderful, but mundane. Sad. The exchange of those stories took us through another lunch. In the end, we reluctantly agreed that we, Stuart and I, had both "grown" during the years of our marriage, while Sam and Paula had not matured at all. Poor Sam and Paula, poor us. What were we to do?

Stuart and I shared another quality, a gift for disloyalty. We spoke about Sam and Paula as if they were innocent children, a little retarded, but not to be blamed for their offenses. Our conspiratorial candor charmed me. I didn't mind about the betrayal. It was necessary if we were to be intimate. During our third lunch, by now good friends, Stuart asked me to have dinner with him on the next night.

"Dinner, that's a different story altogether. What will I tell Sam?" I asked. The surprised look on Stuart's face alerted me. I had gone too far. He would not collaborate with me in lying to my husband. He did, after all, have a sense of honor.

"Oh, don't worry," I quickly assured him, "I'll think of something."

I told Sam I wanted to go back to school, take a few courses. He was delighted. Particularly because I seemed so excited about this venture.

I ordered three cups of coffee after dinner. Stuart smiled understandingly. He was staying at the Waldorf. We walked there from the restaurant, suddenly having nothing at all to say. I could be a business associate, I told myself, entering the elevator, entering his room. Just a business associate.

It was a suite. We sat in the living room; he ordered drinks from room service.

"You are nervous," he observed. "There's nothing to be nervous about."

Of course not. Maybe for other people who are being unfaithful, but not for Stuart and me, who have after all, so much in common.

The drinks came; we drank. We went to bed. He undressed me, but the room was cold and I wanted to be under the covers. I wanted to be under the covers for other reasons as well.

He took time with me. I was more enchanted than excited by his technique. The digital clock kept flipping over the minutes. How long was long enough, I wondered. Three minutes, four. After five minutes, I decided I was ready. Five minutes seemed to me to be about right.

His gold St. Christopher medal lapped against my chest, occasionally hitting my chin. I wondered if his wife had given it to him, and why he didn't take it off. It hung there above me like a hypnotist's charm. I closed my eyes, my body motions indicating that I was ready.

It was not nearly as strange as I had imagined, having another man inside me. I could tell the difference between him and Sam anywhere. Actually, Sam filled me more. Stuart was longer and thinner. Stuart appeared to want to include me in this sex act. After he got settled in, he stopped and asked if I was all right. "Fine," I murmured, "fine." Moved by his concern, I opened my eyes. The medal was now hovering above my cheek, dangerously close to my eye. "Put your legs around me," he said. Pushing the covers up, I complied. The covers formed a kind of tent, my legs the poles holding them aloft. When he came, his body collapsed on me, and I wasn't sure what to do with my legs. After a moment, I slowly unwrapped them, the tent collapsing around us as well.

He stuck with it. Telling me I was beautiful, he loved me, I was wonderful. Still resting on me, he asked, "Would you like a cigarette?" "God, yes." Sam didn't smoke, had no idea of the after-sex cigarette ritual.

He lit two, handing me one. "It will get better, Susan, I promise."

"It was marvelous, Stuart, fantastic. I'm just shaking because it happened at all."

"Darling, darling, we haven't hurt anybody. We're just taking a little happiness for ourselves."

What astonished me the most, of course, was that I was so little affected by the fact of my infidelity. I had been stopped in the past because I was sure I would feel terrible, look different, my life would collapse if I slept with another man.

Instead, I felt better. I was anxious to get home now. Stuart got up to go to the bathroom and order more drinks. I felt fondly toward him too. But fonder still of Sam. I didn't want Stuart to feel bad, perhaps fifteen minutes would be a decent interval before leaving. He came back, still naked, the medal glowing in the dark against his tan chest. He was definitely prouder of his body than I was of mine. I had rearranged the sheets and blankets and smoothed my hair. He sat on the bed like a doctor paying a house call.

"What shall we do, Susan?" he said. "What on earth shall we do?"

I was uncertain if he was talking about right now or life itself. For right now, I would have liked a Coke. As for life, well, it seemed unlikely that Stuart White was going to be the answer to anything at all.

"We'll just have to see," I said ambiguously. He got up to answer the knock on the door from room service. I hoped he'd remember to grab a towel or something.

"Here, darling," he said handing me a drink. "You know, this isn't the first time for me, Susan. I confess I've strayed before."

I wondered if those other women had been as menaced by the medal as I had been.

"But this is different. I guess you know that," he continued.

"Yes, I suppose so."

How was it different? And how impoverished had those other encounters been? For me it had been an approximation of intimacy, in the vicinity of passion, but not at the core.

"You disturb me, Susan, this isn't just a one-night stand, you know."

"When are you leaving?" I asked. It was certainly good enough for a two- or three-night stand.

"In two days, just two days. That doesn't give us much time to make up our minds."

"We can't do anything to hurt Sam or Paula, Stuart. We agreed to that."

"Oh, God, I know. But it's so hard." He began fingering his medal, praying no doubt for divine guidance. "You're so brave, darling. It just kills me when I think of you and Sam together," he said.

He needn't have bothered to agonize over that. The occasion was sufficiently rare, and the contact sufficiently tedious not to cause anyone to become exercised. Some latent loyalty emerged at this, however.

"Stuart, dear, Sam is really a very good husband. And I love him much the same as you love Paula. We'll just have to bear it; perhaps it will be easier with you so far away."

During that last year of my marriage, Stuart would come to New York occasionally. I managed to get out of bed for lunches and dinners with him. He always brought with him a new scheme for a vacation together. He treated our affair as if it really had the possibility of permanency. He wanted to be sure I was his, if he ever chose to leave his wife. I didn't argue. Why be querulous over such a small point?

Intimacy with Stuart stopped short of his telling me how much he earned, and my revealing that I never had an orgasm. As earnest and candid as we were with each other, those bastions of personal privacy were never breached. When I was with Stuart, I lived up to his expectations. I was, if not flawless, certainly charming. And those minor flaws which did emerge he found "delightful." I began to blame Sam for not similarly inspiring me. How could I be so enchanting and captivating with Stuart, and so dour and sullen with Sam? I suspected that if I married Stuart I would stay charming. Stuart would live with the Susan he wanted, the Susan he cultivated. In fact, because of him, even if we divorced I would still be charming.

Speculating on our marriages, a subject we both found endlessly entertaining, I could see that there might be a few obstacles like money and sex. All the other basics would lend themselves to amiable negotiation. We had already settled the problems of shared housework, philosophy of child-rearing, decor, summer versus winter vacations; we were

127

accommodating and compatible on such matters. I gave in on the window being open at night, he conceded on my reading in bed. We would have no minor irritations to disturb our bliss.

Finally, he asked me to join him for a week.

"A whole week together will give us some time to think things out. I promise I'll make a decision after that," he said.

Unfortunately the week never happened. Stuart called from the Coast one morning explaining that he couldn't get away. It seemed that Paula was having an affair.

"Well," I said, "You must feel relieved. I guess this solves your dilemma."

"Relieved? Yeah, I guess I am. I mean it comes as a great shock. I can't tell you how much of a shock. I never imagined she would do such a thing. She's lived an incredibly sheltered life. I could hardly believe it when she told me."

"But it gets you off the hook. You have been feeling so guilty, so confused. Kind of funny when you think about it, she was doing the same thing to you."

"I don't think it's funny at all, Susan."

Was this the same man with whom I had been sharing all that pasta al pesto?

"Oh, well, I didn't mean funny, I just meant you never know, do you?"

"Listen, Susan, I don't think you understand. There are children involved here. And not only that, Paula is very upset herself. She is seeing a psychiatrist, and he feels it is important for us, Paula and me, to go for therapy together."

"But why? I mean you've both found other people, why do you have to go to a psychiatrist?"

"You forgot the children, Susan, the children."

"What about the children, for God's sake."

"You know, Susan, I don't think I realized before how insensitive you can be. These poor kids are suffering."

"Suffering? Because Mommy and Daddy are fucking other people? Your teenage children, who are probably fucking other people too, are suffering?"

"I can understand that you feel threatened, Susan, but please don't get vulgar."

"Vulgar. You're the man who taught me vulgar. You're the one who wants me to be your whore in bed."

Stuart sighed. "Susan, don't do that. Try to understand, it is only temporary. Until Paula and the children are on their feet again. I have to help them. You see that."

"Okay, so help them. Tidy up your life. See you around."

"Susan, I love you. I really do. You believe that, don't you?"

"Sure, I love you, too. Stuart, do me one favor, will you?"

"Anything."

"You know that St. Christopher's medal you wear . . ."

"You'd like it as a memento."

"No, Stuart, I wouldn't like it as a memento. Just take it off when you start going to bed with someone else."

"Susan, I thought we were going to be civilized."

"Sure thing. By all means. Civilized. Goodbye, Stuart."

Having had a suitor of sorts bolstered my marriage for a time. Infidelity was tantalizing. Besides the sex, which I suspected was not really the point, the complications, the administration of an affair were a distraction in themselves, not to the affair, but to the marriage. Nevertheless, having had one, I hesitated about others. By then I didn't want to be distracted from the failure of my marriage; I wanted to end it. And an affair would only postpone that inevitability.

Had Sam suspected nothing? I had laughed at him plenty.

Well, I thought, looking around at his relatives, I'm not laughing now. We were surrounded by half-empty coffee containers and all of us were weary now.

"Poor Sam, even now he's not the star. His mother and I will see to it that he gets second billing at his own death."

For all the times I had laughed at him, hated him, betrayed him, he had been, after all, my first sane family. I was beginning to panic now at the thought of Sam's dying.

18

I have been asked during the course of these last terrible months why I am applying to emigrate to Israel. There are many factors that entered into my decision.

Before 1971, I was deaf to the cries of oppression of the individuals and most particularly of the Jews in the USSR.

In 1971 I was invited by the New York Philharmonic to give a series of guest concerts in New York City. Permission was at first granted and then, at the very last moment, I was told that it was not an "auspicious time for me to go." Several weeks before, Sasha Luborsky had defected while on a concert tour in Canada. "Was this the reason?" I asked. "Oh, no," they said, "it is just an inauspicious time."

For the first time in my life I felt trapped and the beginning of some vague fear.

In the summer of 1973, a visitor from the West brought some music. It was Israeli music and I played it alone, not in my studio but in my flat. It was good music, but I knew that I would never be allowed to perform it. When I heard of the shameful attack on Israel on the evening of October 6, it became clear to me as a Jew that it was time to play that full melody I had for so long denied. I did not think of repercussions, so naive and sheltered had I been.

I did not dream then that I would not be allowed to perform again, that my wife and I would be spied on all the time, picked up and interrogated constantly and threatened with prison. I did not know then that my future life would be one which consisted only of waiting.

I deeply regret the years that I refused to listen to the most important chord of all, that of my own identity as a Jew. Of course, technically I have committed no crime, but seen through their eyes I have committed the worst crime of all and so they level the full force of their hatred against us.

Perhaps by publishing this letter, our plight will be more understandable to the people of the United States. We grasp at the few letters that get through. Our phone has been disconnected but people should know that we hear of their efforts. That is all there is that gives us reason to hope and live.

Leonid Rabinovitz
August 1974

Dear Leonid:

It was wonderful being able to speak with you. I was so relieved to hear your voice. As I mentioned to you on the phone, everyone is working very hard on your behalf. Many senators are now interested in your case. You asked me to tell you about myself. I have enclosed a snapshot taken with my daughter about a year ago. I'm thirty-seven years old and live alone with my daughter because I am divorced from my husband. Most of my days and nights are spent working. I feel very lucky to be involved at a time like this.

In my past I've also had a few hard times. One day when we can sit face to face and drink together, perhaps I can tell you about some of them. For now it must be sufficient to keep writing and speaking on the phone when we can.

I'll send you another cable on September 1, and hope to speak with you then. Please give my love to Lucia.

Sincerely,
Susan

19

Was that only two days ago? Instead of lying here, cozy in my familiar fear, I should be writing a protest for Leonid or learning the Russian alphabet in preparation for the trip. I am ashamed that I put anything before Leonid.

But can I make a difference? My vanity is circular.

I calibrate my life by event, not calendar. I do not remember dates; my time frames have titles. Mother, marriage, June, Jason. My emotions are cumulative and seamless. If I were to rest at the end of the day, review each episode with pleasure or dismay, I would surely lose the sense of mounting emotion at the end of the time frame. A day is a primitive way of counting. It is feeling that defines time. When I was inexperienced, I anticipated endings full of hope. But experience with disappointment has changed that perspective.

It seems reasonable now that the future will be grim. All my nostalgia is remembered despair. Still, memories comfort me. They are, after all, my memories. And if they cause me pain, it is my pain. As long as I can contain it all in my body, I am essentially comforted. Only, do not impose upon me the simple truths of others.

I have missed my morning routine. The time for me to shower is long past. It's cold in this room; I am not inclined to leave my bed again.

I am worn out with fear. My stomach aches with periodic spasms. Cancer? My mouth tastes as if my teeth are rotting. I cup my hand to contain my breath. The putrid smell comforts me. I can feel a slow leak from my cunt. Reaching down, I wipe off some translucent liquid. Who will suck it next?

I have tried to be a good girl. Whatever it was they expected, I tried to accommodate. What a liar I am. I gave nothing. Sam said, "You don't trust anyone." Perhaps. But still I lick the cunt juice from my fingers.

Early in my affair with Jason I was sure of myself. I called him for lunch.

"I can't, Susan. I really can't today. I've had this lunch date set up for weeks."

"Cancel it. It's really important."

"Can't it wait until tonight?"

"I suppose it could but it shouldn't. I don't want it to. Please."

I could hear him weighing the choice. But he loved me.

"Okay, okay. One o'clock, but this better be good."

"Law school. You want to go to law school?"

"You think it's a bad idea?"

"No, no, not at all. You never mentioned you were interested in law school."

"Well, I wasn't. At least until I thought about it. I can go at night, work during the day, and then when I'm finished I'll at least have a trade, a profession. You think it's crazy?"

"No, I don't think it's crazy at all. As a matter of fact it sounds exciting. But you can't work all day and go to school at night. We'll have to think of something better than that."

"Like what?"

"Something better. Let me think about it a little. If it's what you want, if it will make you happy, we'll manage it."

We were seated next to each other in a restaurant.

"I want to touch you," he said. "Move closer to me." He put his arm around my waist and slowly pulled my blouse out of my skirt, all the time talking to me about law school and living together and what an investment in my future it would be. He moved his hand up to my breast, under my blouse. I turned toward him slightly to accommodate him.

"I can't stop touching you. Do you like me to touch you? Tell me you like me to touch you." His fingers were playing with my nipple. I put my hand on him. "Tell me," he said.

"It's okay." I laughed.

I applied to seven law schools and began to study for the law aptitude test. I wrote for my college transcript but could not bring myself to show it to Jason. I had forgotten what a poor student I was. In the mornings, after he left, I straightened the house and settled in to study.

For the first time in many years, I was home when June came in from school. We went to the park, alternating turns riding on her bicycle. I had hated these excursions in the past, watching June playing, sitting alone on a bench with a book unread in my lap, lonely and wretched, waiting only for enough time to pass so that I could whisk her home, away into the solitude of our apartment.

But now I had nothing to fear. I pushed her on the swings and balanced her on the seesaw. Now someone cared. Jason. Now it was all right. In the evenings, after dinner, I could feel Jason watching me as I read. Once in a while my hand moved to make those hair curls. I looked up and saw Jason and smoothed my hair instead.

He knelt in front of me and took the book from my hands.

"You're working too hard. You don't need to study this much. Any of those schools would be lucky to get you." He was unbuttoning my blouse.

"I hope you're right, but it all seems a little too good to be true."

"Not for you. Nothing's too good to be true for you." He was sucking my breasts, his hands pulling me down toward the floor.

"Let's go into the bedroom," I said, setting down my book.

"No. Here."

"No."

"Yes."

He raised my skirt and took my panties off.

"No."

"Yes." And put his mouth on me, his hands strumming my hair.

"No, not here."

"Oh, yes. Here. Now. I love you."

I moved my body to accommodate him.

I took the law aptitude tests and knew they had not gone well. I was afraid to tell Jason. I applied to all the law schools in the New York area. Weeks passed and finally the first rejection came. Then they came one after another. Neatly typed form letters regretting their decision.

When the last one came I called Jason at the office. "Come home," I said. I was still sitting with the letter in my hands when he came into the bedroom.

"Sweet girl, don't care so much. It doesn't matter. If you want to go that badly you can apply again next year and this time we'll pull some strings. It doesn't matter. I love you. I'll always take care of you. It doesn't matter."

For his sake I pretended to be consoled. For his sake, I let him hold me and comfort me. It was necessary to protect him from knowing how deeply I despaired. That was necessary for my sake, for after all, what could he do about it?

By now I was less sure of myself.

"Jason, do you think we're really special?"

"Sure we are. Do you doubt it?"

"I don't know. It seems impossible that this can be happening to me. I never meant to feel so much about anyone. I spend too much time thinking about you."

"That's just because you're not working."

"Do you think about me? I mean during the day?"

"Sometimes. Don't push so hard, Susan. It's all there."

"Do I love you too much?"

"I don't think so. How can anybody love anybody too much?"

"Listen, Jason, you have taught me so much. I want it never to end. Sometimes it's terrible. If I think about losing you I feel such terrible pain. For the first time I know where my heart is, I mean literally. Right there in the left side of my chest, my heart hurts. I always thought that it was just a literary conceit but it isn't."

"Why do you love me so much?" Jason asked.

Actually, that wasn't a bad question. I should have known by his asking it that I was losing him. I had not loved him at first, certainly not at that lunch. When then, did I fall so desperately in love? I tried to place the time but it was elusive. I almost had it, tried to creep up on the moment, but it turned slippery and I lost my grip. It would seem I just found myself here, in love. This place, love, was like a padded cell. Now that I feared losing him. I paced the floor, but there was no distraction. No windows, no light. No escape. When I heard the key, when Jason came, he brought everything I needed with him. So, for a time, I was happy. Then the door closed behind him and I was alone again.

138

Some time, when I wasn't looking, he had become my conduit to the world.

I no longer cared why I loved him. Once, perhaps, there had been good reasons. I only cared that I loved him. The foundation of it was buried deep in the ground. But the building was collapsing, the walls of my cell were caving in, and who had time to look and see if the original material was rotting? I was locked in; I could not go outside to begin an investigation of the site. I had to do whatever I could from the inside. I was trying not to panic.

Lightly, I replied, "Your money?"

"Seriously, why do you love me so much? I'm not so special."

"That makes it even scarier. You're smart and you're funny and you make me feel good about myself. Why do you love me?"

"Well, the thing is, Susan, I've got your number."

"You've got my number?"

"Yep. I know you. I know what you're going to do and say before you do it."

"Makes me sound boringly predictable."

"Not that way, it's just that I know you. I feel you, sense you, know when you're worried, scared, I need you in my life. I can't do without you."

"Hey, Jason. How long do you think people should know each other before they get married?"

"That's what I love about you, sweet girl, you're so subtle."

"Do you want to marry me?"

"I think I do. Give it a little time, Susan."

"Jason, I have a terrific idea. I don't want you to marry me."

"Oh?"

"Nope, I want you to adopt me. Then June will be your granddaughter and we can all live happily ever after."

"Marge, do you think I should tell him about my family?"

"You mean you haven't told him yet?"

"No, I just told him that they were dead."

"You haven't told him about how they died, that they committed suicide?"

"No."

"About how you lived during the war, about your father being in the camp, about Jean dying in the camp. Susan, that is your history, your life. How can you expect him to know you at all if you don't tell him those things? Who does he think you are, Marjorie Morningstar? What are you ashamed of?"

"I'm not ashamed. I just don't want to exploit it."

"For Christ's sake, you two are supposed to be in love. You're supposed to be able to tell him everything. Are you sure you're not afraid of telling him?"

"You mean because he'll think that I'm too different?"

"Something like that. Maybe you think it's a kind of blackmail. Once you tell him, how could he possibly leave you?"

"Well, isn't it?"

"It depends how you tell him. You are too dependent on him anyway. You need to get a job. It will never work if you keep leaning on him so much."

"You don't much like him, do you?"

"He's all right. I don't see quite what you see in him but he's all right."

"I really have to tell him about my parents, my childhood, before we get married."

"Surviving the Holocaust is not a communicable disease. Anyhow, has he asked you to marry him?"

"I'm not sure."

"Then he hasn't."

I didn't need Marge to tell me that I was too dependent on him. I could tell that my calls disturbed him at work. But I couldn't help it. I wanted to hear his voice, even though I would be seeing him in a few hours. I began to call him four and five times a day. Hanging up the phone, I felt shabby, promised myself I wouldn't call again, but picked up the phone a couple of hours later anyway. Over dinner I would tell him about the day's job hunt. He was preoccupied with his own business successes and seemed bored and impatient with my stories.

"I have enough money, Susan. You don't need to get a job now. Relax a little."

"I want to get a job."

"Well then, get one. I just hate to see you so agonized about it."

Once he gave me a check and when I started to protest he said, "Listen, sweet girl, don't think you can force me to marry you just to support you. After all, I'm staying over here most of the time."

I took the check.

I had met his son Mark and on weekends, while Sam had June, I stayed at his place. Jason's apartment was in mint condition. It resembled a department store display of decorator rooms, half completed. A large white modern couch dominated the living room, its pristine condition inhibiting its use. We dined on the gleaming lacquered floor and spread a sheet for a tablecloth. A chrome arc lamp stood alone in one corner, its trembling arm bravely casting about for a picture to illuminate. The walls, however, were bare. A new stereo, with speakers in the bedroom as well, and three bookcases, with a few books, were testimony to the fact that Jason had taken nothing when he left Clarissa. No pictures, no ornaments, no souvenirs of any kind had been claimed from his marriage, his former life.

I meant to leave some impression here and had already begun by filling his kitchen cupboards with odds and ends of my wine glasses and Arabia dishes. I offered prints from my own walls. He accepted three, but they were yet to be hung and stood propped against a wall. I provided ashtrays and some linen. Once I brought over June's latest accomplishment at sculpture. He could hardly refuse such a gift. The multicolored pot that she had crafted stood like a spitoon in another corner.

Mark was nine. A bright boy with sharp eyes and a laconic manner. He arrived with his clothes in a shopping bag; his school uniform always needed pressing. Mark was built into our weekends as June was a part of our weekdays. But I shared no intimacies with Mark, no private jokes, as Jason did with June. I was accepted, it seemed to me, as the first girlfriend of his father's new life. He did not require or desire tucking in or bedtime stories and flinched at hugs. He was polite enough but was making no commitments to this transient female guest. It made me uneasy. But I could hardly ask him to call me Mom. The thing he liked the best about me was my cooking. He fancied himself quite a good cook and we would occasionally become competitors in the kitchen arena. Jason indulged him, we watched Mark's preferred TV shows, went to Mark's choice of movies, ate Mark's favorite food (turkey and corned beef hash) and treated him generally as if he had a terminal disease and we were trying to ease his last remaining days. When we were with Mark, Jason refused to be happy with me. As if that would somehow compound his desertion. "See," he was saying to Mark, "I'm not really happy. You can't hate me for leaving because I'm not happy anyway." Mark seemed unimpressed, one way or the other.

Bedtime was a bit awkward. I would use the bathroom first, and scamper into the bedroom, not wanting to traumatize the boy with the sight of his father's girlfriend in her nightie. Father and son, alone at last, had a whispered conversation in the living room. I imagined Jason was pumping him about Clarissa, among other things. "Listen, Mark, if you don't like Susan, just say the word and I'll get rid of her."

Finally Jason came to bed, firmly closing the bedroom door. Sex was one long sigh. I was not distressed when the weekends were over.

After he took him back home Sunday nights, he was always depressed. "Lousy way for a kid to grow up," he said.

"Would she give you custody?"

"Maybe, I don't really know. As it is, who would take care of him?"

"I would." I was hurt and got up to leave. "I'm going home tonight."

"Oh, come on, not you, too. I'm sorry if I hurt your feelings. Don't leave me on a Sunday night, for Christ's sake."

"If you want custody, why don't you fight for it? I'm sick of you feeling sorry for yourself. If you really wanted custody you could at least try."

"Don't you see, that's what depresses me the most. I know that. It's hard for me to face, but I don't really want custody."

"You know if you got Mark I would . . ."

"I know. I know there's nothing you wouldn't do. I told you, I've got your number. You're not really going to leave, are you?"

Of course, I couldn't leave then. Jason still said and did too many of the right things.

"I love to touch you, Susan. The minute I touch your back, just putting my hand on your back, brings me joy. I need to touch you all the time. Who would have thought that I would have had such a love?"

It was true. He would touch me all the time. In restaurants he would reach out to touch my hand, as if to reassure himself that I would stay.

"You mean you have never taken a bath with anyone?" he asked me.

"No, I never have. It's ridiculous, two people can't fit in a bathtub."

"Sure we can. Come on, I'll show you how."

Jason had a system. With two ponies of brandy on the bathtub ledge, he settled me first in the steaming water and then positioned himself so that our outstretched legs were touching. We would sit there in the tub, soaping and drinking brandy, loving each other, terribly proud and smug. I kept wishing I was thinner so that my stomach didn't stick out so much. But he didn't seem to mind.

The money he gave me was enough for the rent and utilities. I used my unemployment check for food. There were other expenses but I couldn't bring myself to ask him. Couldn't he see that June needed clothes? That the vacuum cleaner didn't work properly?

When we were with other people, he changed slightly. His friends were rich, and I was shy and awed by them. But he was accepted as a kind of savant, allowed to be eccentric.

"You're a goddamned social asset, Jason. Do you know that? All these rich people love you. What do you do to them? You insult them, mock them and they're crazy for you."

"That's why. If I pandered to them, they wouldn't like me at all. I learned a long time ago, if you're clever about it, you can get away with telling them the truth. It makes them feel like insiders to the human race, at the same time that they preserve their holy status as super-rich."

He was hard in business, I could tell that. I wondered that he didn't seem to notice I always wore the same dress, and that we had meatloaf three times a week. "I should tell him, he'd give me more money," I argued with myself. But I didn't. It's not something you should have to ask.

The job hunting was a joke. I formulated a different résumé, lied about my experience. I wanted to work now, more than ever. Too dependent on him. Too damn dependent.

We went away for a vacation, no expense spared there. A suite overlooking the ocean on a small Caribbean island. The last day there, we were sitting at the pool. I, tanned a deep golden brown, pulled the towel over Jason, who was too fair to tan and afraid of being burned.

"Jason, this has been perfect. I never even dreamed anything could be so good. This island, the sun, but most of all to actually be here with you. That's something, all right."

"It's something, sweet girl. Let's stay five more minutes. Five more minutes in the sun. I have a funny feeling about these five minutes. Maybe, some time when we're cold, this extra five minutes will warm us, give us strength." And so we sat, five minutes more, watching the sun turn shades of color man has not yet named, rainbows forming in the sky and on the wet tiles.

After the vacation, some tension came between us.

"You call me too much, sweet girl. It's too distracting. I need time to concentrate at work. You're too intense, Susan, really, you should relax a little."

"It's just that I love you so much."

"Maybe too much, Susan. Sometimes your intensity frightens me."

"But I asked you. I asked you at the beginning, if I could love you too much. You told me I could love you as much as I wanted to or was capable of."

"I didn't know what it meant for you, Susan. So much intensity. I guess I'm confused. I love you. That much I'm sure of, you will always be the love of my life. But you cling to me, need so much. I don't know if I can give you what you need."

"Coward! You should have warned me you were a coward."

"Don't scream, Susan. Stop yelling. Dammit, we need a rest from each other. Maybe it will straighten out if we have a change of pace."

He decided one night a week we would not see each other. Magnanimously, he let me choose the night.

"You're not a prisoner. I don't have to dole out a night for you to be alone. Take them all," I cried, "take all the damn nights you want."

But he took only Thursday.

20

Those Thursday nights. I tried to make plans for myself, to keep busy. But I couldn't keep still. I thought about Jason all the time. I didn't want to be distracted by a movie. Sometimes I would have dinner with Marge. Then I could talk about Jason.

"It's perfectly natural that he would want some time to himself. I mean, he's only been divorced a short time and then I come along like a steamroller. I don't think it means anything about how he feels about me." (Come on, Marge, tell me it doesn't mean anything. Think of all the times I backed you up. Lied to you to make you feel good. What the hell are friends for? Come on. Tell me it doesn't mean anything.)

"Who are you trying to convince, you or me? Do you really care so much for him, Susan? How can you care so much? It's been such a short time."

"I don't know how and I don't know why. We're too old for questions like that. Don't question the premise. You can't question the premise. You just have to accept it and then everything else makes sense. No one questions the premise of great literature or bad movies. The same is true of love."

"I don't love that way. I've always got reasons, my own reasons, at least some rationale," Marge said.

(But we love so differently, you with your reasonable, rational feelings. How can I explain what you miss. I wish I were you. No, I don't.) "After I get all through trying to find a reason for loving Jason, looking at it coldly, with all his faults, even wishing I had never met him, I'm still stuck. It's no good preaching to me. I don't want advice no matter how smart it is. The only thing I want is Jason."

"If you're this intense with him, it's no wonder he needs a night off."

"Maybe, but I think it's my intensity that attracts him."

"And that will drive him away."

"What can I do? I can't just be intense when it seems suitable. There's no such thing as moderately intense."

"But nobody can keep up this level. After a while people have to settle in."

"If I could only be sure of him, I could settle in."

"What would make you sure of him? I mean, he sees you six nights a week, supports you when he doesn't have to, sends you flowers, puts up with your screwy phone calls. What the hell do you want the man to do?"

I didn't answer. She knew the answer.

"Susan, don't you see that the way he is with you now is better than if he married you? This way you know that he's with you because he wants to be with you."

"I'm familiar with the theory but I'll tell you this, I would rather have him obligated. I don't care so much about whether he's with me because he wants to be. I just care that I'm with him."

Marge shook her head. "You have no perspective, no sense of balance; I can understand why you don't. People in your life, your family, didn't have everyday, commonplace

148

problems. Their problems were life and death. I'm trying to tell you that you're having a perfectly normal love affair. It's possible to have a bad day. You know, Susan, I don't think you've ever had just a plain old-fashioned bad day. You know, the kind where you go to sleep at night feeling not so hot, or even crummy, and wake up in the morning feeling better."

"I have plenty of bad days."

"No, you don't. You have disaster days. I'm talking about . . . oh, never mind."

"No, go ahead. What the hell are you talking about?"

"I'm talking about your trying to find a way to gauge Jason in his world, which I might add is my world."

"Why should I? Why shouldn't it be him, and for that matter, you who understand what I want, what I need?"

"We can't play by those rules. I won't. He won't. It's too greedy, Susan, too consuming. It doesn't leave any room for the other guy, for Jason. It's suffocating and stifling and surely leaves him gasping for breath. He seems to have two choices, either he immerses himself totally in you, lives for you every minute, or he's negligent and remiss. Who in hell needs that? Some choice . . ."

"What do you want me to do, pretend? Pretend that I have other things I'm busy with, other things I care about?"

"Yes, if that's the best you can do, then by all means pretend. Exactly. Do it, pretend. And do it right, make him believe he isn't the only thing in your life, pretend you don't need him so desperately. Try it."

"I can't, anyway it wouldn't be honest."

"Screw that, you don't seem similarly conscience-stricken when it comes to telling him about your past. You're not all that fragile, Susan, you're not."

"I'm pretty fragile, Marge, I really need to be handled with care."

"Listen, you can't just turn yourself over to somebody and expect he will take over completely."

"But I've given him so much."

"That's the point. You've given him too much. Take some back. Take some of yourself back. Then at least you'll have him and you'll have some part of yourself left."

"I don't think I can now. I really wouldn't know where to start. What should I say? 'Hey, Jason, I'd like some of myself back'?"

"It isn't his to give. It's only yours to take."

"First you tell me I give him too much. Then you tell me to take it back. Now you tell me he can't give it back to me."

"People can't give themselves away. Sure, you can thrust yourself on somebody, but you can't just give yourself away. Not even if you're an orphan."

"What do you think I ought to do, Marge?"

"I think you ought to have a goal. One little small goal."

"What's that?"

"Have a bad day, Susan. Just have one bad day."

I gave up trying to keep busy on Thursday nights and stayed home. Smoking too much, sipping vodka, I tried to reason with myself.

I had one picture of Jason, taken on the Caribbean vacation. He was climbing out of the pool waving at the camera, self-conscious. Too short, and his wet hair made him look even balder. God knows, I thought, he's not so handsome. It's laughable that he causes me so much pain. I put the picture next to my father's. He looks small next to Daddy. Just a little man.

Stalking around my apartment, smoking, listening for the phone, I heard some laughter outside my window. I leaned out to see a couple holding each other, walking up the street, laughing and stopping to kiss. I hated them. I hated anybody who could laugh on Thursday nights when I was alone. Why should anyone have a good time when I felt this way? I could remember times when people had stopped to look at Jason and me. That was good. Let them look at me, envy me.

On Thursday night, the phone never rang, and I could not imagine what he was doing without me. How he could live without me. Probably it's just his pride that keeps him from calling on Thursday night. Doesn't want to admit it was a lousy idea. But one night I called him, meaning to hang up if he answered, calculating that he might know it was me, but after all a lot of people get wrong numbers and just hang up. But there was no answer. I let it ring,. and pictured him coming in the door rushing for the phone. Went out to get the papers. I let it ring some more. Any instant now, he would pick up the phone; maybe hearing it ring he dropped his key. That always happens when the phone is ringing—and I let it ring some more. Finally, I realized that I had been holding the phone for an hour. The buzz had become a hypnotic comfort, and I hummed along with it. All that night I awoke at intervals, and rang his apartment. There was no answer. I couldn't reach him. "I would have spoken to him if I had," I promised. "I would not hang up. I would tell him I was upset and sick." But all night there was no answer.

At dawn, I reached for the phone again. Better not call, not now. For a moment I didn't care, didn't care if I ever saw him again. I felt positive I would not call him. I'll sleep, I thought, and took a couple of sleeping pills. When I started crying, I was angry at myself.

Why are you crying? What did you expect? Now stop crying. It won't do any good. Don't cry any more. Not over him.

I heard the phone ringing in my sleep, but it stopped by the time I reached for it. No staying power, I thought. A few measly rings, not like some of us who hang on for hours. For a moment, I considered calling him, but turned over to drift back to sleep. The phone rang again, and this time, making my voice sound awake, I answered it.

"Hi, just called you. You didn't answer."

"I was in the shower." (His voice sounds the same. Thank God he'll never know what last night was.)

"Have a big day planned?"

"Oh, sure. Lunch at the White House, that sort of thing."

"You sound discouraged, in fact you sound like a sweet lady who should get taken out to a specially nice dinner tonight. Are you free by any remote chance?"

"Let me check my calendar." (What is this shit? Why don't I tell him to fuck off, that he's killing me?) "Well, I see that my secretary has penciled in a date with Gregory."

"Gregory?"

"Peck."

"Oh, Peck."

"But I'll break it. After all Greg and I are seeing an awful lot of each other and I hardly ever have a chance to see you."

"Good." (He actually sounds glad. You hypocrite, you fink.) "Suppose you meet me at the office. I'll be a little on the late side. About seven-thirty."

"Fine, and Jason . . ."

"Yes."

"Nothing, thanks for calling."

"Don't be silly, Susan. See you later."

There was nothing to do all day. Even if I washed my hair, and cleaned all my closets, there was still nothing to do but wait until seven-thirty. (Stop feeling so happy.) But I couldn't repress it. Seven-thirty would come, and I would be with him. Probably there was some simple explanation for last night. I would be beautiful, and he would love me and, of course, there was some perfectly reasonable explanation for last night. As long as he never knew I had called, I would be all right.

21

TO: COMRADE N. V. PODGORNY, CHAIRMAN OF THE PRESIDIUM
OF THE SUPREME SOVIET OF THE USSR

COPY TO: THE HEAD OF THE LENINGRAD REGIONAL DEPARTMENT
OF THE MINISTRY OF INTERNAL AFFAIRS

On August 11 of this year the head of OVIR in the Leningrad
Regional Department of the Ministry of Internal Affairs informed
me officially of the department chief's refusal for me to emigrate
to the state of Israel for permanent residence. This is my second
refusal.

I am appealing to you to reconsider my application and
respond to it favorably in accordance with the foundations of
Soviet legislation and the Declaration of the Rights of Man.

Since making my decision to emigrate ten months ago, I have
been unable to work due to the fact that all of my concerts have
been canceled. I have been informed by certain officials that if I
do not find employment I will be charged with parasitism.

In addition my wife and I now find ourselves living in a
hostile environment. Even our neighbors have been questioned
about us. We are not receiving our mail and while the telephone
rings we are unable to hear the caller.

I am fully appreciative of the generous training I received from the Soviet Union and I have no wish to harm anyone. I have never been a political person and am not now politically motivated. I do not believe that it does credit to the Soviet Union to deny persons who wish to be reunited with their families permission to do so. My needs are simple. I want to be able to perform, as I have in the past, in many countries of the world, and to join my relatives in Israel.

Although officials have charged me with "anti-Soviet activity" and disseminating propaganda for Zionist ideas, I believe that even they must know these charges are ridiculous. In joining with the thousands of other Soviet Jews who desire to go to the State of Israel, I have identified myself as one who recognizes the most human of all desires—preserving my identity.

What possible benefit can be derived from detaining my wife and myself when all the world knows that we wish to leave?

Leonid Rabinovitz
September 1974

Dear Leonid:

Your letter to Chairman Podgorny has been made public and printed in the newspapers.

We are all very distressed to learn of the harassment you are being subjected to.

In addition to the many artists who are petitioning on your behalf, there are now other groups such as lawyers, who are joining together to try to help you. I call you every week but the operator tells me the phone is out of order. I will send you a telegram October 1, to alert you to a call that I will place to the post office in Leningrad. If they don't deliver the telegram, which by law they must, please go to the post office between 10:00 and 1:00 your time on October 1, and wait because I'll definitely be calling you person-to-person at that time.

It is very foolish of the authorities to withhold your mail and to disconnect your phone. It makes those who work on your behalf feel even more strongly about you.

Try to keep your spirits up and remember you have many friends.

Sincerely,
Susan

156

22

"Hey, Mom, this room is freezing." June walks into my bedroom, interrupting my thoughts, my memories. I have a daughter to care for, and a job to go to. I am embarrassed to be in bed. Why am I lingering so long today?

June looks at the piles of clothes. "Do you want me to help you pack, Mom?"

"Not now, maybe later. Aren't you late for school?"

"I will be if I don't get moving. Are you sick, Mom? Aren't you going to work?"

Her voice is anxious, she has had some experience with a sick mother.

"I'm fine, going to the hospital to see your dad and then to work." *And waiting for Jason to call.*

"Dad's going to be all right, isn't he?"

"Sure, sure he is."

"Give him my love," and I kiss June goodbye.

I wonder how much June knows. Often she has come into my room when I am masturbating. I still my hand and pretend to be asleep, but still, I wonder if she knows. I have tried to conceal from her the harsh realities of my life. They are representative of nothing at all and I doubt that she would learn much from them. I watch her grow, afraid almost to do more than stand at the edge of her life. I had hoped to be a good mother but in the end I don't know what is expected of me. June would like me to be happy or at least not to cry. Do children really want to know their parents' anguish? I think not. I will not be a mother who tells her daughter everything.

With June gone, I relax back into my bed. This bed that I have shared with Sam and Jason.

I know now what I'm waiting for. I'm waiting to react. I'm waiting for something to happen, Jason to call, Sam to die. Something to respond to. I'm waiting to be prompted, provoked, stimulated, aroused.

I have a bag of tricks for that. Reactions up my sleeve, a magic act of resiliency.

I whipped it out for Jason, after he took his Thursdays. I told him every detail of my past. He would have to love me for my tragic past.

He was stunned when I told him. He took me in his arms.

"Susan, sweet girl, why didn't you tell me before? My God, I never dreamed that these things had happened to you. Why didn't you tell me before?"

"I didn't want you to feel sorry for me or think I was peculiar. I've always wanted to forget. Please don't tell anyone else."

"For God's sake, it's nothing to be ashamed of."

"I just don't want anyone else to know. I've only told you now because we're so close and I love you so much, I don't want to hide anything from you."

"I wish you had told me before. I understand now why you need so much."

After that he was gentle with me for a while. Passionate and loving again. I could see telling him had made a difference. I felt freer to demand more of him and he was less able to deny me.

But we began to quarrel again too soon. Was he tiring of my pose of orphan-victim-survivor? By telling him, I had strengthened the threads between us, but was I stretching them too far? If so, they were bound to snap.

One night we had dinner with Jason's business colleague and his wife. Jason whispered to me that he was sorry but they had insisted we join them. The wife was small, young and rich. I, wearing my best black dress, felt shabby and large. I recognized the clothes the wife was wearing. Designer clothes. Expensive clothes. Clothes not made in sizes over ten.

I had met the couple before and hadn't liked them. Now I hated them. We went to a private club where the couple and Jason were greeted warmly and people stopped by our table to talk to us. I had nothing to say. I didn't know these people. I took Jason's hand under the table, but he smiled at me and shook it off. They started talking about private schools. I ridiculed everything they said, smug in my poverty. I launched a frontal attack on private schools in general and their own pet school in particular. Jason was quiet. Gripping the stem of his wine glass, he was plainly angry. *Christ, this is a test. Stop it. You're really fucking it up.* But I couldn't stop. Not now. And finally, when the wife said politely, "Susan, my dear. You sound like a communist," I looked her right in her perfectly arranged face and said, "Well, I am."

That was too much for Jason, who finally roused himself and with great irritation asked me to shut up.

Later, back at his apartment, I tried to get him to laugh at it with me. But he was in no laughing mood.

"You deliberately embarrassed me, you know that. I don't understand you, Susan. You know these people are important

159

to me, and you go right ahead with your goddamned stupid, insulting speech, which you don't believe for a minute, and pretend you're a communist. Why, you'd give your eyeteeth if June could go to that school, and I guess you'd give a whole lot more if you had one ounce of the class Amanda has."

"Class. So that's what it's called. Class. My, my. All along I'd mistaken it for snobbery and bigotry and now I find it's class. You know you can't stand them. You've told me their values stink."

"Well, maybe I was wrong. They are a hell of a lot better than your values. Oh, shit, let's drop it. I'm tired."

Go home. Just get up and go home. But more than pride was at stake now and I could only meekly follow Jason into the bedroom.

Later that night I tried to rouse him. But he was too tired and mumbled that he wanted to sleep. My only comfort was that in his sleep he still reached for me and locked me in his arms.

My job hunting took a more serious turn. My relations with Jason were troubled and allowed no respite from the continuum of rejection. Always before job hunting represented an escape from an arena in which I was entrapped. But this was different. The arena, my relationship with Jason, was what I wanted. If anything, I wanted to go backward in time. My strength had always come from a belief that the future would be better than the past. Now, I no longer believed that. Life without Jason would be intolerable. It could not happen.

For several weeks we muddled through our time together, each more conscious of what was not being said than what we spoke about.

My strategy called for appeasement and I was careful not to provoke any quarrels. But the deadly silences that permeated our conversation were provocative in themselves. I plotted to keep things on neutral ground, then grew weary of my own defenses. Soldiers in wars of attrition are frequently undermined by their own anxiety to get it over with. Unable to bear the suspense of waiting it out in the foxhole, they rush the enemy. It is a suicidal impulse. Frequently they get their heads shot off. I had confined myself to a bunker outfitted with provisions for a long battle. Circumspect and cautious, I meant to wait it out.

I rehearsed our meetings during the day, looking at myself in the mirror to see how I looked when I smiled. I watched him for any sign of change, good or bad. Was he touching me less? Then I would touch him, just a little more. He was tired all the time; I was considerate. He talked endlessly about business; I was fascinated. Mark was sad; I was hurt for him. His ex-wife was a bitch; I was angry at her too. He was part of a new organization, the Committee to Unsell the War; I said it was terrific, would have impact. I was too heavy; I would lose some weight. He hated all the new movies; I agreed they were trash. Our favorite French restaurant was poisoning its customers; we would certainly never go there again. Maybe I should lower my sights and take an ordinary job; I would look into secretarial work. We should eat at home more; I would cook. We should eat out more; I would research new restaurants. He was no good for me; he was perfect, I loved him more than ever.

And in this way, we survived a few more weeks.

In the middle of dinner one Friday night, the trivia exhausted, I poked around at my food and said, quite without meaning to, "Jason, are you seeing someone else?" Before he could answer, I said, "You know today's the anniversary of my mother's death. I lit the candle tonight before I left the house."

He frowned. "Susan, why do you bring that up now? When you first told me about your family I knew I couldn't begin to really understand how painful it is for you and I certainly didn't believe I could make it up to you. But when you bring it up like this it makes me angry. I don't want to have to feel so sorry for you. From what you tell me your mother considered your father responsible for Jean's death. In a way you are doing the same thing. You know where we're at. You know it's no good. You've made it impossible for me to break up with you but you're turning me into a brute. I don't want to be cruel. You make me cruel. Can't you take some responsibility for the reality of what's happened?"

"Wow, what an outburst! What have I done now to displease you? You make me sorry I ever told you anything. Is that it? Would you rather I hadn't ever told you anything?"

"No . . . maybe. Maybe I am sorry you told me. You don't listen, Susan. You don't listen to anything I say. I guess you don't want to hear." His face had hardened. Snap. More threads breaking. "You asked me a question, Susan. You asked me if I was seeing someone else."

"Never mind."

"I want to tell you."

"Never mind. Don't tell me everything."

"I did meet someone at a party and I have seen her once or twice."

I smiled and nodded my head. I waited for more. There was no more. Cutting a piece of meat, I began to talk. *That's it, move away from it. Keep talking about anything. Just slowly move away from it.* I viewed the information as I would a lethal snake. It had the power to dart out and kill me, but if I made no sudden moves, allowed it to pass me by, shifting away from its darting fangs, I would survive.

It was nearly a week before I asked him if he was sleeping with her. The words just came out, in an unguarded moment. Slipped out of me while I was concentrating on something else. (Whose voice was that? Did I say it? Maybe I just thought it.) But Jason was answering me and I was attending to his reply.

"Susan, we've got to end. I can't go on this way. I know you're trying, I can see how bottled up you are. But it's no good, you can't take it and neither can I. Wouldn't it be better if we just stopped seeing each other for a while?"

Obviously, he didn't know what he was saying. Didn't he realize that seeing him was all I lived for? What the hell did he think I did with my days? Nothing, just nothing, except wait until enough hours had passed after the first phone call so I could call him again. Just what the hell did he think I would do with my life if he stopped seeing me? This time, however, I just thought these things, and minutes passed before I spoke.

"I know this has been a difficult time, Jason. I really know that. I mean, I've tried very hard to make it better."

"Susan, please don't cry here."

"I'm not crying, am I?" I reached up to touch my face. By God, I was crying. He handed me a handkkerchief. I saw he was looking around the retaurant to see if we were being watched.

"Susan, don't make a scene, you know I hate it."

"Oh, I won't make a scene, I won't do anything. But you didn't really mean it, did you?"

He was silent. He didn't speak. I imagined he had lost his

voice. I kept telling him I understood; he didn't have to talk. I understood perfectly. He didn't know what the hell I was talking about.

"Don't worry about it, I know how you feel. You don't have to talk." I was repeating myself, chanting, "I understand, you don't have to talk." And when I saw he was going to speak, saw his mouth opening and his lips starting to move, I screamed at him, "Don't talk. You can't talk. Stop it. Stop it."

Everything had disintegrated into endless phone conversations. Jason wouldn't hang up on me but he implored me to let him work. I called him a dozen times a day. I refused to believe that he didn't love me. "Tell me that you don't love me. Just tell me that to my face and I'll go away." But he didn't want to see me. He was afraid of me.

"Susan, I do love you, but I can't take the relationship. Maybe it's me, maybe I'm crazy. Please, let's just let it go, for a little while."

All I heard was that he loved me. I had stopped looking for work. I followed him at lunchtime, and waited outside the restaurant until he was finished. If he saw me he didn't acknowledge it. Once I entered the restaurant and walked up to his table. He was lunching with two women.

"Susan, what are you . . ." he started and then his face turned to stone as he introduced me to the women.

"Aren't you going to invite me to join you?" I asked.

"I'm sorry, Susan, but we are discussing some business matters. I'm sure you understand."

Humiliated, I left. But why was I smiling?

Later that week, I wrapped up all his presents to me, all the cards that had accompanied his flowers and took them to his apartment. And his key as well. Leaving my house in a cold fury, I arrived at his apartment and rang the bell.

"Who is it?"

"It's me."

"I can't let you in, Susan, you should have called."

I heard a dog bark. He doesn't have a dog, I thought, he doesn't have a dog. But *she* must. A memory of childbirth came to me when I was in labor, gasping for breath, for water, for some relief that was still hours away, begging the nurse for water, squirming to move away from my body pain, but unable to leave it. And so I stood in front of his door, forcing myself to breathe, to swallow, to move away from the pain. But instead, like that other time, I begged.

"Please, please let me in." I was crying.

"Susan," his muffled voice came through the door, "Susan, go away." The pain was worse, a beam of pain, my head hurt, the pain jumped around, a bursting in my head, then my chest exploded with it and then my legs were numb, my face distorted and wet and weak, imploring.

"Please, let me in."

Oh, Susan, Susan. Comfort yourself. Don't do this.

But everything visceral moved me further. Finally, in a frenzied exhaustion, I sat down and, finding the only thing I could write upon, I tore out checks from my checkbook and slipped them under the door. Fifteen checks, on the back of which I tried to make him remember, cursed him and *her* and even the dog. I kept slipping them under the door until my supply was gone. Quietly, I left my parcel, walking down the six flights of stairs, drained now not of pain but of hope. Jason was gone to me. Some mad woman in me had driven him away. All I was left with as I walked home across the park, and touched a tree, maybe that same one we had sat beneath at the beginning, were those extra five minutes in the sun.

I looked for him in familiar restaurants. Maybe he would take Mark to the park on Sunday. I sat on a bench, waiting. I never saw him. Even the anticipation of seeing him helped me live through those months. The ringing of the phone (let it ring three times; maybe it's Jason). I hated to be anywhere which made me inaccessible to him. I stoically bore all disappointments. Later I relished them. A Sunday outing to the park, waiting for four hours not seeing him and then some satisfaction, at least, that I had not given up. The very routine of looking for him carried its own reward. At night I talked to him, long conversations, orchestrating his part.

The timbre of his voice was clear to me; for a long time I closed myself off, waiting for him. He would not find me faithless when he returned.

"Susan," Marge said, "you must really give up, he's not coming back, you know that. Get out a little. It'll help. You're becoming boring, really. Your behavior is inappropriate and excessive. You're not all that tragic. Try and act a little civilized. I mean, we all live through this."

"No, Marge, we don't all live through it. I don't believe you've ever lived through it. If you had, you wouldn't use words like 'appropriate' and 'civilized'. I don't care about that. I don't want to be appropriate and civilized. I never did understand all that crap. It's just some bill of goods that we've been sold on. The psychiatrists, everyone conspires to get us to restrain ourselves. For whose sake? I want to know who it helps? Not me, that's for sure. I'm a hurt animal, and maybe I'll kill and maybe I'll just take my own sweet time to lick my wounds. But I won't be civilized and God knows I won't be appropriate."

"You're only hurting yourself more."

"Maybe that's the only way to cleanse the wounds."

My grieving took a quieter tone. I slipped into this new phase luxuriously, like sinking into the sumptuous cushion of a huge down comforter, soft and pliant. Unable and unwilling to rouse myself from its seductive comfort, I lingered there a while. I understood that it was self-indulgent but could not fault myself for that. What I had felt for Jason deserved more than some ordinary burial; it was worthy of the vigorous crusade I had waged. There would be enough time to forget, all the time in the world for forgetting. It was keeping it twitching and throbbing that separated me from the rest of those who would have chosen to forget too soon.

Obsessed people are ridiculous. There are no dignified obsessions. Which is not to say they are not splendid. How pallid and ultimately deprived are those who have never been so humbled.

Why was I surprised at such betrayal? My mother told me everything.

SUSAN: Who is that in the picture, Mother?

MOTHER: You mean the beautiful young girl with the white hat? Why, that's me.

SUSAN: You?

MOTHER: You look so surprised. I was once young and beautiful.

SUSAN: You're still beautiful, Mother.

MOTHER: You know your father doesn't like to admit it but he really adored me.

SUSAN: He still does.

MOTHER: You know how we met? Our family doctor was sick and asked if we minded if he sent his young assistant. My father had gout. He suffered terribly. When I heard the doorbell ring and ran for it, even before the maid could get to it, there was your father. I was only nineteen. He was much older. He told me later he was nervous. Father was his first patient. Just before he left the house he asked me if he could call upon me. Imagine. My father didn't really approve. Oh, it was nothing against your father. It's just that he didn't think anyone was good enough for me.

SUSAN: Tell me about how you used to sneak out to meet him.

MOTHER: Did I tell you about that? I shouldn't have. Well, as long as I've already told you. Your father was busy until eight or nine at night in his dispensary, and sometimes I would sneak out the back door and down the garden just to stand and talk to him a while. He said the most extravagant things. Of course, all my girlfriends were jealous of me.

SUSAN: I'll bet they were, Mother. You were so beautiful and you had a beautiful home and you even had Daddy. I'll just bet they were jealous of you.

MOTHER: Oh, they were. My best friend, her name was Anne, she was especially jealous. She tried to hide it, but I could see. We were very close, Anne and I. She would come and sleep at my house and we would giggle a lot. I wish I could remember what was so funny.

SUSAN: She sounds nice, Mother.

MOTHER: Oh, yes, she was very nice. She was very pretty too. Not quite as pretty as I was but pretty. Anne was my best friend. She was my maid of honor at the wedding and when you were born, I asked her to be your godmother.

SUSAN: It's too bad you never hear from her.

MOTHER: I have a picture of her somewhere. One day, I think it was just after we heard that Poland had been invaded, we were having coffee. Really, I was kidding at the time, or maybe I wasn't. I asked her if she would hide you and Jean and me if the Nazis invaded France. Well, of

168

course by that time we all knew that the Nazis planned to kill all the Jews.

SUSAN: What did she say?

MOTHER: She said no.

SUSAN: You don't mean that.

MOTHER: Oh, yes I do. I would have said exactly the same thing. There would have been one difference. I wouldn't have felt guilty about it.

23

June seemed only slightly surprised when I told her Jason was gone. A far cry from the shattered child whose father had left several years ago.

They had had a good thing, Jason and June. Weekdays at my house, it looked like a family. Jason helped with homework, played Monopoly. We vied for his attention, June and I. It was easy to cede to her; after all, it was me he was fucking.

With Jason in my home and in my bed, I was released from my vows. Having fallen from grace, I experienced an epiphany: lapsed martyrs make better mothers.

With Jason in my life, June and I grew side by side. She was not a burden then. I was expansive in my love for her, patient and gentle, even as Jason was with me. Her child demands, which used to make me angry, were nothing then. We were a geometric pattern, June and Jason and me. A triangle with a tensile strength.

I loved June no less, of course, when Jason left. I was not indifferent to her needs. It was just that I was ill, with feverish dreams and headaches. And perhaps I did not listen quite as keenly to her child jokes. I was, after all, waiting for the phone to ring. My eyes burned; I kept them closed, for safety's sake. My throat was dry; I didn't want to talk. She was there, where once he stood. In my bedroom, in my bed. June was there now, occupying all the space. I poured her cereal and washed her clothes, braided her hair and kissed her bruises. I loved her no less. Better though to remain aloof. To keep her separated from this grief, this affliction of loss. I did not want to taint her with my own plagued heart.

I had no money, and I was forgetful about going to the unemployment office. The apartment was too large and I really only felt safe in the bedroom. Mornings I would take a stack of cookies and some cans of tomato juice and go back to my bedroom. There, at least, I could think clearly and make plans.

The family pictures on the dresser shared space with an array of pills. Over-the-counter pills that said on their labels "this may cause drowsiness" and some prescription pills I had stolen from other people. I always took pills from the medicine chests of people I visited. Trying to remember what they were so I could label them, but usually just ending up with a collection of oddly shaped and varicolored pills. I never knew, therefore, what the effect might be or how strong the pill was. I had some good pills though, even some Demerol, but unfortunately, I didn't know which one it was.

One excursion I did make daily was to the mailbox. There, small envelopes arrived with pink or yellow slips inside them. After a while, I didn't bother to open them, just held them up to the light to see the color. They all said the same thing: "You promised to meet your obligations. Unless you do so immediately, we must refuse you more credit."

One oblong one came from the telephone company warning me that my phone would be disconnected.

I composed a letter.

To Whom It May Concern:
I have no money at the moment. When I have money, I will certainly pay you.

Thank you,
Susan Warner

I gave June the letter and told her to get it Xeroxed. Sending the letter out to my creditors, I was proud of myself. But to my great disappointment, they didn't understand at all, and the small envelopes kept coming.

I called Sam. But Sam was writing a book and was broke himself. And anyway, I wanted the divorce so badly, I could damn well pull myself together and get a job. Of course, when he had money, he would give me some, but at the moment he couldn't do a thing.

"I'm worried about you, Susan," he said.

"Listen, Sam, just give me some money and don't worry about me, I'm fine."

"I wish I could, but no can do. What about all your rich friends? Can't they help?"

"There are no rich friends, Sam."

"What about that guy you're so crazy about?" he asked, but he must have known from June it was over.

"There is no guy, Sam. Please, just give me a little money."

"Sorry, Susan, you'll be all right. I told you it would be hard. Just pull yourself together."

I called him again.

"Help me. How can you let us starve?" I screamed at him.

Calmly he told me, "Susan, you're sick, you should see a doctor."

"You made me sick. Take care of us. Take a job, drive a taxi, anything. Don't let us starve."

"Bullshit," he said. "You were so quick to throw away our eight years, so sure you could make it. Go make it. I can't save you. I can't even save myself. You were always the one pushing me, get a better job, do better. I was never enough then. Why the hell should I be enough now, when it no longer counts?"

Then he hung up the phone, softly, not even slamming it down. I held the dead buzzing phone in my hand, staring at it, wanting it to become alive again with Sam on the other end so I could scream some more.

The next time I went to call him, I discovered my phone had been disconnected. I was relieved. Really, all this fighting with Sam was ridiculous. I noticed the crumbs of cookies on my bed, they comforted me. The room was messy. It smelled of stale cigarettes and tomato juice. The only neat place was the dresser where the line-up of pictures and pills alternated. A collage of all that mattered to me, I rearranged it, taking the pills out of their bottles and forming patterns with them around the pictures. My artistic work finished, I carefully selected one. "Surprise, what will this make me feel," I wondered, and lay down to wait.

June was staying with her father now. I had told her I was sick. I missed June, but when I saw her all I could do was cry and tell her to go to her father's.

One morning I awoke and got straight out of bed. "Today's the day," I said aloud. "I'll get a job today." I considered cleaning the room first, but was afraid to lose the impetus. I showered and dressed and went to an employment agency. I took the typing test. Sitting alone in a small room, I looked at the paper I was to type. It had numbers on the side of each line. The words didn't make any sense at all. But I typed them anyway, typed as hard and fast as I could until a little bell went off and the employment agency lady came to tell me the time was up. Ha, I thought, I typed at least one more line after the bell. I waited on a bench, with my hands folded while the woman marked the test.

I had failed. "Perhaps you should take a refresher course," the woman said kindly. "But I'm afraid this won't do at all."

It was then that I took to bed. Then it was my only asylum.

Sam still had a key to my apartment. Sometimes he came over. I could see how it looked to him.

He stood with his hands on his hips surveying the mess. "This place is a garbage pail, a shithouse. What are you doing to yourself, Susan?" I was combing the tangles out of my hair with one hand while pulling the sheets and covers over me with the other.

"You don't have to come here, Sam. You have no business here. If you don't like it, get out. In fact, get out anyway."

I could see that there were cellophane wrappers from cookies, empty cans of tomato juice and piles of ashes and cigarette butts all over the room. Clothes, unopened mail and newspapers mingled with the other debris. It comforted me.

"What do you want here?" I asked him sharply. "What the hell are you doing here anyway? Do you have any money for me?"

"For God's sake, Susan, get up, get out of bed, do something for yourself. How can you let June see you this way?"

174

"What way? I'm resting," I said imperiously. "Leave me alone."

"Resting! Susan, you're sick. Look around at this place. It's not fit for an animal. How could you let yourself get this low?"

He walked toward me kicking aside clothes and papers.

"Get out of here!" I yelled at him. "Get out of here! It's all your goddamned fault. Everything's your fault. Leave me alone. Don't ever come here again. You never understood me. No one does. But you most of all. So just get the hell out of here. You're not making my bed any more. You're not lying in it either."

He continued walking toward me. (What if he killed me? Maybe he would take out his knife and kill me.) He wouldn't stop walking toward me.

"Susan, Susan," he was saying, "don't do this to yourself."

Now I knew definitely that he meant to kill me.

"Get out, get out or I'll call the police."

"Susan, I didn't realize things were this way. Look, I'll help, really, just get out of bed. I'll help you clean up." He started to pick up some of the newspapers. (He must not disturb anything.)

"Don't touch anything. It all has a place. Please, you'll just mess it all up. Leave it alone." (If he moves anything, I won't know where to find it.) "Sam, stop picking up the papers."

"Susan, let me call a doctor."

"I don't need a doctor. I suppose you think I'll just go away quietly, like Mother, taking family pictures with me. Well, I won't. I can talk. Listen to me, I can talk. I'm not like her, stupid woman, refusing to talk just because my father blew his head off. I can speak perfectly clearly." And indeed I could hear myself enunciating each word. "I don't have to be sent away."

"I just want you to get some help. You're not rational. You're not making any sense."

"Sense, dollars and cents. That's what I need, I need some dollars and cents. Please give me some dollars and cents. If you give me some dollars and cents, I'll have sense. If you give me dollars and cents, I'll give you my scents." Now I knew what he wanted. Of course. I flung the covers off and spread my legs and beckoned him. "Is that what you want, Sam? You want to smell it a little, lick it a little, put your thing in it?" How stupid of me not to realize what he wanted. I pulled up my nightgown and started to play with myself. So comforting. "Come on, Sam, I don't mind. Really."

Sam looked horrified. I liked that.

"Stop it. Susan, stop it. I loved you. I can't stand to see you this way."

"You always told me it would end up like this. I would end up alone playing with my own cunt. I'll bet you're glad. I'll bet that cold part of you is glad. Don't you feel justified now? Come on, for old time's sake. Just shove it in the way you used to."

I saw him leave the room out of the corner of my eye and sprang up to shut the door. (Safe. That was close. He'll probably kill me the next time.) I opened the door and called, "Sam, hey Sam. Don't leave, don't leave me. I'll do whatever you want. You can't leave me, you love me."

I ran through the apartment. He was gone. Rushing to the window, I saw him walking slowly up the street. I started calling to him but no sound came out. I was yelling his name

176

inside me and my throat burned from the strain of my screams but no sounds came out.

The leaves I noticed were beginning to drop to the ground. I closed my mouth and sat on the windowsill, feeling happy to see the trees shedding their first leaves. Nice, I thought, a lovely neat system. How perfect to be a leaf. There is a time to fall. Fall is the time to fall. Spring is the time to spring.

I sat there for a long time. There was nothing to hurry for now. I knew what I had to do. How remarkable that I had not seen the solution before.

I straightened up. I made my bed, neatly this time. Changed into a clean nightgown. Not a sexy one but one that was flannel and old-fashioned with a little lace on the sleeves and at the neck. I combed my long hair and washed my face. I threw the clothes and papers and books into the closet and closed the door. I took the dirty dishes into the kitchen. I hummed. I felt satisfied. My bedroom was neat.

I locked my bedroom door and got a glass of water from the bathroom sink, letting it run from the tap, making it clear and cool. Walking back to bed, I slipped between the fresh cool sheets and covered myself so that the overlap of the sheet was precisely two inches over the blanket. The sun was flickering around the room, brightening it a little. I had collected all the pills from the dresser. A wonderful collection, all different in shape and form. I began to take them slowly, by twos, trying to match them up so that they were color-coordinated. I felt no fear now. Only relief.

Out, out—the most crucial thing now was to get out. I took more pills and rested a moment thinking what a gracious host death would be; I would be welcome.

I noticed a wrinkle in a fold of the top sheet and tried to

smooth it out. The trouble is, I thought, there are too many wrinkles. Holding the pills in one hand, I used the other, trying to press firmly on the wrinkle. But the minute I took my hand away, the wrinkle returned. It was important to get that wrinkle straightened out and I pressed again. Wrinkles. Sheets wrinkled, Mother's face wrinkled, wrinkles slowly began to appear on the fresh crisp lines of the sheet.

See, I'm going to take care of that now. I'm going to take care of all that now. I'll iron out all the wrinkles.

But it was hopeless. The sheet continued to frown at me.

(All right. Stay that way. You want to wrinkle, then wrinkle. You won't spoil this for me.)

I swallowed a few more pills.

Drowsy now, I thought for the first time about June. She would be better off without me. Without such a mother. I knew what mothers were supposed to do, they were supposed to put their children's needs before their own. But I was too broken for that. Too bereft myself to recover. Too humiliated by my various supplications. Too much bowing and scraping for too long. I would curtsy no more before the powerful and the cruel who dispensed of jobs, money, love.

I understood my mother and father better now. Instead of a trust fund or grand lineage, I had the tradition, the legacy of family suicide. They had left me that, their approval of this final way out. It was reassuring to know that they would have approved, that I would be reunited at last with my own kind. I would leave no note for June, as none had been left for me. Perhaps the impulse for this solution will skip her generation. In any event, she must make her own choices. I will not involve her in this with the pathetic words of a suicide, she has no part in this. I will not tie her to me, or this act, with a plea for forgiveness or understanding or other such hypocritical defenses.

Much better to think of happy things. It's all over. What a ghastly party it was. How chic to leave it early. I feel floaty. Hey, I'm floating. Still grasping the remaining pills in my right hand I slowly moved my left hand to my face. No tears. Of course not. Why should I cry? *Sweet girl, you deserve this.* My eyes are closed. That's good. I won't have to see the wrinkles any more.

An instant of chaos when two thoughts collide. Every-thing is neat—I'm frightened.

I felt sick. My throat and stomach hurt. Was I in a bathroom? All that white tile.

"She's awake," someone said. Did they mean me? Was I she? A face appeared over mine.

"Susan, do you know where you are?"

"Crap. Oh, shit." I turned my head away from the face toward the tile wall and could see tubing going into my arm.

"Susan, you're in the emergency room of Roosevelt Hospital."

"Crap. Dammit. Leave me alone."

"I know you feel terrible. You've been through quite a lot. We had to pump your stomach out. Now you are getting fluids intravenously. I repeat, you are safe. You are in the emergency room of Roosevelt Hospital. We are going to take care of you."

The son-of-a-bitch doctor was talking to me as if I were crazy. He spoke slowly, like Sam.

"Please leave me alone."

The doctor was explaining how I had been found and where I was and how much trouble I had caused everybody.

I actually had a lot to say to the son-of-a-bitch doctor with his agonizing slow talk. But all I could manage through my tears was, "Goddammit, leave me alone."

I smelled like vomit, as if I had thrown up through my nose. The son-of-a-bitch doctor was still talking at me with that perfect intonation one uses when reading a children's story. He kept repeating himself but then again, so did I.

"I need a tissue. For Christ's sake, can I have a tissue?" (I can't stop crying. What the hell am I crying about?)

He wiped my face and held the tissue so that I could blow my nose. God, that was painful. Everything hurt. Mostly my stomach hurt and I was thirsty. I fell asleep again. When I woke up I was in another room. There were bars in the window and I wasn't tied any more. The nurse came in and told me to ring if I wanted anything and not to try to get off the bed.

It was a white room. I was worried about what I would think about for the time I had to be there. I didn't want to think about anything. I wished the son-of-a-bitch doctor would come back to talk to me. I wished I had a book. A friendly book that I had read before. I was awfully worried about what I would do to pass the time.

When I awoke it was night. I rang the bell. Now there seemed something sinister about the room. I felt very nervous. I could hear a key in the door. (Why did they lock me up?)

"How are you feeling, Susan?" the doctor asked, a different one. He took my pulse and blood pressure. I was glad to have him touch me. Maybe he would stay and talk to me. I probably looked pretty bad. Maybe not too bad.

"I feel okay. I'm thirsty. Can I have something to drink?"

"Sure. Would you like some tea and toast?"

"Yes, I would. How long will I be here?"

"Oh, just tonight. Tomorrow you will be in a regular room."

I started to cry again. "Doctor"—I sounded so meek—"I can't stop crying."

He'd been nearly out of the room making notations on a pad. "Well, Susan, you're alive, and you tried to kill yourself and mad that you didn't and maybe, just maybe, you're mad that you are relieved that you're not dead. We'll talk tomorrow, you're safe now. Try to relax, try not to worry. There will be time to talk tomorrow."

I had forgotten to ask him what time it was. I didn't know when tomorrow was. I didn't know what to think about. I would have to remember to ask the nurse what time it was when she brought me the tea.

My mother told me everything:

MOTHER: I'm glad you came this week, Susan. Did you bring me some cookies?

SUSAN: Sure I did. Right here. The kind with the marshmallow inside. Would you like me to come every week, Mother, instead of every two weeks?

MOTHER: Oh, I like these cookies. Don't you have any now. You can have all you want out there. You leave these for me.

SUSAN: Mother, do you want me to come every week?

MOTHER: One reason I like these cookies is because it doesn't hurt my teeth to bite into them. You know the white marshmallow part is nice and soft. See? Just take a little bite of one, Susan, and give me the rest. I just want you to see how soft it is when you bite into it.

SUSAN: I'm doing very well in school, Mother, I've been thinking that maybe I would like to be a writer. You once told me that you wanted to write. Maybe I could write about some of the experiences that we had.

MOTHER: The last time you were here, I had one of the boxes of cookies in my room, but they found it. Somebody took the cookies. Do you think I should hide each cookie in a separate place? What experiences?

SUSAN: Well, you know, about the war and living in the basement and Daddy . . .

MOTHER: I don't like to tell you this, Susan, but my roommate's daughter, she gets chocolate cupcakes. Do you think you can manage to bring me some chocolate cupcakes? One thing they do for you up here, Susan, I mean they do a lot of things for you, but one thing they do for you is they keep telling you what a terrific person you are. Till I got up here, I never realized what a terrific person I was.

SUSAN: Oh, you are, Mother. You are.

MOTHER: Oh, I know I am. I just never realized it before. There isn't a single thing that I've ever done that I have to feel bad about. Not one single thing. I'm a really terrific person. It's just that I haven't always believed that. So, if you could bring me some chocolate cupcakes and manage the marshmallow cookies, too, that would be really special.

SUSAN: I'll try. I'm glad you are feeling better, Mother. You can imagine how much I'm looking forward to you getting out of here and our being together.

MOTHER: You see, before I was here, I thought I was a terrible person. You know what I mean, don't you, Susan?

SUSAN: Well, not exactly, Mother. I always thought you were a good person.

MOTHER: Oh. I am, I am. But before they explained it to me, I thought it was wrong that I was doing it with the farmer when they killed my mother. Did you know that, Susan? I figured it out. At the very moment that they pushed her into the oven I was doing it with the farmer. These are very good cookies.

SUSAN: Mother, you can't possibly know what happened to Grandma. We're not even sure how she died.

MOTHER: That's where you're wrong. As you know, I have spent a lot of time on this. My mother died on May 14, 1943, at six-twenty in the morning.

SUSAN: Mother, there's no way to know that.

MOTHER: She was very thin by that time, and sick. And she walked naked, dazed, with the other women into the gas chambers. She was very proper, my mother. It bothered her very much that she was naked. When the gas started pouring out from the ceiling and everyone started scream-ing and clawing at the walls, my mother was the one who was comforting them. She must have been very upset at being naked.

SUSAN: Are you feeling well, Mother? Are you over your cold?

MOTHER: The farmer liked to do it in the morning before you were awake. Of course, I would try to stop him, but no, he had to have his way. We hung a blanket between your bed and mine. I was always worried that you would hear us. I wouldn't have ever done it, but you know men. Anyway, that morning when my mother was being gassed, he made me do it.

SUSAN: Listen, Mother, I brought you some cards. People are asking for you. Everyone hopes that you will be well soon.

MOTHER: I still remember that morning and what I felt like inside me. I knew that my mother was being gassed and I begged him not to do it, but no, he did it anyway.

SUSAN: I have to go now, Mother. Our time is up. I wish you wouldn't think those things. Please try. Please try to think about how it will be when you're out and we're together.

MOTHER: Oh, I don't think about that any more. I just told you that because now I know what a good person I am. Don't forget the cupcakes.

25

Observation. That's what they call it. "She's under observation."

All kinds of images come to mind involving glass and mirrors, reflections and fishbowls. I have always wondered exactly who was observing whom. For my part, I felt as if I was observing the rest of them, with their peculiar ways and strange language.

I was transferred to a room with four daybeds. My roommates were friendly. All of them were alcoholics. I had my own sink and closet and the ledge built along the bed served as a bookshelf. There was a dining room that converted into a dayroom. A kitchen. Patients could make coffee or tea, buy ice cream or fruit or keep special food for themselves. The bathrooms and showers were clean. The linen was cheap. It had a rough texture.

The nurses' station, that mysterious enclave at the end of the hall, was the only obvious medical trapping. There, once a day, our vital signs were taken and our medicine, if any, was dispensed. Otherwise, a schedule was set for various forms of therapy. Art therapy, occupational therapy, group therapy, outings, private therapy. Nurses around just to talk to. There was another room, glass-enclosed, where the staff met in the mornings. The patients could see them meeting and gesticulating, knowing that we were being talked about. Walking around that morning, I felt no sense of belonging. As I saw the other patients, I eyed them suspiciously. Perhaps they were crazy, but I was not. I felt clever, and then I began to cry again. All because some kindly older woman had come over to me and put her hand on my shoulder and said, "Hello." I was crying again, damn it, and a nurse took me back to my room and I rested awhile, feeling not so clever now.

Later Sam came and brought me some clothes.

"How are you, Susan? I hope I brought the right things."

"I'm all right. Did you bring any books?"

"No, I'm sorry. Just some clothes. I didn't think you would be up for reading."

Looking around the room he commented, "Certainly doesn't look like a psychiatric ward. Looks more like a resort. Doesn't anybody wear uniforms?"

"I don't think so. A new kind of treatment, I guess. If we all wear the same clothes you can't tell the crazies from the staff. I think it's supposed to make us crazies think we're not inferior."

"Boy, you really gave me a scare."

"Did I? Inconsiderate. I'm sorry."

"You looked as if you were asleep. . ."

"I was."

"But your room was so clean. First I thought to myself, my God, you actually listened to me, you cleaned your room, you were all right."

"The cleaned room pleased you, did it?"

"Well, it took me a few seconds to realize everything seemed like a stage setting. Nothing seemed quite real.

186

Finally I realized what was missing. The pills were missing."

"Why didn't you ever think of taking them away before?"

"Why, that was your business. But I never thought you would do anything like this. You were a lump of sleep. I actually slapped you across the face. Christ, I was scared then. I dropped you back on the bed and ran next door to call the police."

"You saved my life. Thanks."

"Are you being sarcastic or something?"

"No, no, I mean it."

"Well, anyway, as I was rushing back to you June ran in dropping her books on the dining room table. I couldn't help it, I screamed at her to get out."

"Poor kid. She's not used to you screaming. It's usually me who does all the yelling."

"Yeah, well, she kept wanting to know if you were sick."

"Listen, Sam, I'm kind of tired. Thanks for bringing the clothes."

"You know, it's amazing, the first thing June noticed was how clean your room was."

"You need to finish this story, don't you, Sam? You need to tell me everything."

"Listen, Susan. It was a real mess. I mean, a nightmare. The police dragging you out on a stretcher, a doctor slapping your face. I was crying. They wheeled you right past June. She just stood quietly watching. It was a real mess. The police and radio equipment. You could hear, 'Apparent attempted suicide. White female about thirty-five.' Shit, that was something for June to hear all right."

"I know I should have thought about those things. I'm sorry."

"June was talking to you, trying to tell you everything would be all right. Then she started to cry, too. She ran to try to hold your hand. Jesus Christ, you had pills in them. They dropped like jacks, scattering all over the floor."

"I appreciate you coming to cheer me up like this, Sam. I'm kind of tired now. Give June my love, will you? Tell her I'm all right. I'll be home soon."

"She doesn't blame you. She blames me. She said to me, 'Mommy's been sick so long and no one took care of her.' I tried to explain that it wasn't my fault but she blames me. You made a real mess of things, Susan. You should have listened to me. That's your trouble. You never listen to anybody. I would have helped you."

"I asked you for help. You wouldn't do anything."

"You always wanted it all your way."

"Well, I'm sorry. I'm sorry it was such a mess and so much trouble."

"It's all right. Don't worry about that. I'll take care of things now. I'll see you in a few days, okay?"

"Sure. I guess so."

"You didn't really want to die, did you, Susan? I mean, not really."

What I really wanted to do was tell the son of a bitch what I thought of him. Loudly and obscenely. But all my energies had to be focused on being a good patient. I did not think the staff would regard it as reasonable if I gave vent to what I was feeling about Sam. Not reasonable at all.

"Oh, go away, Sam. Go away for now."

My therapist was a young woman, very young. What have I come to, I thought, that I have to be helped by someone younger? It seemed important then. The therapist, Dr. Jane Howard, wore her hair in a pony tail. She was pretty, the kind of prettiness that I envied. Small-boned, delicate. She had no visible makeup on, just a trace of pale lipstick.

She didn't need any, not with that complexion. I knew this woman. As a young girl she had long, straight hair and a closet full of frilly dresses, and drawers full of different-colored Danskins. In college she tormented me with her perfect complexion, tiny waist (still had long straight hair). Later, she was the woman who owned the perfect silk lounging pajamas (showing off her trim figure) in which she served her home-cooked gourmet dinners.

Immediately upon seeing her I felt as if I had forgotten to brush my teeth. My stomach, never flat, was a balloon, my nails ragged, my hair dull (and far too curly).

She wore a white jacket over her light blue blouse. A gold chain with a small diamond circled her neck, small gold earrings twinkled at her ears. Her watch, with its black lizard band, emphasized her petite wrist. She looked dry and cool. The hospital was overheated, I was sweating all the time. They had given me a kind of housecoat to wear, striped. It hung loosely, except for the fit under the arms, which was tight.

"I wonder, Dr. Howard, " I asked, "how old are you?"

"Why do you ask?" she replied.

"Well, you seem so young. Are you a medical doctor or a social worker?"

"Does it make a difference?"

"I don't know, but I am curious."

She thought for a minute, obviously trying to decide what deeper meaning my question had.

"Look," I said, "you're a total stranger to me. You know about me from these records, but I don't know a thing about you. Now I'm not asking you about your personal life, not yet at least, just your credentials."

"I'm a physician."

"A physician. Well, you are certainly a young one. You must be a genius to have gone through medical school . . . you are a graduate physician? Not just an intern?"

"Susan, I'm a fully qualified psychiatrist. I'm not quite as young as you may think."

"Well, how old are you?"

"It's not that I mind telling you, but we are here to talk about you, not me."

"Sure. But I would have guessed you're about twenty-eight."

She smiled at this. "I've always looked younger, actually I'm thirty-four."

"Lucky you. I've always looked older; it's nice when you're sixteen, but it catches up with you. So, you're younger than me. Married?"

"Susan, this is turning into an interrogation."

"Please don't take it like that, I just want to know about you. If you're going to help me, I have to know how much you can understand. If you've been married, for example, well, you'll understand things about marriage that you wouldn't if you're single. That's only reasonable, isn't it?" I noticed she wasn't wearing a wedding ring. "I assume you're not married, no ring."

"I was married." She flushed slightly. "I'm divorced. So you can be sure that I'll understand the problems of marriage."

"You look a little upset. Was it a painful divorce?"

I couldn't imagine anyone leaving this trim physician. Surely she had thrown him out. But maybe not. Maybe the bastard just left her. It was impossible to imagine her small frame trembling, her eyes glistening with tears. Hysterical, even.

"Susan, this is silly. You're resisting talking about yourself. Why would you think my divorce was painful? Was yours very hard for you?"

"No."

She was fidgeting with a pen; so far I hadn't given her much to take notes about.

"Well, we can talk about that more at another time. For now I'd like to explain how things work around here."

She began by outlining how often she would see me and explaining the various other kinds of therapy that I would be having. There was also a twice-a-week group meeting of staff and patients. At this meeting patient gripes and requests for passes to leave the floor were considered and voted upon. But you had to submit your request two days before the Tuesday and Thursday meetings.

"We don't want you to push yourself, Susan, that is important. Just take it easy. Try to get used to the schedule."

"And how do I get out of here?" I asked.

"Oh, we won't worry about that right now. It takes time, time to get adjusted, time to heal. Don't be in a rush to get out of here, Susan. It's much more important to make sure you're ready to cope with the world than to leave here unprepared."

"How long?" I persisted.

"It's impossible to say, right now. Technically you can check yourself out, you're not a prisoner. But for discharge you'll have to wait until we think you're ready. The faster you adjust to things here, the faster you'll get out."

"But the people here are disturbed. The whole system here is one for disturbed people. Why should I adjust to a system for disturbed people? That doesn't make much sense to me. Shouldn't I be adjusting to the world out there, where there are no therapy schedules, no lights out at ten, no arbitrary institutional restraints?"

"The point of all this is just that—to help you to adjust in the world. But you have to live here, with these rules, with these schedules. We'll have plenty of time to talk about your adapting to the world, where you failed and how you can do better." After Dr. Howard explained these things, she sat back and asked me to tell her about myself.

I was self-conscious, fidgeting in my chair. It was a dingy, impermanent room. Everyone used it, it wasn't like a regular office, there was no couch. Window shades blocked the sun. Dr. Howard had a folder with her. She seemed to travel with her folders.

"You ought to have an office where you can leave your things," I said.

"Oh, I don't mind," Dr. Howard answered.

"Well, I do. I think it's outrageous that you don't have a regular office. It's demoralizing for the patients. Never knowing what office we'll be meeting in. I don't like that at all."

Neither of us spoke. Shit, I thought, what the hell am I doing here? I have nothing to say to this woman.

"Susan, I'm sorry if the office disturbs you. Do you like permanent homes?"

"I really don't give a shit. Look"—I moved forward in my chair—"let me try to explain all this." My voice was earnest. "I know you people think suicide is crazy. Well, there is another way to look at it. It happens that I believe suicide to be a real option. Do you understand that? A real, personal option. It's my business, It's not necessarily sick. I know you think it is, but I don't. People either understand suicide as an option or they don't," I went on, warming to my subject. "It's very interesting. Some people can't even imagine it, would never allow themselves to even think about it. But there are others, it's kind of a club, who accept it with absolute equanimity. Maybe we're born with it, with that extra insight which allows us to view it as one of many options. The way I see it, I wouldn't be here if I had decided on one of my other options, say, robbing a bank. I'd be in jail then, but no one would think I was crazy. That would be a solution, too, but instead I decided on suicide."

I couldn't tell what Dr. Howard was thinking. Her face was impassive. "Do you understand at all?"

"Yes, I think I do. I don't agree with you, but I know what you're talking about. In your case, however, I think it was sick to try to kill yourself. I don't think you understand yourself why you did it. and perhaps if you did understand your own motives you wouldn't have wanted to."

"There's only one motive, Dr. Howard, and that's to get out. To get away from everything that hurts, from all the fear and the pain. That's all there is, that's all that's important."

"There are other ways to deal with pain and hurt and anger and fear, Susan, and I would like to help you find the other ways. The problem is, you don't see options, not really. You see only getting your own way or killing yourself. But in between there are other things, maybe they aren't perfect, but you don't see them at all. Of course suicide is an option, but at least consider some of the others before you take such a drastic step."

I had walked to the window; reluctantly I was listening to her.

"Susan, let's begin at the beginning. Tell me about yourself, about how you feel. I'll try to help you. I don't want you to kill yourself."

I turned around angrily. "You don't want me to kill myself, you don't even know me. Why the hell should you give a shit?"

"Why not? You're a young, bright woman with a lot to

live for. You have a child, and you have had, apparently, more than your share of pain. Why shouldn't I care about you?"

I had answers for that but remained silent. I knew damn well that this woman didn't give a damn, but I also knew I wasn't going to get out of here unless I played the game. I returned to my seat. "Okay, doctor, take out your pencil, I'm about to deliver into your capable hands the story of my life."

"I'm sorry, Susan, but it will have to wait. Our time is up today."

"Hey, what is this?" I was furious. "I'm ready now."

"But I'm not. There are other patients, Susan."

"The hell with them, I'm all set to tell you and you walk out."

"You have options here, Susan, you can be furious, you can hate me, or you can try to understand that while I care about you, I also care about my other patients. They're ready, too. I can't force you to choose what to feel, but think about it. You're frustrated because I can't stay right this minute. Think about what that is doing to you. We'll talk about it next time." And with that, leaving me open-mouthed and miserable, Dr. Howard walked over to me and said, "We really do have to end for today. I'll see you tomorrow."

We left the room together. Back in my room, one of the women, Marci, was dusting her area, humming.

"Anything I can do for you?" she asked sweetly. "You poor thing. I know how it feels, the first time."

"No thanks, I'm okay."

"I'm drying out," she said. "Is that why you are here, too?" Suddenly tired, I just wanted to rest. "Who knows, maybe. Maybe I am drying out."

Marci nodded. In this place, who knew anything? I knew I was going to have trouble with Dr. Howard. She was smarter and smaller than me. She sat behind the desk, she held the pen, she had the degrees, the credentials, the pedigree. She looked like a satisfied woman. Why not? If I were small, I'd be satisfied, too. She must have been adorable in medical school, all those young boys making room for her at the cadaver. I could well imagine the feeling she had when people said, "You're a doctor? Pretty little you, smart enough to be a doctor!" God, how I would like that feeling. There wasn't one thing I could think of that I had over Jane Howard. Not one thing. This was just what I needed now in my life. Regular sessions with a thirty-four-year-old (looks like twenty-eight) petite physician who had it all. Where in hell were the overweight, bearded male psychiatrists who, at least, might have lusted after me? That's what I needed. Even a young male shrink, who could eventually be reduced to serious discussions about "transference" and "counter-transference." Someone to dress up for, to impress. The least they could have done was given me an older woman. Gray hair pulled back at the nape of the neck in a bun, very large, maternal woman, graduated medical school in 1932. And sympathetic, and every once in a while I could see that "if only I were your age again" look in her eye and know that I had something she wanted, at least.

26

The couch that converted into my bed was narrow. Since they would give me no medication, except for a mild tranquilizer, I couldn't sleep. I couldn't turn or toss, the damn bed was too narrow. I listened to the other women breathing, one of them snored. Sam had snored, but at least I could roll him over and he would stop for a while. But trapped in this narrow bed, all I could do was listen. I wanted to masturbate but was afraid of the constant bed checks the night nurse made. A flashlight illuminated each bed at regular intervals; I pretended to be asleep.

Everyone in Tower 10 was very intense about therapy. As if simply talking, or drawing pictures or acting out roles could solve their problems. The day revolved around the scheduling of various forms of therapy. Checking the schedule in the morning, you carefully noted the times you were due in therapy sessions. I had a full schedule, private sessions with Dr. Howard, art therapy, play therapy, physical therapy, music therapy. The staff was thrilled with themselves, providing so much therapy. I was never quite sure where the patients stood; they certainly seemed to take it all seriously.

The big question, of course, was how to get the hell out of there. Not that the sessions with Dr. Howard weren't interesting, they were. I watched Dr. Howard carefully as I recounted the story of my life. I told it accurately and quickly, not dwelling on any particular moment. It was all prelude, anyway, I wanted to get to the main event. The words seemed so naked. There was no way I knew to make it real for Dr. Howard. The words themselves were nothing. "Mother killed herself," meaningless words. I felt as if I were lying to Dr. Howard, and that was very strange because I was just telling the simple truth. But still, I had the uncomfortable feeling that I was lying. Deceiving her.

Dr. Howard kept asking me how I felt about this or that. Dumb questions. Just another who doesn't understand. There are no words for those feelings either, and I despised the ones that were ordinary. Everyone feels grief, pain, sadness, fear . . . these were not adequate words to describe my feelings. If I used those words I would be like everyone else. How could Dr. Howard distinguish between my grief and someone else's if there was only the word to explain the feeling. It was no use, no use at all. Everyone wanted to hear my words, wanted me to speak in a language with which they were comfortable. But I had no language for my emotions.

The hospital routine was absorbing and kept me busy. God, it felt good to be busy, to have a purpose even if it was all this therapy.

The art therapy wasn't half bad. There I stood and drew pictures on a large paper attached to the wall. At least no words were needed there. I drew a lot of circles, but left them incomplete. I liked that, lots of circles that did not close. I drew them in all colors, taking up the large paper with different-sized circles. Sometimes I drew circles within circles, careful to position the openings on opposite sides.

Admiring my work I wondered what the hell anyone would make of that. But anyway, I liked it. The art therapist asked me what I thought they meant. I just looked at her and shrugged. After the circles, I drew boxes, boxes that didn't close. It wasn't as much fun as the circles, but it was okay.

In play therapy I was asked to improvise a woman who wanted to kill herself. I stood in the middle of the circle of patients and thought for a couple of minutes. Then, I held up my hand, indicating that it held a dagger and thrust it toward myself. (Shit, that would have to do. How the hell would I know how to play someone who wanted to kill herself?)

Occupational therapy was really awful. I hated working with my hands, and finally asked if I could write. The therapist was delighted and gave me heavy bond typing paper and unlocked the typewriter. I wrote a poem:

> *To be deprived of death yet*
> *Foster that burden still*
> *Is but the greater loss.*
>
> *At night down on the drive*
> *I dream of life. Then*
> *At the whisper of stirring leaves*
> *I tremble back in death . . .*

I liked that. And wrote another:

> *It is the precious paradox of life*
> *That I should have been a child.*
> *Fulfillment is an anxious seed,*
> *There are no tranquil passions.*
>
> *"Step on a line, break your mother's spine."*

Cruelly I stepped. Crack. Pausing then
On the wrinkled pavement, I wondered if I would be grown
When the kind hot grass consumed the gaps.

Impatient blossoms flared and fell
Leaving dark mosaic on an aging tree;
I counted only the interludes—
Child's play. Grownups total essentials . . .

Such as these were not. But I, alive
Now only to mature grotesqueries,
Feel eyes tiring to all
Bright fantasy or infant illusion.

And then one more:

Drops from a dropper
Tell the time.

Why must my life inevitably slip out
When at my will I can release my thumb
And cease the flow of drops, the seconds
Cruelly captured in translucency.

There is no need to rush,
I still have time to decide
What moment I cherish enough
To halt the pattern of those lethal drops.

The occupational therapist asked me what the poems meant.
I stopped writing that day.

I was sleeping better. Dr. Howard explained that she was
a behaviorist. That meant, I gathered, that we were going to

talk about how I behaved. Well, that was okay,"I have a question, Dr. Howard. I have this surplus of guilt, and pain and anger. So the thing is, what do I do with it?"

"Do with it?" Dr. Howard repeated.

"Yes, how do I get rid of it, where can I park it, leave it, drop it off?"

"Susan, it's more complicated than that. You can't rid yourself of all of those things like taking off a coat. You have to work them all through—to understand all the feelings—and then there will be appropriate ways to deal with the feelings."

I was listening intently. (Appropriate? That again. Oh, no, not again.)

"Listen, Dr. Howard, I don't believe in appropriate."

"Why not, Susan, we've made a good start. Why can't you take each one of those things and work with me so that you can deal with the things that made you want to kill yourself?"

I sighed. God knows this lady meant well. She was waiting for an answer. What'll we tell her to make her understand? Dr. Howard looked at her watch. The session was coming to a close. I knew the signs.

"Dr. Howard, I don't want to kill myself any more. Really, I feel pretty good. I'm very grateful for that. You've helped a lot."

"Well, I'm glad you feel that way, Susan. But you haven't answered my question. Why do you feel we can't talk these things out? You're very intelligent, it won't be easy. Susan, why are you shaking your head? Why can't we talk about your feelings?"

(You're hearing all this, Mother, they are still doing it. They haven't learned much.)

"Dr. Howard," I said very gently, "we can't talk about my

feelings because we don't speak the same language. Nobody's invented the right words."

"Then you invent them, Susan. Use any words you want."

"Oh, no, no," I said fervently, "I couldn't do that."

"Why not? Make them up. We'll find the right way to communicate."

"No, Dr. Howard, you don't understand. This isn't a game. It's not for me to invent the words. You want me to speak gibberish, to pretend that some strange letters put together will approximate my feelings? There is no idiom, no vernacular for what I feel." I stood up to leave. I extended my hand to Dr. Howard. "I'm really grateful for all your help. You're a terrific psychiatrist. I mean it. You mustn't feel bad about this. It's not your fault. And I really don't want to kill myself any more. The whole experience has taught me a lot." I was pumping Dr. Howard's hand as I spoke. Dropping it, I walked behind the desk and kissed Dr. Howard on the cheek. "I'm fine, now, Dr. Howard."

On Sunday, I noticed an ad in the *Times* that was not through an agency: "Public Relations, writing skills necessary, self-starter call 876–5979."

I showed it to Marge when she came to visit me.

"Well," she said doubtfully, "what do you know about public relations?"

"Nothing, but it's one of the few ads in the paper that isn't through an agency. What's there to know about public relations, anyway?"

"True, so what do you want me to do?"

"Lie for me. I thought I'd do a résumé and give your firm as a reference. Say I worked there for five years, doing public relations for a few of your accounts."

"And why did you leave again, I forget?"

"Oh, that. How about painful staff retrenchments due to the recession?"

"You think it will work?"

"Why not, anyway, it's all I've got. If he calls, just give me a buildup, sorry to lose me, and don't forget to mention I'm a self-starter."

"Listen, I really do need someone in the office. I was thinking of asking you if you would like to . . ."

"No."

"I need someone, I really do."

"Then hire someone. Not me, thanks, I know what you're trying to do, but no. Let's try it this way."

I typed a résumé in writing therapy and called for an appointment.

A man answered, and after a few questions gave me an appointment for Wednesday. I was stunned. I hadn't said much about myself, just that I was very interested in the job and was a self-starter. I had sounded inane. But I had an appointment. I tried to find Dr. Howard, left word for her to see me as soon as she got to the floor. I went to write my request for a pass. One of my roommates was in the room.

"You'll vote to give me a pass, won't you?"

"Well, I don't know. You've only been here a week."

"Please," I begged, "please vote for me."

Dr. Howard came in and I told her the news.

"You don't think it's a little soon, another chance to fail a typing test?"

"Oh, no, it's not too soon. I must go on this interview."

"We'll see," Dr. Howard said.

I called Sam. "Listen, Sam, I'm going on a job interview. Bring me my suit, my good shoes, and new stockings. No, I don't want to see you. Please just bring those things."

I discussed the interview with Dr. Howard in my private session. "Trying to kill myself wasn't crazy. I think it was sensible. At least at the time, it was a way out. And look what I achieved. I got here, I have been helped. I've begun to see I can't change other people, or wait for a miracle. You're always after me to help myself. Well, dammit, isn't this a beginning?"

"Susan, I wonder if even you realize how raw you still are. You keep asking me if you are different. Well, in some ways you are. You really have a great drive for health. But I wonder how you will feel if this is another rejection. I have a lot of faith in you, but I want you to think the realities through. Are you qualified for this job? You don't even know what it is. Isn't there a little bit of fantasy there? Never mind proving you can get a job. You can get a job, but maybe not this one."

"Let me try. Just let me try."

By this time, I had settled into a routine. I was polite, a good patient, cooperative and thoroughly revolted. Meal-times were particularly revolting. And never being alone, and the sobbing and sometimes the screaming of the other patients unnerved me. No question about it, this place might be safe, but it was depressing as hell.

At Tuesday's group meeting, I waited to present my request for a pass. *Don't appear too anxious.* At last in my most reasonable tone, I asked for two hours off on Wednesday. Immediately one patient said, "I think it's too soon. Anyone who tried to kill herself a week ago, it's too soon."

I kept silent. The patients bickered with each other, but I saw something. They were worried about me, really worried. Not just trying to deprive me of an opportunity, but really worried. The chief psychiatrist asked Dr. Howard how she felt. She was examining her small delicate hands as she spoke.

"For a lot of patients it would be too soon, but I think Susan can handle this. I vote yes."

It was a near thing. The chief psychiatrist voted no, as did many patients. But I had my majority. After the vote, I thanked the group for their confidence. When I was finished, Dr. Mailman, the chief, looked me straight in the eyes and said, "Susan, I've rarely met anyone who talked a better game, but I think you're full of shit." He said it very matter-of-factly, and I smiled. A good-looking son of a bitch, he had my number.

27

"You haven't any experience in Jewish life?" David asked, his cigar resting on the ashtray. I longed to tap the ash off.

"No, no experience but I'm very interested," I replied.

David Hirsch was looking skeptically at my résumé. "Why do you want to work here? The pay isn't very much, and after an advertising agency it may not seem very exciting."

"Well, as you can see, I was with them for five years. If they hadn't had some reverses, I probably would have stayed, but now that I have the chance to start something new, I'd like to try something that makes me feel useful."

I was warming to this now. I lowered my voice, just a little. "You see, I am a survivor myself. My family was killed by the Nazis. I know what it means to be Jewish and persecuted for it."

I glanced at him to see how this was being received. His face was tight, grim. For once being a member of this club was useful.

David nodded his head as if he understood my explanation. He was so earnest himself, it all seemed perfectly reasonable.

"I can't pay much, that's the problem. Our budget is very small. How much do you need?"

"How much can you pay? I realize I'll have to take a cut in salary, but if you're doing something meaningful, well, that's worth more than money."

I would learn later that this was a common theme told to people who work in nonprofit agencies. For the privilege of using your talents to help people, you naturally got paid less.

"All I can offer, at the start anyway, is two hundred dollars a week. For openers, anyway."

I hesitated for just a moment; he mustn't think I was too eager.

"That would be okay," I said carefully, "for openers."

With that settled, David relaxed. I noticed that the paint in his office was peeling, the windows which looked out over an alley were dirty, opaque with grime. His desk was metal, painted over green. Similar to the ones the state provided in the employment office.

Nevertheless, it was not depressing. He had added a few touches of his own, a radio, a lamp, and posters from home. And the work on his desk was in neat piles, pencils sharpened. He was a man making the best of it. It was time I learned to do the same.

"When can you start?" he asked.

"A week from Monday, if that's all right."

He paused. I pulled in my stomach.

"Let me be honest, Susan. I had hoped that I would find someone who was experienced. We have a small budget; we're understaffed. But if you're willing to try, well, I'm willing to give it a chance, too. Actually, there aren't many people around with experience in Soviet Jewry. I don't suppose you know any reporters at the *Times*?"

"No, I don't. I'm sure I can get to know them. I will get to know them."

"You'll have help. There are a couple of top PR guys at other Jewish agencies. Use them. They can be valuable. Now, let me fill you in, just a little." He smiled at me then, tapping his cigar ash. "Don't be nervous," he said kindly, "we all have to start somewhere."

My fellow patients were excited for me. Dr. Howard was all smiles.

"Sounds good, but why did you agree to start so soon?"

"It still gives me another week here."

"That's not enough."

"For other people it isn't, but for me it is. Don't you believe me?"

"Yes, I do. And you seem to have gotten a lot from your week here, but we need to see if you really understand. You need some time to solidify this experience."

"I don't have the time. I know I'm all right. I need this job. It's like an omen. I mean, who the hell gets a job from the psychiatric ward of a hospital, a real job?"

"Susan, I'm glad about the job, but I won't release you, not yet. At least plan to stay another week. Then you'll have to sign out AMA."

"What's that?"

"That's 'against medical advice.' It means that we don't think you're ready."

"But I am ready. I got a job, and I'm ready."

"Well, that's up to you. I can't force you to stay here."

I was afraid she knew what she was talking about. Afraid that if I didn't have her sanction, I wouldn't make it. She was the authority here, my breakdown was her business, what did I know about it?

"I'm different, I can do it. Don't just label me because I tried to kill myself. Look at me. Who I am. I got a job, from a locked ward of a psychiatric hospital. I got a job. Surely that's different."

"Susan, you want my approval for something and I can't give it to you. I think it's too soon. This isn't like starting a new grade in school, where the notebook is clean and all the kids are new. You're carrying some pretty heavy problems with you. You should allow yourself more time to understand them."

"No. I need this job. I know what you're saying is right for other people, but not for me. I'll be careful, very careful. I won't allow myself to get depressed, or rejected, I won't even screw around. I'll work hard, I can do it. I don't have any more time to waste. I've spent too much time, all my life, trying to understand all these things. I need to have some success now, to feel some good feelings."

"They can come from inside you, Susan. They are not dependent on a job."

"Bullshit, you can talk, you a doctor who can feel good about yourself every minute, always someone needing you. You are necessary. I want that, too. And I'm not going to blow it because you think I should stay another week. I've been looking for a job for months, and now I've got one, a good one. Another week, what's that?"

Dr. Howard was kind, but would not change her mind. I signed myself out AMA, hating Dr. Howard for clouding the beginning of my new life. And doubting, wondering if I was making the right move. But looking around the floor, I saw that most of the patients had been there before, chronic inmates. (It's a make-or-break situation. Either I make it or

I'll be back, just like them. With all that patronizing shit about how *this* time I can make it, this time being visit three or six. Not for me. I won't be back. The food stinks anyway.)

Sam came to visit. I told him about the job.

"I guess you'll be needing help for a while. I thought it might be a good idea if I moved back in."

"Moved back in, to my apartment?"

"Well, yes, then I could help with June while you're starting work. Nothing permanent, just until you get on your feet."

"Sam, I'm on my feet, and if I was laid out forever, I wouldn't agree to that. You bastard, you can only really like me when you think I'm sick. Well, I've got news for you. I may have ended up in here, but you're the one who should be here. You're sick. We're divorced, divorced"—I am starting to shout—"You would have let us starve. Me, June, just to prove something for yourself. You can't take it when I'm strong. And I'm so fucking stupid I fell right into that trap again. No more trays in bed, Sam, no more sick. No more hiding in the basement. You can get the hell out. Just have June home on Sunday at eleven. I'll be there and I'll take over. And stay out of my life, except, of course, if you'd care to have some self-respect and help support June. Otherwise, stay out. Do you want to know what I dreamed the first night I was here? The dream I was so afraid to have all these years, that I took pills to keep it away. I dreamed you were dead, and that I found your body in a parking lot and took a hatchet and methodically cut you apart. I kept cutting you apart, your legs, your balls, your head, and throwing you in the Hudson River. It doesn't take any genius to figure that one out. And for that lousy dream, that one I've been too afraid to have, I kept myself numbed with pills."

Sam was stunned. He had come with flowers for me, a box of candy and with plans to be gentle.

"You bitch. You sick bitch. I've got a chicken roasting in the oven for dinner, I cleaned your apartment, I did the laundry. I polished the mirrors, and straightened your God-damned books, I created order for you. You have all that to go home to." He threw the flowers on the floor, and tossed the candy on the bed. "Bitch," he said again softly, as he left, "sick bitch."

Is it because we have been so cruel that I must ask him to come back? Is there safety in familiar cruelty? Is it too frightening to seek out a relationship of kindness?

28

On Monday morning I walked down the corridor to the small office that was assigned to me. The walls of the dingy halls were covered with posters. One famous one was just opposite my office. A photograph of a boy about four or five, hands raised, prodded by Nazi soldiers holding bayonets. The boy's eyes were bright with fear. We were children at the same time, I thought, he might have been my friend. *Staring at his picture isn't going to help anyone.*

My office was littered. Piles of mimeographed material on the floor, pamphlets and brochures. I wrote a press release, filling in information from a file card. I made up a quote for David expressing his "outrage."

David smiled as he read the release. "It's okay, except for the quote. I don't make statements, our chairman does. I forgot to explain the most important thing. There are two kinds of people in Jewish life: professionals, that's what we are"—he jabbed his finger at me indicating I was one of them—"and lay people. The lay people are wealthy. One of our jobs is to make them look good. Okay, now we process this and send it out to the papers. We have a clipping service so we'll know if it gets picked up. You might call it into the foreign desk at the *Times*, AP and UPI. Introduce yourself; you'll be talking with them a lot. Sometimes they call us for confirmation of a story. Most often we call them. If we get something really important they'll cable their Moscow correspondent for confirmation. It's important to have a good relationship with them. When you're finished, come back. We're meeting with representatives of our constituent agencies to plan a demonstration. You'll be part of that."

I called the *Times*, AP and UPI. They weren't too interested. "Send it over," they said, "we'll see."

Back in David's office, a lively meeting was in progress. David motioned for me to sit down and interrupted the man who was speaking to introduce me. Later, I didn't remember any of them. Not one name stayed with me. They were discussing a mass demonstration that was being planned for the first time. New York was expected to turn out one hundred thousand people marching down Fifth Avenue to the United Nations, where they would hear a program of speakers. It would be the first "Solidarity Day with Soviet Jews" ever held. No one knew if they could actually get one hundred thousand people to march. It had never been tried before. The budget for advertising was miniscule. Moishe Kaplan was frantic that it would fail. He was an orthodox Jew, one of several in the room wearing *yarmulkes*. As he spoke, he kept patting it, as if making sure it was there. Nervous and worried, he asked the others to "get their people out." "The troops," he called them. People who belonged to synagogues, anyone who had any affiliation with a Jewish organization should be exhorted to march. Buses would be provided from the boroughs to Fifth Avenue.

Sandwiches and coffee were brought in but nobody stopped talking to eat. I was trying to listen, but there were too many distractions. I was worried that my fresh white blouse was soiled.

Listen to them, damn it, Susan. Just listen. But the room was charged with too much intensity for me. I was tired of intensity. The conversation of the group sounded distant to me. I didn't belong among these zealous planners. Planning to save Jews. Indeed. Save Jews with a hundred thousand people marching on Fifth Avenue, floats depicting Soviet labor camps, teenagers dressed in uniforms with toy guns, signs and slogans and songs that began "Let my people go. . ." *Hey, what do you know, anyway.*

I had run out of cigarettes. I was anxious to leave. Occasionally someone said, "Find out the best time for the parade to start," "Check who is covering for the *Times*," "Will the 'Today' show interview some key people involved in the movement?" I made notes of all the things to check.

It was nearly six o'clock when they got up to leave. They left still talking; it seemed to me they hadn't stopped for a minute.

Moishe Kaplan stayed behind to talk to David.

"You think it will work, David?" he asked.

David shrugged. "God, I hope so. We'll look like idiots if it doesn't. We'll have to make it work."

"You mean I'll have to make it work," Moishe said. "I'm the only one with enough people in this area to make it look good."

"So?"

"So, I want the New York Coalition for Soviet Jewry to have equal billing. On everything, ads, radio spots, everything."

"No way," David said.

"Why not? You know damn well you can't do it by yourself."

"It's a national event," David insisted.

"But happening in New York—in New York, and it will be my people there. Listen, I need it, I need the publicity. It will help me get them out, I'll get you a hundred thousand people. But I need the cosponsorship."

"I'll think about it."

"Good, think about it. Think about my hundred thousand people. Call me in the morning."

Moishe turned to me. "What do you think about this, Susan?"

"Leave her alone, it's her first day," David said. "For God's sake go home."

Moishe laughed. "Okay, I'm going. If you need any help Susan, just call me."

After he left I asked David about Moishe.

"He's terrific. An orthodox Jew with political ambitions. I'm afraid you'll find that this business is competitive, too."

"Are you going to give him equal sponsorship?" I asked.

"Not equal, but we'll work out something. He does need it, and he can get his people out. He'd get them out anyway, but if he's asking, it means he needs the *kovid.*"

"Tired?" David asked.

"Yes, as a matter of fact, I am."

"Well, it's a lot for a first day. It's hard work, Susan." Checking his watch he noted, "I won't leave here until nine or ten tonight. These damn meetings take up all my days. Then the only time I have to work is at night."

I could see he was pleased with the idea that he would work half the night. The piles on his desk, his late work, all proved that he was vital to his humanitarian effort.

I felt shaky. Maybe this wasn't such a hot idea, after all. Maybe these Soviet Jews needed David Hirsch, with his noble intentions and self-sacrificing spirit. But they didn't need me. And I didn't need them. I was the last person that needed to be reminded of persecution. I needed a movement all for myself, a committee to save Susan Warner.

"Well," I said, collecting my papers, "I really am tired. Is there anything more you want me to do before I leave?"

"No, you did just fine today, Susan."

"Thanks." I had done nothing. Maybe this would be all right after all, if he was pleased with so little. I had listened, and nodded and made notes, and contributed nothing. I had been frightened all day that they would find out how little I knew. Waiting for someone to object to me, to confront me with my ignorance. Instead, they had accepted me. And now David was telling me I had done well. It was crazy, a lot crazier than Tower 10.

I walked home that night because I was lonely. The lonelier I felt, the more necessary it was for me to be alone.

I had serious doubts as to whether I would return.

Reaching Central Park, I felt better. Safer. I stopped to rest. The rock I leaned against was cool and smooth. I reached down and pulled up a handful of grass and smelled the rich earth, holding it close to my nose for a long time to wipe out the stench of my body fear. Relaxing into the rock, that hardened slate seemed to accommodate my body. The lights of the city flickered on as I stood up. On three sides of the park the tall buildings contested to see which would be lighted first. One runner, I thought, for each side, sprinting across the buildings with a torch, igniting lights east and west and south.

And the photograph of the boy came to me. He's been dead too long for me to cry. They've all been dead too long.

I might have been standing next to him, hands in the air, a whimpering child of four. The terror, the confusion, what would I have done? Nothing. There was nothing to do. I would have been prodded onto the train, and screamed with all my might believing that someone would save me from it, but I would have died. Nobody would have saved me. Nobody saved him. And if I were his mother and saw the gun at his head, then the pain would have been unendurable. I would have tried to run to him, and they would have held me back, perhaps hitting me with their guns. But still I would have tried to go to him. What if I remained conscious and had to watch as they dragged him away?

Walking in the midst of the glittering city, I had no answer for that. What do you do when the pain is unendurable and you are totally helpless? Smash yourself against the wall and beat yourself to death, or run into the bayonet of a eager murderer? Or curse God and damn him? What if you live? But does one have to live? There is always a way, if it is bad enough, not to live. Did that mother live? Did she choose to live knowing what she knew? No, surely not. But perhaps she did. Maybe, she lived through the unendurable and no longer cried for her son because he, after all, had been dead for a very long time.

It was months before I came to know the Soviet Jews as people, sitting alone at night in my office reading through their grim stories. Each of them finally became real to me.

It was not unlike the lessons I learned at my mother's knee when she would pick up one picture of an aunt or another of a cousin and tell me again what camp they had been in and how she imagined they had died. In place of the specific facts of their deaths, she had only the survivors' tales dredged up from horrified fantasy. In order for her to keep her family real, she needed to play out each of their deaths. How she selected one death tale and matched it to one of her

216

family, I never knew. Finally, in the end she herself was convinced of the particulars of each of their deaths. It seemed to bring her some relief.

Sometimes, as she would complete her dossier on one of our murdered relations, she would pause for a moment to remember where she herself had been at that time.

"Hiding," she said to me, staring at me then with questioning eyes, "we were hiding. We were safe. What day was it, I wonder? What movement was I making? Was I feeling glad because we were safe hiding?"

Sometimes I would ask her, "Would you rather that we had died, too?" And in her passive way she would nod at me, and shrug her shoulders, only acknowledging that I had asked a meaningless question.

Now in place of those dead relatives, I had manila folders with neatly typed biographies of Russian Jews in trouble. I knew them, too, only secondhand. I wanted to believe that I cared about them. For the time being at least it seemed sufficient to go on pretending.

That was a year ago.

I'm still waiting to be found out, unmasked. I was accepted eagerly; no one questioned my credentials. I was supposed to know what I was doing; they wanted to believe that. I was their public relations person, their legimate expert on press matters. They endowed me with the qualities they needed; all I did was follow their lead. Somewhere in this past year, I began to feel, occasionally, authentic. I have piles of paper on my desk, and frequently work late. I am needed.

29

TO: L.I. BREZHNEV SECRETARY GENERAL OF THE CENTRAL COMMITTEE OF THE CPSU

Dear Leonid Ilyich:

It has been many months since I applied for permission to emigrate to Israel. Not only have my wife and I been refused permission to emigrate, but we have been told that we will never be allowed to leave the Soviet Union.

Surely this cannot be true? Surely this great country will not continue to deprive me of my livelihood? Since it is impossible for me to play in concert halls I have been performing in my apartment for small groups of friends. You understand, of course, that for a performer it is necessary, indeed it is life-sustaining, to perform. Last week during one of these informal performances at my apartment, officers of the KGB entered. They arrested six people and took me to their headquarters for interrogation. I was held there overnight, not permitted to sleep and given nothing to eat.

My wife, Lucia, who is in a highly nervous state as a result of all that has happened over the past months, was subjected to many hours of interrogation during my absence. The officers accused us of "anti-Soviet activity." I assure you that my pale efforts to play Tchaikovsky are not anti-Soviet. From the time I was a young boy I had only one interest and that was my music. I am not a political person and I seek now only to be permitted to go to Israel to rejoin my relatives there.

One reason for my refusal has been based on the fact that my relative is a distant aunt, an aunt whom I have never seen but who shares my blood, my heritage and is in fact the only family remaining for me.

My father, Piotor Rabinovitz, was killed during the Great Patriotic War defending the Soviet Union. We have always been proud of him and even as we mourned him, believed his death to be a victory for freedom and patriotism.

My wife and I are followed all of the time, pointed out to shopkeepers who then refuse to sell us food. My former colleagues are afraid to visit me because of the possibility of arrest. Spies are everywhere. Our situation is intolerable. I implore you to reconsider and permit my wife and myself to go to our historic homeland.

Leonid Rabinovitz
October 1974

Dear Leonid,

I am very concerned that I was not able to reach you. Did you get my cable? I called all day, but was told you were not at the post office. Perhaps there has been some mix-up. But please do not think that I did not try. I am afraid that you are being prevented from going to the post office.

Of course we have all heard of the crackdown last month during the Jewish holidays. What a shame that Soviet authorities would not allow Jews to peacefully congregate in a home to observe a religious holiday. Of course it saddens us all when we read of such repression.

There is, however, still much to hope for. Persons very high up in the United States government are interested in your case. There is a great deal of pressure from all kinds of groups, not just artists, to demand your freedom.

It is very strange, because we only know each other through these letters and the few telephone calls, but I feel as close to you and Lucia as I do toward my own family. I look forward to the day when we will meet, but I feel as if I know you both so well there will be no strangeness. Please always remember that we will never stop working until you are free. Don't despair, it cannot be too long.

Sincerely,
Susan

"A little favor. One lousy favor. What are you making such a fuss about?"

I was trying to persuade Marge to call Jason's apartment to see if "she" would answer.

"Because it's ridiculous. I don't care about doing it but what would you find out?"

"At least I'll know if she is living with him."

"Susan, you have been out of the hospital for three months. You're doing well at work. You're paying off your bills. Do you really need this?"

"I can't forget him."

"Nobody says you have to forget him. It doesn't mean you have to do something about it. Jason is a smart man, Susan. If he wanted to reach you he would know how to find you."

"It will be different if he hears my voice. He'll remember."

"He'll remember what? Was it so pleasant for him that you really want him to remember?"

"Just make the call, will you? If she answers tell her you

221

want her to be the building organizer for Muscular Dystrophy."

"Oh, God! All right."

"Mrs. Lampert? Oh. Well, my name is Sarah Smedley and I'm calling for Muscular Dystrophy and I wondered if you would agree to be the organizer for the present drive in your building. I see. Yes, perhaps next year. Thank you very much."

"What did she say?" I asked as she put down the phone.

"Well, I'm not sure what she said. When I said 'Mrs. Lampert,' she hesitated, which makes me wonder if she is Mrs. Lampert. Then she said that she and Mr. Lampert were leaving for Europe and she didn't feel that she could take on the responsibility at this time. Nice proper voice she has. 'Perhaps next year,' she said. Looks pretty solid, Susan."

"It means nothing. I can still get him back."

I'd been marking the days off on the calendar. Each day a small victory of not calling Jason. I knew, of course, that inevitably I would. It was exciting to know that it was in my power to pick up the phone and call.

Some days I had no inclination to do it at all. A couple of times my name had been in the newspaper as a spokesperson for the I.C.S.J. Had he seen it? Surely not. I could hardly send him the clipping. I wanted him to know that I was well and whole again.

And I wanted to hear his voice.

And I wanted him to love me.

"Mr. Lampert, please."

"May I tell him who's calling?"

(Bitch secretary. She knows my voice.) "Mrs. Warner."

"One moment, Mrs. Warner. I'll see if he's in."

222

(He's in. He's in alright. Don't humiliate me in front of your secretary, Jason. Take the call.)

"Susan?"

I thought I'd remembered his voice, but still it stunned me.

"Hello," I said.

"It's nice to hear from you. How are you?"

"I'm well. How are you?"

"I'm well, too. Busy, but very well, thank you."

(I remember when you were between my legs licking my cunt. How can you be so formal now?) "I was ill for a while, but I got better. I have a good job."

"I'm very glad for you."

"This doesn't sound like the old us, Jason."

"Susan, there isn't any us any more. I'm glad you're better. I'm glad you've got a good job. But there isn't any us any more."

"You don't mean that."

"Susan. Let's just let it be. I'm sorry. Sorrier than I can ever say for all the pain I've caused you. But there's nothing that can be done about it now. Just let it be."

"Are you married?"

"No. Not yet."

"You're getting married?"

"Probably."

"You're not sure?"

"Susan, I really can't talk now. Not like this."

"See me then."

"No. There's no point to it."

"Please. You owe me that at least."

"All right. I'll call you."

"Jason. I love you."

"I know that. Thank you."

"Do you love me?"

"I care for you. Goodbye for now. Keep doing good work, sweet girl."

Three weeks passed with no call from him.

"Mr. Lampert please."

"May I tell him who's calling?"

"Mrs. Warner. That's spelled W-a-r-n-e-r."

"One moment, Mrs. Warner."

"Hello, Susan."

"I've been waiting for your call."

"I've been busy."

"Nobody's that busy. You don't want to see me?"

"I suppose I'm a little afraid to see you. Hold for a second. I have to take another call."

I was tired of being put on hold and suddenly I was enraged, furious. He'd promised. He did love me. My anger made me strong.

"Would you tell Mr. Lampert that Mrs. Warner is here to see him?"

Picking up the intercom she said, "Mr. Lampert, Mrs. Warner is here. No, no. Here, in the office. Mrs. Warner, would you just have a seat? He'll be with you in a moment."

I sat close to the potted palm. I wanted to take a sniff under my armpits to see if I smelled. I must have because I was sweating terribly. But how could I sneak a sniff in with the secretary watching. I crossed my legs. (God, I have good legs.) A leaf of the palm was brushing against my arm. (I just hope I don't smell too much.)

The massive oak door to the inner offices opened and Jason appeared. How ordinary he looked.

"Come in, Susan." He held the door open and I preceded

him through it. Entering his office, I closed the door behind us. We stood very close. "You just . . . came?" he asked.

"What else could I do?"

He was shaking his head, denying that I was there at all. He reached out to touch my hair. "You're beautiful. You're even more beautiful than I remember."

I was kissing his face. "What else could I do? I had to come so you would remember."

"Come sit down, Susan."

We sat on the couch. He was staring at me.

"I hadn't planned to come today. I really hadn't. If I had I would have worn a much nicer dress."

"Your dress is lovely."

"Thanks. You should remember it. I used to wear it all the time."

"I remember it. The trouble is, I remember everything."

"All the bad things?"

"No. The good things. I can't believe I'm really seeing you, touching you."

"Jason, I'm not asking for much. I know you've got a girl. I'm sure she's wonderful, but I know she can't be to you what I can be. She can't possibly love you as much as I love you. I'm not asking for much. Just another chance. I know I was crazy. I'm sorry for all the terrible things but we had so much. Just give me a chance. Give us a chance. Come and play with me for a while. The way we used to play. Why are you staring at me?"

"I'm sorry. I don't mean to stare. It's just that . . . I'm looking at the only woman that I'll ever really love."

"Can you leave with me now?" I asked.

"Give me ten minutes. I'll meet you on the corner in ten minutes."

We took a taxi to his apartment. When he went to the

bathroom I looked in the closets. A few of her things were there. (She must still keep her own apartment.) I sat on the bed.

He came in and took off his watch. He looked at me all the time he was undressing. I just sat on the bed. I could see the dust particles in the light fluttering near the Venetian blinds.

"Are you frightened, sweet girl? You look terrified."

"It's been so long."

He sat on the bed next to me, stroking my hair, touching my face, unzipping my dress. "Susan, do you think it's wrong to kiss on the first date?"

"Oh, yes, I don't believe in kissing on the first date."

"What about fucking?"

"Oh, that's different. Fucking is creative. Jason, we're us again, aren't we?"

"I don't know. I just know that when I touch your back, just touching the skin on your back is so incredible. Come here, sweet girl. Come here and love me."

"You don't mind if we rest a little, do you, sweet girl? I would like to rest with you just for a little while. Perhaps we could sleep."

"I don't mind." But I did mind. Time was running out. I wanted to talk. (Talk to me, Jason.) "I don't mind. Just rest."

"Are you weeping?" He felt my face. "Why are you weeping? Have I made you sad again?"

"No, no, of course not. It's just that it's been so long. It's such a relief. I love you so much. You do love me, don't you, Jason?"

"Why do I have to say the words?"

"You're right. The words don't make any difference. It's just that it would be nice to hear them."

"What do you want, Susan?"

"I want to be your girl."

"You'll always be my girl. You're going to have to leave soon, Susan."

"What time does she get home?"

"About six."

"What is it she has that I don't?"

"Nothing. Well, perhaps one thing. She's soft."

"Soft? Soft?"

"Yes. She has a softness that you don't have. She doesn't frighten me."

"I can be soft. I can be everything you want."

"You are everything I want."

"We don't have to be a Greek tragedy, Jason. We can just be two normal people who love each other and live together."

"It doesn't seem to work that way, Susan."

"Does she know about me?"

"Yes. You are not exactly her favorite topic of conversation."

"Does she know you would rather sleep with me?"

"I think she knows that. I think that's something she probably knows."

"All right, I'm going to leave now. I'm going to prove I can go away quietly. We're old friends, aren't we, Jason?"

"We'll always be that. The funny thing, Susan, nobody has ever been as good to me as you. And you're right. No one has ever loved me as much. Just looking at you I wonder what kind of an idiot I am to let you leave." He was watching me dress. "You really are beautiful. With your hair grown long, you are even more beautiful."

I sat down on the bed. "Do we have a pact then, Jason? A contract?"

"A contract?"

"A simple one. That I'm your best girl. That we'll give it a chance. That we'll play a little."

"You're not asking me to make a choice?"

"No, I wouldn't do that. I may be crazy but I'm not stupid. I want you to watch, Jason."

"Watch?" he asked. I was getting dressed.

"Yes, just watch, because now I'm going to go away quietly."

So it began again, this beginning more like a postscript, a tersely scribbled afterthought.

Jason postponed his wedding plans, but he did not tell her he was seeing me. I am always calm now, soft and reasonable. There are no more arguments, I make few demands.

Jason is sad. There is no way I can talk to him about his sadness without sounding self-serving. So, I let him talk. About his business worries, and Mark and all the rest.

We meet for a drink, talk about the day, and then go to bed. Hotels now, neutral ground. Our apartments would be too close to the bone, we might be reminded then of other days and nights. Hotels are fine, crisp and anonymous. I insist on standing near him when he registers. In such petty ways do I declare my existence.

Jason is pleased with my new attitude. He is sad for me, too. He assumes that I still feel the same hysterical depth of love. What else can he assume? And I will not explain it any differently. To moderate it, to deny it, to shave just a little off would sound so foolish. He thinks I behave as I do so as not to lose him again. Perhaps that is true.

But lately I've begun to notice a few things. He is worried about growing older. He is aging in a totally conventional way. Too bad. Not graying, but balding. And his slumped shoulders, his bowed stance, once charming, are the forerunner

228

of an old man's shuffle. His body is not firm. It bothers him. Not me, of course, and I compliment him and tell him I love his body. Which I do. If I despise the sag in him, what will I feel about my own slack?

When I loved him before, I saw him as strong. At least that must have been part of it. Now I see he is weak, unable to make a decision, unable to accept a new safe life with her, or what he views as a dangerous one with me. We play at our old roles. That is the only way possible to survive. His flaws gnaw at me. I would like to talk about them. The simple truths are not so terrible. I feel he could not stand them. I cannot bear to voice them.

The other real difference is my work. I come to him now, strong from a day's work, excited, keyed up, nervous and concerned. When I tell him about it, I wonder if he thinks I am making it up. He patronizes me. Everything is cast in that light. He thinks I am trying to entertain him. Entertain him with the stories of the Soviet Jews, of Leonid in particular. All for his entertainment.

We meet in a paneled bar, and I trot out the day's anguish. He inspects my report card (graded solely on my calm-soft-independent qualities). Once I have established that I will not shout at him or make demands, he is impatient to go to bed.

His patronizing manner angers me. I order another drink, prolonging our time in the bar. "Jason, I feel as if you're not interested at all, as if this routine of meeting for a drink is mere social foreplay. If you'd prefer we can just go straight to the room, skip the drinks and the requisite fifteen minute summary of my day and just fuck. You're obviously bored to death with what I do."

Jason flushes and orders another drink, too. "I'm not bored, exactly, just a little skeptical," he says.

"Of what?"

"You can hardly blame me for wondering. One minute you're killing yourself and the next you've found this passionate vocation for saving Jews. You don't treat it like a job; you act as if you had a calling. You've heard the Word, something's been revealed to you. Special Susan. Redeemed by good works. While the rest of us poor suckers toil at commerce missing all the fun of salvation. Well, let me tell you something. I'm Jewish, too, but I don't like the idea of singling out Jews as being the only persecuted people in the world. Millions of people are being persecuted worse than Soviet Jews. And there's something else; I like my job, my very lucrative job. I can see that you don't care for it any more, nothing but contempt now for the likes of me. Well, sweet girl, you take care of the petitions and rallies—and just maybe I'll contribute some of my money. Because if I don't, and people like me don't, you won't have a job. And all your dedication and purpose will go down the tube. You won't have the paper for the petitions. So maybe, please, you could stop being so damned sanctimonious. If you forgive my saying so, you lack a little seasoning to qualify as some kind of Golda Meir."

Our drinks had arrived, and Jason lifted his in a toast.

"To us?" he asks.

"To us," I reply.

"You're not angry with me?"

"Yes I'm angry. Damn right I am. But that's got nothing to do with us, and, if you're wondering, nothing to do with fucking. I'm impressed as hell with your money, Jason, I always have been. You're good at making money and you're fairly generous. I hope to hell you do give some money to Soviet Jews; I need the job and they need the help. And I guess you will, that is, if something else doesn't strike your fancy, like migrant workers or crippled children."

"What's wrong with that? I'll give where I think it's most needed."

"But your money is needed everywhere, a thousand causes. How do you decide?"

Jason is silent for a moment. I wonder, in fact, if he does give any money to any cause.

"You decide in favor of what's chic and trendy," I say. "What your partners are giving to, what your friends and clients think is worthwhile. That's how you decide. Oh, you're Jewish all right. After all, you just said so. And I've seen the pictures of your bar mitzvah. You would certainly never deny it. That doesn't mean you haven't rejected it. Actually, you find it, and therefore me, slightly unsanitary and certainly unseemly. Croissants instead of bagels. Perrier instead of seltzer. You cringe at Jewish weddings, vacations at Grossinger's, loud-shirted and loud-mouthed tourists. Barbados instead of Miami . . ."

"I notice you didn't object to Barbados when we went there."

"And I wouldn't now. Ask me, I'll go. But not because I aspire to be a non-Jew. Not because deep down I loathe Jews or half believe that all those stereotypes are right, that just maybe where there's smoke, there's fire."

"I don't like Jewish weddings, and I do prefer the Islands. After all, there is such a thing as taste and personal preference. So what? That doesn't make me anti-Semitic."

"I never said you were."

"Right," he insists.

"Well, what does it make you? So you're not anti-Semitic exactly. But, you sure as hell aren't pro-Semitic. The fact that Soviet Jews don't suffer as much as other people doesn't change another fact."

"Which is?"

"Which is that in this monumental task you have of

deciding which oppressed people are worthy of your generosity, it doesn't occur to you to give it to Jews because you are Jewish. Because no one else ever helps, at least not in time. Roosevelt, Churchill and those great heroes of freedom. The Jews still had to prowl the oceans of the world with no port open to them. And now, even with you, Jews have to compete in pain for your largesse."

"Right. I'm a member of the human race, my responsibilities are not just Jewish, they are broader than that."

"Okay, good for you. We'll limp along without you. The Jewish people will manage without you. It's a great loss, what with your intelligence and earning power, but we'll just have to make do."

"Yes, well, luckily for the Jewish people, they have you."

"Indeed. Win some, lose some."

We were both silent for a moment.

What has this quarrel to do with us, I wonder. Do I really mind that Jason does not share my ideological passion? I think not. I prefer it this way. It equalizes things. Before this it was assumed he was right, I took my cues from him. Now, at least, on this one I have no doubt.

"Jason," I say softly.

"Yes."

"Do you think I'm cute when I'm mad?"

"Cute as hell."

Good.

There are all kinds of fights lovers can have. Some can be devastating, ruining everything. Others, like this, are stimulating. We had been cautious not to attack those things that really counted. Jason didn't care about being Jewish, not enough so that my accusations cut deep. And I was flattered to be considered a fanatic. Although we had spoken angrily, it was a sham.

We were shadow-boxing, jabbing a little, exciting each other, mere foreplay masquerading as a lovers' quarrel. We had accused each other of the very things we wanted to be. Even better than affirming those things, we proved them by condemning them. We were, in the end, grateful to each other for the reassurance this fraudulent quarrel provided.

He signals the waiter for a check. "Are you ready to leave, Susan?"

He's losing his hair and his impatience diminishes me.

I, too, am impatient. His business concerns irritate me. How can he be so worried about "deals"? People and money are manipulated; he wins or loses, it is all the same. I care nothing for his deals, for his people and their money. He cares nothing for my work. More than anything else, it is that which separates us. Sometimes we talk politics. He is more knowledgeable than I. He dances over the issues, light-footed and facile, very facile.

"Energy, the most crucial domestic issue of our time."

"Big business is immoral but it must be served."

"Russia, a question of economics, all the rest will follow."

He is pragmatic, but he will boycott lettuce, march to Washington, sign the latest petition. He is also, after all, a humanitarian.

Our political conversations do not go well. I do not contradict or raise questions. I patronize his pompousness. Besides, my political instincts are of another kind.

I am considered a political romantic, Jason a realist. In all other ways, in other parts of our lives, this is reversed. It is I who am the real pragmatist and he who is the romantic. It's all nonsense, of course. Anyway, neither our personal conversations nor our political debates are gratifying.

In bed it is much the same as before. He receives the bounty of my sexual energy. I'm used to the power now. I have assimilated it and no longer brandish it. Which is not to say I don't play at it. I do.

I must be fair. Disdainful as I may be of everything else, when we are in bed, it is good. Sex with Jason is shockingly intimate. Lust has become the name of this game. In his passivity Jason is the most sexually complaisant man I have ever known. We make love two or three times. In between, we lie about, drinking wine, smoking, free to touch and sometimes even laugh. We tell each other our dreams. I am interested only when I appear in his. Once in a while I cry, weep, as Jason says. But he doesn't mind. He knows I will not go out of control. We congratulate each other for having survived. There is no continuation of our intimacy once outside that room.

In the hotel corridor later, I see him adjust his tie as we wait for the elevator. Aloof now and distant.

"God," I remark, "it's over so soon."

"Yes," he says matter-of-factly, "it is indeed." He looks to see if I will challenge this or object, but I simply shrug. He will find no satisfaction there.

We have been more awkward with each other in the last few weeks. First, when I told him I was going to Russia.

"That's ridiculous, Susan, really. I'm astounded. It's one thing to play around here, but going there alone is really stupid."

"Why? I'm not going to do anything illegal. Just see Leonid and some of the others. Take some pictures if I can. I thought you'd be pleased."

"Well, I'm not pleased. If you're doing it to please me, don't. You're getting in too deep. Whose idea was this anyway?"

"Mine, all mine."

"I thought so. Well, I can't stop you. But I really think

you shouldn't go. You have other responsibilities—June, for example."

"Nothing is going to happen to me there."

"How do you know? You're not the most emotionally stable person in the world. I'm surprised you'd even consider this."

"Shit, let's drop it. I'm going. Nothing will happen. I'll come back in one piece, just as fuckable as ever."

"Don't be crude."

"All right, I won't be crude. I want to go. To me it's important."

"Because you think it will make you important, Joan of Arc or something. I can't stand that about you. Always so different. Poor martyred Susan. I swear I won't be at all surprised if I pick up the paper to find you swinging from a rope in Red Square."

"They don't do that any more. It's strictly electrodes and drugs in Lubyanka's basement."

"Very funny, ha ha."

We are silent for a moment. He, peering into his drink, I, fumbling for a match.

"Do you have a light?" I ask.

"Yes." He pokes in his pockets and comes up with a lighter. It flickers, and he tries once again. "Damn it, the fluid is low, catch it next time." He cups his hand around mine, drawing it closer to the lighter. The light holds long enough to take a drag. Our heads are bowed forward over the table, our eyes meet. I think for a moment he is going to tell me he loves me.

"Look," he says stiffly, "I'm sorry. It's really none of my business. You know what you're doing. I've got no right to talk to you that way. I'm really very sorry, Susan."

"None of your business?" I repeat.

"None of my business at all," he says firmly.

What with Sam's sickness and everything he is careful not to get involved. My life has become complicated again. Jason wants none of it.

My mother told me everything:

MOTHER: All men stink!

31

The telephone is ringing, it's eight-thirty. I thought it was later. Like a good meal, memories are a long time in the preparation and quickly devoured.

"Susan, hi, it's Phyllis."

"Hi, anything wrong?"

"David just called me, he got word that Leonid is going on a hunger strike. He wanted to know if you're going to be in today."

"Sure, I'll just stop by the hospital for a minute to see Sam, and then I'll be in. How did David find out?"

"AP called. They have a letter from Leonid. Their correspondent called to say he's been in some kind of accident. His hand is bandaged. Leonid said he is going to starve to death if necessary. I suppose he thinks it will attract world attention and embarrass the Russians. Anyway, there's going to be a meeting this morning on Leonid. Also, you have a letter from Leonid. One of the tourists I briefed a couple of weeks ago brought it out."

"Okay, thanks for calling. I'll see you later."

I remembered the first time, about a year ago, one prominent Soviet Jew went on a hunger strike. It lasted for three days, and I was trying to get the media to cover the story. One smart-ass from a network said something to me: "He isn't exactly Mahatma Gandhi, is he?" Vulture. It was true of course. A gesture. But Leonid's life is now reduced to such gestures. He composes his appeals, phrasing them carefully so they cannot be interpreted as slander against the Soviet state. Now he will go on a hunger strike, waiting for something to happen. I suspect he didn't know what he was getting into when he first applied. Now, there is no way out. No going back. He may even regret it, but it is too late for that. He lives at the whim of the Soviet government. He has become a symbol, and we exploit his gestures. But what he is and what will become of him has nothing to do with symbols.

If he is allowed to leave, or if they keep him, it is more than symbolic. Personally, in the flesh what will become of him and his body has more than just symbolic meaning. His future is the life of one man. The body count in this war is fanatically kept. There are no missing in action, no unknown soldiers.

I resent his gesture, it intrudes on my life. But it is real, and for the one moment, transcends the disarray of my life.

My peripheral vision has improved, my eyes have grown accustomed to the darkness. In the foreground there is me, murky memories, chaotic core, insatiable appetite for centrality. Too bad it is not elegant and orderly at the center, easily satisfied. Too bad it can't be set aside entirely, dislodged by virtue and nobility. Those venal vices are not so easily renounced.

In the background, illuminated now, there are other images I must yield to. They beckon with a peremptory finger, demanding that I take a break from vanity and illusion.

So I'll go to Leningrad. I've sucked the memory teat dry; it's shriveled and needs replenishing. My father was wrong, I think. Maintaining my observer status is not enough.

It's definitely time to get up.

In the bathroom I notice Jason's shaving mug, a gift from me to him lying consecrated on a shelf in the bathroom. I notice, too, that he hasn't called.

What the hell, he has to eat.

"Mr. Lampert, please."

"May I tell him who's calling?"

"Mrs. Warner."

"Susan? How are you?" Jason asks.

"Calling with the latest medical bulletin." (What can he do? He has to pretend he's interested in Sam's recovery.)

"Oh. How is Sam?" (He's too polite.)

"No change really."

"Well, perhaps he'll be better today."

(Cold, cold, he's so cold. I used to smell my diaphragm when I took it out after making love with him. I would hold it up to the light to check it for holes and smell it. Sometimes I would put my tongue around the rim and lick it inside. Now he's so cold.) "I have to go over there later but I was wondering if you were free for lunch." (He's annoyed but what can he do?)

"Hold on a moment, Susan. Let me see if I can cancel my appointment." (He'll cancel. I think he'll cancel.) "Sorry to have held you so long. Yes, where would you like to eat?"

"Doesn't matter. You choose it."

"One-thirty at Orsini's."

I stop by the hospital to see Sam.

His eyes are closed. I hope he's sleeping. He looks small; the white sheets, like a shroud, swallow his bulk.

He opens his eyes, nothing else moves, just his eyes.

Slowly, as from a small crack in a massive dam, tears leak down his cheek.

"Are you in pain?" I ask.

"Not too bad, they gave me morphine."

His voice is shaky, weak.

"Am I crying, Susan?" he asks. "I think I'm crying."

"Just a little," I said and take out a tissue to wipe away his tears.

"I sweat so much, Susan. I always sweated too much. I guess that repulsed you."

"Oh, please, Sam, not now."

"No, it's just that I sweat so much. I want you to know that I always have known that I sweated too much. Sometimes I would get up and change my pajamas so you didn't have to be near all that sweat. Funny thing is, I'm not sweating now, I'm cold."

"Do you want a blanket?"

(Please God, just give me something useful to do now and I'll never curse at him again.)

"No, I'm just cold, I think I'm cold inside."

"Sam," I took his hand. "Really, it will be all right."

He wasn't listening. Would he ever hear me?

"Susan, you know I did love you, really loved you, too much maybe. I'm sorry for all the things that didn't work out. I'm so sorry. I just wish you could explain to me what I did wrong. Whatever it is, I'm sorry for it. In case anything goes wrong . . ."

"Sam." (Am I shouting?) "Sam, stop it." I had to be out of that room now. In the presence of his simple truths, I wanted to be able to cling to my version.

"Now look," I said, patting his hand, "I am going to work. Do you think I would go to work if I thought you were dying? Never mind me, do you think your mother would? She

240

wouldn't miss it. It would be the highlight of all the crises in her totally crisis-ridden life. Nothing is going to happen, Sam."

"I need to pee."

"Wait and I'll call the nurse."

"No, I'll tell you what to do. There's a bottle over there. Just get it for me. See that funny-shaped bottle, like a milk bottle but curved at the end." I walked over to pick up the bottle.

(Please, God, just let me get out of here now. I promise I won't ask any more.)

"Help me sit up, Susan."

I fold the white sheets back and around to the other side of the bed so I can help him sit up. He leans on me, his legs dangling over the edge of the bed, and I hand him the bottle.

He holds his limp penis and pushes it into the mouth of the bottle. It has been years since I have seen his penis. I remembered that penis when it was hard. When he would put his hands at the back of my neck, pressing on the pressure points there, hurting me, but keeping me still while he thrust it into me.

That penis, that very same one. Built more or less like all the other cocks. And they all worry so much. Is it big enough? Is it hard enough? Did I come too fast? Did I come too slow? They worry so about their cocks.

"Oh, you're wonderful," I squealed.

"Oh, it feels so good," I groaned.

"I love it," I purred.

"Don't stop," I begged.

"I want more," I demanded.

"You're the best," I rhapsodized.

"I never knew it could be like this," I marveled.

"It's really different," I lied.

The tributes I paid to all those insecure cocks.

He was sitting there holding his limp penis in a bottle.

Should I go over and suck it? If I suck it and make it hard, will he get well?

Nothing is happening. He grimaces slightly, almost a smile. "It's hard to pee," he says, "because of all the spasm. It's very hard to pee." Finally, a few drops came out. "Okay." He is pleased with himself. "I guess that's it," he says. "Thank you, Susan."

I take the bottle and put it in the sink and cover him. I bend to kiss him on the forehead. His face is wet with sweat. He has exerted so much for those few drops, I can see his body is drenched. "I'll call the nurse, Sam, she'll make you more comfortable. And then I'm going. I'll be back tomorrow."

(Please give me permission to leave. Please let me leave.)

I can see in his eyes he does not want me to go. But I have to now. I can't bear it another minute. When I leave the room, I lean against the wall. A nurse asks, "Are you all right, Mrs. Warner? You look tired."

"I'm all right, I'm fine" (but maybe . . . maybe I should have sucked his penis).

32

Through the closed door of the conference room, I hear raised voices, the meeting in progress. I stop in my office to get my messages. There are three messages from Joel, all urgent, and several from people on the Committee to Free Leonid.

I like Phyllis. Over the past year we have had to make peace with our respective positions at the I.C.S.J. She worked for David in the job he had before this and is devoted to him. She has a prior claim. At first we jockeyed for position, a little back-biting here, a little slander there. But as with Marge, once we staked out our territories we settled into a warm relationship.

"Hey, I'm glad to see you," she said, handing me my mail, including the letter from Leonid. "Joel is trying to reach you, he called three times."

"I know," pointing at the telephone messages. "He can wait. I'm anxious to read Leonid's letter."

My dear Susan,

I have given this letter to a visitor who I hope will see to it that you will receive it.

There is one incident that I have been afraid to publicize. We are confused now. It is difficult to know if all the publicity surrounding our case is helpful or simply stimulates more anger toward us. But I trust you, and someone must know of this incident.

Last week Col. Boris Arbatov, chief of the KGB in Leningrad, had me brought to his office. I had met Col. Arbatov several times before at parties after my concerts, but now I was to see him in a new light. Where once he had toasted my good health, in this meeting he reviled me.

His office is austere and it was late at night, nearly midnight. There was only one light on—his desk light—and I could see that he had been drinking. He got up to greet me, almost as a friend, a big man, lumbering across the room, staggering just slightly. I myself was in a state of exhaustion since we have been visited by the KGB for four nights before this evening. He sat down at his desk again and began to talk. He was still smiling at me. He told me something of his own life. I see now that it was to explain his repugnance toward me. I will relate to you the things he told me of himself because I suppose it is always good to have some insight into your enemy.

Col. Arbatov was thirteen when the Great Patriotic War began. Like many others he was half starved and frozen but longed to join the army. He was prevented from doing so by his mother who had already lost two sons.

Taking a glass of vodka and offering me some, which I declined, he told me of his view of the centuries of indomitable spirit, of indivisible civic dignity which dominated the aspirations of the survivors of the siege of Leningrad. "We would not just rebuild the shattered ruins," he said. "We were determined to restore the intellectual and artistic heritage that was the splendor of Leningrad. Do you understand?" he asked me. "A

generation of people still trembling over their loss, under-
nourished and weak, diseased and chronically sick from the
privations of war, overcame impossible obstacles to begin again."

Fumbling in his pocket, he took out the pictures of his dead
brothers. "I carry them with me always," he said.

His tone was benign, conversational, as he explained the
painstaking reconstruction process. "You understand," he said,
"that for all the architectural miracles we performed, it was the
soul of the people that was the real strength of Leningrad."

He stood up then and began to pace. He looked at me with
some surprise. "Did you really mean to betray all this?"

I was tired. "No," I said, "I understand the miracle of our
city. I love Leningrad. I will always love it, even when I am
allowed to leave I will miss it."

"You will not be allowed to leave," he replied. "You were
given to us, a small child, a remnant of promise in a desolate
city, and now you betray all of us. It is an act more criminal than
even the Germans."

He picked up my file, although surely he must have known it
by heart. He commented on my thinness and I told him then
that I had lost weight, as indeed my wife was now suffering from
serious anemia. "Too bad," he said indifferently. "You should
take care of yourself."

I explained that each time my wife goes to the market, she is
followed. People leer at her and she is pushed to the end of the
line or shopkeepers tell her there is no food available.

"A pity," he replied, "such a pity." And he asked me what I
had expected. Did I think that I would be a hero? "No," I said, "I
never meant to be a hero. I only want to leave."

He took another drink and sat down again at his desk, his
smile gone, now replaced by a cold bitter hatred.

The colonel explained that he had been authorized to offer
me an arrangement. If I would withdraw my application to
emigrate, all would be restored to me. He made it very clear that
he did not approve of this decision. I told him that I could not

withdraw any more than I could decide not to be a Jew. He called me a fool and told me it was my last chance. That I would never be allowed to leave. "That," he said, "had been decided a long time ago."

"You have nothing to look forward to," he told me. "Nothing."

I said to him that I have friends in the West who are helping. That decisions can be reversed and that I will still continue to hope.

He repeated, "There is no hope." He told me he spits on my friends in the West. He sneered at boxes of petitions signed by "American movie stars." "What are they to us?" he said. "And what are you to them? Soon, when they see it as hopeless, they will give up. Americans have no will to perservere in a struggle. You are a fad and they become bored with fads." He called me a "toy" for "American bleeding hearts" to take up and play with.

I was very tired. I wanted to leave. But he wasn't finished with me yet. He spoke to me about how Jews are scorned and loathed everywhere. He told me, even if I were allowed to leave, my Jewish sins would precede me wherever I went. "Perhaps it's in the blood," he said. "Some perverted Jewish gene causes you Jewish men to profane all that good men hold dear." I tried to protest but he continued.

"Israel," he said, "that fraud of a Jewish state, is stolen from others who have moral and legal claims. Like cockroaches the Jews poached on that land and like cockroaches they will be stamped out, crushed."

Never before had I heard anyone enunciate such vitriolic anti-Semitism. I was numbed, shattered. I wanted only to be done with the interview.

The colonel left his office and returned with two men. "They will drive you home," he said.

"It is not necessary," I replied.

"They will drive you home," he insisted. "We will meet again, Leonid."

246

The two men escorted me in silence. A large, black official car was waiting at the curb. Driven home in style, I thought. The men walked close to me, their bodies pushing against me. I was caged in by human forms. I walked in step with them to the car. One opened the car door near the curb, the other motioned for me to climb in. As I bent over to enter the car, the man behind me grabbed my arm. I had no time to struggle. My hands was held against the frame of the car door while the other man slammed it shut. I saw the door coming, and screamed even before I felt the searing hot pain. The flesh torn from my hand, my fingers were numb at first, then throbbing. The one who had held me, released me. "What a terrible accident, perhaps you should see a doctor," he said.

Susan, my dear friend, whom I've never met, will you think it shameful if I, a grown man, tell you that now I am frightened all the time.

Leonid Rabinovitz
January 1975

My phone rings. It's Joel.

"Where the fuck have you been?" He was nothing if not gracious.

"I have been the fuck in the hospital with my fucking ex-husband, who may be dying. Fuck you."

"Shit, are you putting me on?"

"Nope, that's the whole truth. I've just spent the last fourteen hours playing wife, playing frightened wife."

"Shit."

"Joel, dear, do you think you could start a sentence without saying shit?"

"Is this going to interfere with your trip to Leningrad?"

"I'm touched by your deep concern for me and what I have been through."

"Tonight, tonight I'll show you how concerned I am. Right now all I want to know is, is this going to make any difference in your going to Leningrad?"

"Well, I don't know. If he dies, even you should be able to see it would be wrong to leave."

"You're only his ex-wife."

"At times like this, Joel, the marriage vows are resurrected."

"When will you know if he is going to be all right?"

"Joel, I have to go. Believe me, if he dies, you will be one of the first ones to know. I'm too tired to see you tonight. Besides, I am keeping myself chaste."

"Oh, shit."

"On that note, if you don't mind, let's hang up. I'll talk to you later. I'll know more then."

Joel is an example of what you can pick up in New York if you're not careful.

I write a press release on Leonid's hunger strike. The words look stilted, the language of despair is commonplace now.

David comes in and reads the release. "I know," I tell him, "it's crummy." I hand him Leonid's letter.

"I wish we could print this," he said. "Just this."

"Do you think it would make a difference if we could?"

"I don't know." He shrugs. "Sometimes I wonder if anything will make a difference."

"What happened at the meeting?"

"The usual. We're supposed to try to get some celebrities to go on a hunger strike in sympathy with Leonid."

"You know they won't," I said.

"It would make good press. We'll have to try. Let Phyllis call some of the members of the Committee to Free Leonid. Maybe they will."

248

"I'll give her the list, but they won't. We can get them to make public statements on it though, that certainly."

"If he stays on it for a few days, we'll call a press conference. Suppose he's on it when I get there, what do you want me to tell him?"

"You mean advise him?"

"Yes. Suppose he asks me if he should continue it. What the hell do I say?"

David thinks a minute. "You can't give him that kind of advice. He has to make that judgment for himself."

"But if I'm there and he asks me, I'll have to say something. I can't just not respond."

"Then tell him to stop. Tell him not to make himself sick, not to hurt himself just for the publicity. It's wrong. It's not the Jewish way. He doesn't have the right to starve himself, to kill himself. Nobody does. All life is sacred. Tell him, aside from the politics, aside from the publicity value, that it's wrong. It's a sin, a crime in Jewish law. The whole point of this is that he's Jewish. He may not even know that himself. But that's the goddamn point of it all. Because he's Jewish, they won't let him leave. Because he's Jewish, we Jews are trying to help him. And because he's Jewish, he can't starve himself. Being Jewish is not convenient, if it were, I'd sure as hell be in another business."

I rewrite the press release. It's better, a little better.

People ask me, sometimes, why this work. It's true I stumbled in, not knowing or caring what the job was. But I do not continue in this work from inertia. And I do not stay because I think Soviet Jews are particularly deserving or brave. Some are, and some are not. They are no different from anyone else. But that is all beside the point. In this work we do whatever we can do, endure the apathy of outsiders, the cynicism, the contempt, the disdain of people who simply don't care, and often even of ourselves. We do not kid ourselves. We understand very well that others do not have to care. They do not have to help. Their emotions are roused by other matters, they resonate to different instincts.

Russian Jews are no different; most of us who work on their behalf are no different either. The skepticism of others is often contagious. Often we see ourselves through their eyes. Professional Jews. Certainly there is little sense of nobility in what we do. Often we feel foolish. Grown people playing at rallies, student demonstrations. Surrogate politics. Our constituents are Hebrew school students bused in to march on Fifth Avenue. What it is, primarily, is the need to persevere. To hang in. Because despite all the idiocy and daily foolishness there are real problems that reach out. There is real pain that preempts attention. Leonid's anguish exists. We did not make it up.

Marge calls.

"I won't be free for dinner, but I thought I'd come over late, around eleven. Is that okay?" she asks.

"Sure, I'll be up, packing."

"You okay?"

"Fine."

"What's your schedule?"

"I'm having lunch with Jason, and an offer for dinner and fucking from Joel."

"Sounds busy. If you're dining and fucking with Joel, how will you be home by eleven?"

"I'm not. I declined his offer. Beside, I have the feeling I'm going to be fucked quite enough at lunch."

"Then, why did you ask him? You did ask him, I take it."

"Because I'm in the mood."

"The mood for what?"

"For a small confrontation. Just a tiny one. Nothing fatal."

"He'll eat you alive, hell, you know Jason. If you press him, you need him, he'll run the other way."

"Maybe not this time."

"Okay, I hope you know what you're doing."

"Some things you just do on instinct, hunch."

"In other words, impulsive."

"Maybe, maybe impulsive. But also maybe it's time."

"It doesn't sound well thought out to me, not well planned at all."

"Wrong. After I got the hunch, I waited maybe a full minute before I called him."

"Not well thought out at all. You sure you have something to gain from this . . . small confrontation, as you call it?"

"Well, one way or the other, I think I do. It's just possible, you know, that he loves me."

"Do you still love him? After everything that's happened?"

"Oh, I love him all right. I sound pretty good now, but my knees will turn to jelly when he walks into the restaurant. Who knows, maybe I'll just be nice, no confrontation, just nice. That's the way he likes me to be. And if he's tired, or in a bad mood, God knows I won't burden him with my small confrontation. We'll have a good lunch, maybe he'll tell me he loves me, that he'll miss me, that he's worried about me. Maybe he'll cancel his afternoon meetings, and we'll go to bed. Not at his place, however, because What's-her-name might walk in."

"I'm beginning to see your point. It just surprises me, it's not your style."

"True. It's probably time I changed that too, my style, that is. I'll see you at eleven. You'll get a full report."

"Susan, wait a minute, what if it doesn't work out, what if he doesn't love you, or love you enough."

"Well, Marge, I guess I'll have one hell of a lousy day."

33

It used to annoy me that I always arrived first. Even when I'm late I arrive before him. I go to the table, order a drink, nervously check my makeup, surreptitiously dab a little perfume from the flask which I open under the table. I usually am ashamed to anoint myself openly, but it's a comforting ritual.

Jason always arrives five minutes after I do. No matter how early or late I am, he comes in five minutes later. Once he made a point of telling me how much he looked forward to being there to see me arrive. He said he enjoyed watching me enter a restaurant, rushing, peering anxiously around the darkened room. Ever since he told me that, I try to arrive last. It never happens.

I feel beautiful today. My hair is particularly lovely. It flows long and dark on my shoulders. (Who would ever guess it sticks up in those hideous curlicues most of the time?)

The restaurant is empty. It's two o'clock. As I see Jason enter, I stand up. I have never stood to greet him before.

He smiles as he leans across the table to kiss me on the cheek and I smile back.

"Hello. How are you?" he says.

Soft, a caress, his voice. I have never heard him shout or yell. Even when his words are cruel his tone is so gentle, it hurts even more. The waiter hovers. We spend a moment ordering wine.

"You look tired. Your eyes are tired," I say. And indeed he does look tired.

"I am tired," he says.

"Are you sleeping?"

"Yes. But there isn't enough sleep."

"Well, then. Maybe you're not tired. Maybe you're weary."

Nodding in a weary way he pours a little wine.

"I really am tired, Susan. I wish I could go somewhere and cry. It's all got me down. It's all too much. Clarissa, Mark . . ." He lets his sentence wander off, not wanting to mention *her* name.

"And me."

"I guess so. All I have are appointments in life. Appointments for business, appointments to see my ex-wife, appointments to pay my bills . . ."

"And appointments for lunch. Listen," I say kindly, "why don't you just go away and cry for a while."

He smiled. "They won't let me. I don't have an appointment for crying."

"I just spent the week crying. They'll let you. Just do it."

"I'm such a simple fellow, really." (Oh, Lord, when he begins like that I know I'm in for it. Simple fellow, indeed. Lately his small conceits are unbearable.) He glances at his watch.

"What time do you have to leave?" I ask.

"I have an appointment in an hour." (That means we're not going to make love today.) "Sorry, things are kind of busy at the office," he explains. (Feeling harassed is his hobby.)

"I'm not complaining. Just asking."

We drop it.

"Did you want to see me about something special? I know you must need cheering up. It must be very hard on you, what with Sam sick and you getting ready to leave. You are going, aren't you?"

"It has been hard. I'm worried about Sam, and worried about the trip. Leonid is on a hunger strike."

"A publicity stunt?"

"If you can call any hunger strike a publicity stunt, I guess so."

The waiter serves the food, Jason pours more wine.

"And Sam," he asks, "how is he?"

"You can't imagine how pathetic he is. The hospital has become my world. Everybody treats me like his wife."

"Well, you're behaving like a wife."

"What else can I do? What would you do?"

"There's nothing else you can do."

"I've been thinking of asking Sam to come back."

"Have you really? How extraordinary."

"How do you feel about that?"

"I don't know. If it's what you want."

"It's not what I want. You know what I want."

He peers at me over his glass of wine and hesitates before he speaks. "Do you really want to do this now, Susan? I mean right now with all the pressure you're under. You want to have this conversation?"

The waiter comes and we order lunch.

(He's right. It's too big a conversation. I can feel he's too strong. The balance is weighted in his favor. I will lose everything.)

"Do you remember a few months ago, Jason, I told you I had the feeling I'd never be important enough to you? Do you remember what you said?"

"No. What did I say?"

"You said, 'But you're going to try, aren't you?' I took that as an invitation. I've tried. So the question is, am I enough for you?"

"That isn't the question. You've missed the point. I have other commitments. You know that. I can't give you what you want, Susan. I can't give it to anybody. But at least nobody else asks quite the same way that you do. Does it ever occur to you that I just don't have it to give?"

"It occurred to me, but I remember . . ."

"Oh, remember. Well, that was a long time ago. I was happy with you. You made me laugh. It was a long time ago. Now I can't give you what you want."

"What do you think I want?"

"You want me to throw over everything and put you first. You want me to rearrange my priorities. I can't do it."

"What are we, then?"

"Not much. A lost opportunity maybe."

"Why did you start with me again if you knew you couldn't give me what I need?" I ask this curiously; my voice is even.

"You said you were different. I thought maybe it would work."

"On what terms?"

"I thought we would have an affair. But you keep pulling at me. I just wanted an affair."

"Affair? You wanted to fuck me?"

He grimaces at this. "Sweet girl, you want this conversation now? I'm going to rain on your parade."

"Is that what you want? You want to fuck me?" I persist.

"Yes. No matter what else, there's something, something extraordinary about our sex. I guess it's kind of an obsession with me."

"For an obsessed man you don't seem to want to fuck me very often."

"It's all too difficult. I do want to but I know what comes along with it. The other needs you have. What I'd like to do is put you in a room, locked away. Only I would have the key. I could come and go any time I wanted and you would always be there."

"So, you would be out in the world and I would be tucked away, just waiting for you. Tell me, would I be allowed to read?"

"Come on, Susan. It's just a fantasy. You asked me what I wanted. Well, that's what I want."

"It's ridiculous."

"Of course."

"It's worse than ridiculous. What does it say about me, that that's all you want? To put me away in some room naked so you can come and fuck me. I thought there was more left than that."

"Oh, don't make a thing of it. Christ, we're old friends. You know there's more than that. You know what I feel for you."

I can feel my face getting hot. (Probably makes me look even prettier.) "Listen, let me get this straight. I need to know now. Is what's left just fucking? It would be okay with you if we just fucked now and then? Never talking or going to the movies or anything else? That would be okay with you?"

"Don't make me sound brutish."

"I'm not making you anything. Just tell me. Would it be okay?"

"It would be okay. I love to go to bed with you. Right now I would love to go to bed with you, but it would be okay if that's all there was."

I sit back in my chair. (I'm usually leaning toward him.) I

see it's going to end here, but out of habit, I give it a little more space.

"Well, I guess I'm not giving you what you want either," I say. "You want to be such a good fuck that I'll put aside every other human need I have just so you'll fuck me. Jesus, you want to be a sex object and I don't give you that."

Jason smiles wryly and says, "I know I'm an unlikely figure for a sex object (By God, that's the truth) but you're right. I wish you felt the way I do about making love. I wish you wanted it the way I want it. Just for itself."

It's ending here. The fragile threads are snapping right now. I want to hold him, to remind him of that first lunch, of the flowers, of the baths together.

"Listen," I say quietly, "you're the lawyer. You think this is negotiable?"

We're leaning across the table toward each other now, friends again.

I touch his hand. For a moment everything is possible.

"Look at our hands," I say, and we both look at them. "Jason," I ask again, "can we negotiate?"

Still smiling he takes my hand and places it against his cheek. "I don't think so. I don't think I can change, Susan."

I take my hand back and point to the wine. He pours me some. I want to tell him that I'll do it all his way. I want to tell him I'm frightened all the time. He can lock me in his fantasy room.

But my hair is lovely, long and dark on my shoulders. I am anointed with sweet fragrance. And in my purse, jammed in between my face powder and hairbrush, between the lipstick and eye shadow, mingling with the minutiae of my vanity, is Leonid's letter.

I begin to laugh. I can't help myself.

"What's funny, sweet girl?"

"It isn't really funny. You know, it's not really funny at all. God, I wish we were what we used to be. It was such an unbearable wonderful love we had. I nearly killed myself for you. It was all so unbearable."

"And now?"

"Now you've got your appointments, your commitments, and I guess I've got mine." I take his hand again, I smile.

"Jason," I say in a friendly way, "you're just not that good a fuck."

34

As I walked to the hospital, I replayed parts of the conversation with Jason, a kind of mental palpation to see if anything is broken. It would seem I am intact. Bruised, definitely bruised, but intact.

I walk slowly, breathing slowly, in no rush for the next encounter. I know now that I will not ask Sam to come back. I will not let either Sam or Jason lock me in.

Life with Sam is not so safe as it seems. There is clear jeopardy in that predictable security. Neither Sam nor Jason knows me at all. Neither one wanted to know me. The image was enough, the image they fashioned for themselves of who I am.

Jason, contemptuous of my credentials, would purge me of my history; an accommodating cunt would be enough. Sam, poor Sam, desperate to prove himself by having a proper wife, requires only that I keep breathing.

I have allowed myself to be cast in their life dramas, disguised by costumes they choose.

I want connections, ties, links, fusion.

260

I'll have to take my chances; it's a risky business, living.

Sam looks better. He is listening attentively to Dr. Rappoport as I enter the room. "Ah, Mrs. Warner"—the doctor seems relieved to see me—"I was just explaining to Sam that he is better, much better. He developed a fever." Rappoport is smiling. "So," I say, "is that good?"

"Yes, oh, yes. Tumors don't cause fevers, infections do. All along I felt there was a chance this might be a virus attacking his spinal cord. Now that he's got a fever, I'm almost sure that's what it is. Uncommon, but not rare. A course of antibiotics and he should be fine."

Rappoport was smiling. He expected to be complimented, thanked.

"Well," I said, "I guess we understand. It sounds as if you'll be fine, Sam. Thank you, Dr. Rappoport."

"I'll be in tomorrow, Sam. I'll leave you two alone now."

"I brought you a new James Bond, Sam."

Sam has turned his face to the window.

"Listen, Sam, it sounds all right. Thank God, it's not more serious. You look pretty well. How do you feel?"

"Bitter. That's how I feel. I don't believe him. They don't know what they're talking about. First it's one diagnosis and then another. I'll probably never get out of here."

"He sounded pretty sure, Sam."

"But I've got the pain, not you and not him. I've got the pain."

"It will get better."

"I doubt it. It's just like everything else in my life."

"You really do look very well, Sam. I guess you've lost weight."

"A little. How's June? Can you sneak her in to see me?"

"Maybe. You know I'm leaving for Leningrad in a couple

of days. She's going to be staying with Marge. I'd hate for her to be upset just before I leave. She's never been in a hospital before, and you'll be getting out soon."

"You're going to Leningrad?"

"You knew that, I told you before you got sick."

"But I didn't think you'd go now. What about June?"

"Marge will take care of her. She'll be all right. You'll be all right too, Sam."

"I guess I'll never learn. I honestly didn't think you'd go now. It can't be that important. As usual you're determined to do what you want and the hell with everybody else. The hell with me."

"Sam, it is important, at least to me. I had hoped you'd be pleased, happy that I've found work which is meaningful. These past few years have been terrible. You were right about some things. Right about how hard it is to be alone, and right that nobody really cares out there."

"Well, I've waited a long time to hear you admit that. All these years I've been waiting for you to come to your senses, to see that what we had was good enough. Maybe not great, but good enough. You had such big ideas, you were convinced you were so special. Let me tell you something, I had a long time to think, too. And in the meantime what I discovered is that I can live without you. I still love you but not the way I used to. When you kicked me out, I used to follow you, watch you, you didn't know that, did you? I was nuts."

"I'm sorry, Sam, sorry that I hurt you."

"Well, you should have thought of that years ago. You were everything to me, you and June and our home. Everything. You didn't have the right to destroy our lives the way you did. You were selfish then and I see you haven't changed much. You know I need you now. For Christ's sake, we were married, doesn't that mean anything to you?"

"Yes, it does. But not what you want it to mean. We shared years together, we have June. We ought to stop blaming each other."

"Sure, as long as you get it all your way. Shit, Susan, go to Leningrad, be special, you'll never change. You live your life as if it were a rehearsal. Well, my pain is real, my need is real, I'm asking you to see me through this. Just this once, see me through this."

"I can't, Sam. I'm sorry, but I can't."

"Won't, not can't, won't. You mean you won't."

"Have it your way. See it any way you want to. I'm telling you I'm going. I'm sorry for you, sorry for me too, for that matter. Sorry I hurt you years ago. But I can't make up for it now, even if I wanted to, I can't. It's too late. We have history between us, Sam, not love." Sam has turned away from me. I can't see his face. Is he crying?

"Sam, look, I don't want to leave like this. Please try to understand." But Sam doesn't move.

"Sam, won't you say goodbye?"

He turns his face toward the window, resolute for once.

"Sam, I'm leaving now." I hesitate for just a moment.

His face still turned toward the window, his voice angry, I hear him say, "Just get out, Susan, get out."

35

I walk to a small French restaurant near the hospital that I had been frequenting. They have a jukebox with French music. I sit at the bar and order a drink. Attractive. An attractive woman alone, having a drink by herself. A little sad maybe. That's the image I want to project. In a little while I will think about this strange day. Right now I need a drink. I hold the drink tightly.

(There are choices to be made here.)

There are always choices.

(You don't understand. Everybody always leaves. I don't want to be alone.)

You leave, too, and anyway, admit it, you're relieved after they're gone.

(That's not true. I've tried to do the right thing.)

Oh, the right thing. That again. Don't tell me you're still looking for simple truth.

(I am. It must be there somewhere.)

You're a fine one to talk about simple truth. You lie all the time.

(I don't, do I?)

All the time.

It's all really bearable, isn't it, Susan?

(What? What's bearable?)

Everything. You'd like it to be unbearable because of them, for your mother and father.

(I don't want to be like them.)

Then admit it. Admit that it's all bearable.

(I don't owe you anything. Why should I try to impress you? I wish you would go away.)

The bar is filling up. I sit straight on the bar stool, eyes closed, slim legs crossed, swaying to the music.

Another pose, This one for the man sitting next to me. (Now I'll laugh quietly to myself and he'll ask me what's funny.)

"What's so funny?" he says.

An attractive man, well, more a boy, really. "Oh, nothing, just a little joke I was telling myself."

"You're much too pretty to be telling yourself jokes."

(Is he really saying that?) I smother a laugh. "Yes, well, just the same I often tell myself jokes."

"Buy you a drink?"

"Sure."

"Well"—he moves over to the bar stool next to mine— "are you going to tell me what's so funny? By the way, my name is Paul Morgan."

I shake his outstretched hand. "Hi, mine's Susan Warner. Actually, I've had a bad day. Standard problems, rejecting lover, difficult ex-husband. A lousy day. Everybody is giving me a bad time."

"Honey, I can't imagine anybody giving you a hard time. Is that what you're laughing about? What did you all do, get together on a conference call?"

"Something like that."

Paul shakes his head. "I think you're putting me on. Do you come here often?"

"Only since my ex-husband's been hospitalized with a mysterious ailment."

"Say, you're some kidder, you are. I'm an accountant. Well, a junior accountant. What do you do?"

"I lie a lot."

"What?"

"I'm just kidding. I work for a Jewish organization."

"Is that so? What do you do, raise money?"

"No, we try to help Russian Jews."

"Oh. They in some kind of trouble?"

"A lot of them would like to get out of Russia."

"Yeah. I can understand that. It's cold there."

"No, they don't mind the cold. They mind the anti-Semitism."

"Yeah, I read a little about that. Personally the way I feel about it, it's all the same to me. I know a lot of Jewish people. A few. This guy who sits next to me at the office, he's Jewish. Doesn't make one bit of difference to me. Are you Jewish?"

"Yes."

"See? Doesn't make one bit of difference. I'm even going to buy you another drink. But if I do, you have to promise me something."

"What's that?"

"I don't want you telling yourself any more jokes. You're too serious. You think of something funny you tell me and we'll both laugh at it. Now, is anything else worrying you?"

"Not a thing."

"Not still worrying about those Jews over there, are you?"

"Would you mind if I were?"

"I can understand that. You're a person that cares about people. Must be like a civil rights worker with the Negroes.

Can't just put it aside because some man in a bar says to. I guess it's part of your life. I just wonder if we can have a good time anyway. If you want to tell me more about your work, you go right ahead."

"Actually, you seem to understand pretty well without my saying anything. Do you want to hear a simple truth?"

"Sure."

"It's all bearable. It's all bearable, and I'm just the same as everybody else. Just the same. I have lousy days, and go to a bar to get a little drunk and then get up the next day to go to work. I'm not so special, after all. And you know something else, it's not so bad."

"You look special to me, I don't understand a word you're saying."

"You don't have to understand. I do."

"You're laughing again. Did you tell yourself another joke?" he asks.

Ignoring his question I ask him if he would like to dance.

We dance a little to some Piaf; he kisses my neck. (God, I'm really turned on. I stop in the middle of the dance and take his hand. "Paul," I say, "let's go." He tries not to look surprised. We go to a midtown hotel. He has bought a bottle of champagne. I don't care about talking. As the door closes I have a fleeting thought about murder. But the bottle of champagne reassures me. Murderers don't buy bottles of champagne.

He undresses me. I am swaying a little from the vodka. Every time he touches me, I feel good.

"Paul, you know I don't usually do this kind of thing." (Am I really saying that?)

"Who cares, Susan. Who cares if you do or don't."

Right. And he touches me some more. When he has me undressed completely, I want him so badly that I can't wait for him to take his clothes off. I lie on the bed watching him. Slowly he removes his clothes. He opens the champagne and begins to pour it between my breasts. He licks it off. He still has his shorts on. Boxer shorts. He is licking my breast with real dedication. Soon, he pours some more champagne and licks more of me. I stop thinking altogether. He takes the bottle and starts to play with my cunt, pouring a little of the cool champagne around it. "Lick it there," I say, "lick it there," and he does, without any of the reservations I was so used to with other men who just sort of circled around it in their heroic attempt not to mind what they were doing. He enters me with his tongue. All the way in, and around and more and more. I am howling when I come.

"Good," he says.

We make love for hours. This one is for me.

He turns me over and explores my ass. Until he began with his tongue and his fingers, I didn't know I had an ass.

"Do it to me that way."

"Are you sure? It will hurt."

"Do it. I want it all now." (Goddammit, I'm thirty-seven and I want it all.)

He enters me slowly. He had prepared me with his fingers, softly, moving inside my ass. Then he enters me and I begin to resist; he forces himself in.

"God, it does hurt."

"Want me to stop?"

"No. Don't stop. Do it."

And when he slides his hand under my cunt, pulling at my cunt hair, I come again.

We had dozed a little. We shower. He is affectionate. The affectionate aftermath of sex, not a caring affection.

"Look, we have to see each other again. Do you have an apartment?" he asks.

"Yes, but I also have a child."

"Well, we'll arrange it. You want to, don't you, baby?"

"Of course." (But do I? All I want to do now is go home.)

I ride through the empty city streets in the taxi. Salvation is not near at hand. I am tired of my own excesses, diminished by all of them. I cared too much for Jason and not at all for Paul. Neither works. I had thought that anonymous sex might be the answer, but all it is is anonymous sex. Satisfying for a moment the nervous twitch of lust, those urgent primal needs. There must be other choices.

In two days I leave for Leningrad.

36

I'm packing. The suitcase lies open on the bed. From various piles of clothes that are candidates for travel, I pluck a sweater here, a pair of slacks there. Folding them haphazardly, I hand them to Marge, who characteristically refolds them.

"You know," Marge says, "you should put light stuff like underpants and nightgowns on top. I'll finish here. You go make the coffee."

Alone in the kitchen I wash the coffee pot although it is already clean. I measure out four scoops and one for the pot. Every movement I make is painstakingly sweet. It's unlike me to take such care. I set a tray—two cups and a small dish of cookies.

The counters have been wiped clean. I sponge them down again. The coffee perks to a perfect brown and I mix Marge's with the one teaspoon of sugar she likes and add milk to mine.

As I walk through the door I realize I've forgotten napkins. I neatly fold two and place them on the tray.

Marge is inserting tissue paper between the layers of my clothes. "The coffee smells good. I'm tired," she says.

"So, what happened," I ask. "You're smiling, so I take it you won."

"For the moment. I won for the time being."

"He agreed to the shopping list?"

"He had all the right answers; actually he was rather splendid, including the part about how I shouldn't have had to ask him, how he should have known it himself. How sorry he was that I had been, well, reduced to these pitifully small demands. He had all the right answers, except one."

"Namely?"

"Namely, as you perfectly well know, the burning question that consumes us all, permanency, forever, all the time . . . me not her. For that one, he didn't have an answer."

"But you didn't ask that one, did you?"

"Hell, no. That would have been indiscreet. But that is the question, all right, the only one that matters."

"Well, why in hell didn't you put it to him, then? I don't get it. If that's the only thing that will ever matter, why don't you just tell him straight out."

"Because when I do, and one day I will, I'll be completely ready for his answer, which, as we all know, will be a regretful no. If it wasn't going to be no, there'd be no problem in the first place. I don't have to ask that particular question; he answers it every time he leaves my apartment at eleven, still buttoning his pants. Every time he checks his watch at dinner, every hushed weekend call. Those are his answers. I'll ask the question when I'm damn good and ready for the answer. Now that he's been slapped on the wrist, so to speak, we'll have a few good months. Then something else will happen, something or other, but by that time I'll be ready.

Because I'll use these months to scrutinize him, to dissect him, to expose everything he does and says to the harshest possible light. By the time I get around to actually asking him, I expect I won't want him any more. But he'll never know that, I won't give him that. I'll sit there, in the bar at the plaza, biting my lip slightly, blinking my eyes a couple of times to hold back the tears, and ask him to please stay and finish his drink. I'll gather up my gloves, fumble for my purse, put my coat on unassisted and walk out. I haven't decided whether or not to turn around, just once, as I leave."

"I don't believe you, Marge. You're not that ruthless, not that devious."

"Believe it, Susan. In fact you might learn a thing or two from it. It's a necessary precaution. You could have used a little of that with Jason, if I may say so. You invite risk. I reduce it. You seem to enjoy living every minute as a cliffhanger, I don't. Look, I love Gary. He knows that, he knows he can have me. He is making the choice, not me. Somebody is going to get hurt here. Him, Marsha, me. Somebody for sure. You'd rather it was me?"

"No, but your present combat plan seems to lack a little spontaneity. You're in love with him, right now, and planning, plotting the end of your affair."

"I don't have to plan on the end; it's going to end. The only question is how it ends. And I vote for me. The only thing I mind more than losing Gary, is losing him slowly."

"The way I lost Jason."

"Yes, the way you lost Jason. Speaking of Jason, how was your summit meeting?"

We both realize there's no place to sit, place the tray on the floor between us and settle ourselves into the rug. I tell her about Jason, Sam and, finally, Paul.

"You had yourself quite a busy day . . . and night," she

says. "You took a hell of a chance with the junior accountant, What's-his-name."

"Paul."

"Yeah, Paul. For a graduate of one of the finest consciousness-raising groups in this country you seem to be doing an awful lot of male-related rushing around. Do you think it's really over with Jason?"

"With Jason, with Sam and with the Pauls of this world. Over."

"Really? All men? Good for you, I wish I had your strength, your deep conviction. God, I envy you, finished with all that dirty sex stuff."

"You're getting nasty."

"Damn right. It's not finished, Susan, and you know it. Okay, a clean sweep yesterday, Jason, Sam, and the junior accountant. Three up, three out, no strikes, maybe some balls, but no hits and one error."

"Error?"

"The accountant, definitely an error."

"Okay, okay, I wanted to try it, to see if I could get off on anonymous sex."

"And did you?"

"Sure, the fucking was technically terrific. He's a mechanical marvel, and while he was touching all the right parts of me, I felt excited, sexy. Hell, with Jason, I used to worry about how my hair looked, and whether my mascara was running."

"During sex, you worry about that?"

"Yes, during sex. And with Sam, well with Sam I didn't even bother to worry about that. I just closed my eyes and counted."

"Counted?"

"To about fifteen, by then it was all over. If I was lucky,

thirteen, but the mean average was about fifteen."

"Okay, so you've had lousy sex. This may come as a shock to you, but once in a while I, too, have lousy sex. But I'll be damned if I'm going to give up on it. Because when it works, and sometimes it does work, it ain't bad."

"Yes, well, maybe. But the difference between us is that I take it as it comes, whereas you come as you take it."

"Meaning?"

"Meaning, that I was whatever they wanted me to be. Even with the junior accountant, I couldn't quite break the habit of pretending."

"But you said the sex was good."

"Not about the sex, about after. After, I felt cold, really empty, felt like just walking out, not even talking to him. The minute it was over, the instant it was over, I felt, well, lessened. It was nothing, nothing. Some jerk I picked up in a bar. But I was nice, kind, even let him think I might see him again. And with Jason I was worse, Shit. I never told him the sex was no good, I perfected that orgasm shudder, you know the one they all think is the real thing, until I had myself fooled."

Marge laughs. "You do that too?"

"Sure. Actually I took quite a lot of pride in that shudder. And then the exhaustion, the relaxing of the body, and sometimes, when the moment is right, a single tear."

"My God, what hypocrites we are. What the hell is the answer?" Marge says.

"Who knows. I don't even know what the question is. But I learned a couple of things. I've got a partial answer. All that shuddering, for example, didn't do me any good, didn't do Jason any good. In the end I didn't even hold Jason. There's got to be more than just bouncing off of men, or on them. More than just lying every minute so they won't leave.

Well, I guess that's both the question and the answer. There has got to be more, but what is it?"

"Well, what?"

I fumble in my purse for Leonid's letter. Marge reads it. "God, how rotten, what bastards they are," she says. "This is what you mean? This is the more?" she asks skeptically.

"Probably not, but it's something anyway. It's real. And I have a hunch if I attend to this work, focus on it, do a good job, I'll feel satisfied. Not the same satisfied as when I'm loved, when I'm in love. But satisfied," I reply.

Marge looks around the room, still piled with clothes. "What are you taking with you?" she asks, "All of this?"

"No, I'll sort it out. I don't think I'll need a bathing suit."

She looks at the pictures on the dresser. "And those, what about those?"

"Those I take. The memories I take. They're real too. They hurt like hell, but they're real."

We are both quiet for a moment.

"How do you feel?" Marge asks me.

For a moment I want to tell her to stay. Something hurts me, I have some pain and I want to be tended to. I want to tell her that I'm frightened all the time.

But I've made the coffee too carefully and the counters are clean. My friend and I are sitting on my bedroom rug as she helps me pack to leave on a journey. My hair is pulled back neatly in a rubber band (later, will I make the curlicues?).

Sometime during this past year I slipped inside, under the stanchions into the main arena, into the chaos of the center ring. They have made room for me, the acrobats and the clowns. Casually, I have been assigned a role. Although I am unskilled labor, I suppose they need all the help they can get. Now that I'm in, I can't just stand around brushing the tears from my face. There's some work to be done, or people will fall from their high wires, we're all worried about those on the tightropes.

Leonid and June are up there, hanging on. I am mother and friend, they look to me for ballast.

Too bad if there is turmoil, if I am frightened all the time. Too bad if I am tired and resent their demands. They have a claim, each of them, upon me. Mother and friend, I have some obligations here. But I see I am not alone. All around there are people securing the ropes, holding fast to the moorings. I need not be ashamed, I notice that some, like me, are still sucking their thumbs.

Marge wants to know how I feel?

"Good," I reply, "I feel good."

Marge looks at me curiously. "You do?" she asks. "You wouldn't kid me, would you?"

"No, I feel good. Excited, nervous, but basically good." Marge gets up to finish my packing. I move toward her and hug her. "Go on home. I'm going to finish this."

"You mean it?" she sighs. "I really am tired. You won't forget the tissues?"

"No, I won't forget the tissues."

We stand and look at each other for a moment, that awkwardness of parting having set in.

"Hey," she says hugging me again, "good luck. I know you'll do good work on this trip. Be careful. I love you."

Bone-tired, I fall into bed. I move my hand to my hair but catch myself and just stroke it to enjoy its thickness.

I imagine for a moment what it will be like to walk into Leonid's apartment.

They are waiting for me.